THE MAGICIAN'S DECEPTION

Also by Carol Miller

The Moonshine Mysteries

MURDER AND MOONSHINE
A NIP OF MURDER
AN OLD-FASHIONED MURDER

The Fortune Telling Mysteries

THE FOOL DIES LAST *
DEATH RIDES A PONY *
MURDER OF A HERMIT *

* *available from Severn House*

THE MAGICIAN'S DECEPTION

Carol Miller

SEVERN HOUSE

First world edition published in Great Britain and the USA in 2025
by Severn House, an imprint of Canongate Books Ltd,
14 High Street, Edinburgh EH1 1TE.

severnhouse.com

Copyright © Carol Miller, 2025

Cover and jacket design by Nick May at bluegecko22.com

All rights reserved including the right of reproduction in whole or in part in any form. The right of Carol Miller to be identified as the author of this work has been asserted in accordance with the Copyright, Designs & Patents Act 1988.

British Library Cataloguing-in-Publication Data
A CIP catalogue record for this title is available from the British Library.

ISBN-13: 978-1-4483-1056-2 (cased)
ISBN-13: 978-1-4483-1669-4 (e-book)

This is a work of fiction. Names, characters, places and incidents are either the product of the author's imagination or are used fictitiously. Except where actual historical events and characters are being described for the storyline of this novel, all situations in this publication are fictitious and any resemblance to actual persons, living or dead, business establishments, events or locales is purely coincidental.

No part of this book may be used or reproduced in any manner for the purpose of training artificial intelligence technologies or systems. This work is reserved from text and data mining (Article 4(3) Directive (EU) 2019/790).

All Severn House titles are printed on acid-free paper.

Typeset by Palimpsest Book Production Ltd., Falkirk, Stirlingshire, Scotland.
Printed and bound in Great Britain by TJ Books, Padstow, Cornwall.

The manufacturer's authorised representative in the EU for product safety is Authorised Rep Compliance Ltd, 71 Lower Baggot Street, Dublin D02 P593 Ireland (arccompliance.com).

Praise for the Fortune Telling Mysteries

"An entertaining plot, colorful characters, light romance, and a satisfying ending make this a pleasant and engaging read"
Booklist on *Death Rides a Pony*

"Fans of Steven Hockensmith's Tarot mystery series may want to check out this cozy"
Publishers Weekly on *The Fool Dies Last*

"Ghosts in the attic, smokescreens, wacky characters, and a vengeful killer add up to good fun for cozy fans"
Booklist on *The Fool Dies Last*

"Pleasing characters spark the first entry in an often amusing mystery/romance series"
Kirkus Reviews on *The Fool Dies Last*

"Fans of humorous cozies with a little mysticism will want to try this one"
Library Journal on *The Fool Dies Last*

About the author

Carol Miller is the author of the Fortune Telling Mysteries and the Moonshine Mysteries. She is an attorney and lives in Virginia.

www.carolmillerauthor.com

For Margarete and Karl

ONE

The pair of suitcases thumped down the stairs of the brownstone one step at a time.

'Does your bag feel as though it's filled with bricks?' Hope Bailey asked her sister, Summer, as they paused on the landing to catch their breath.

'Mine is either a complete set of 1950s encyclopedias or a dead body.' Summer turned toward their maternal grandmother, Olivia Bailey, who was waiting for them – or, more accurately, for her suitcases – at the bottom of the stairway. 'Are you truly going to Morris's fiftieth-year high school reunion, Gram, or is it only a ruse? Did you in actuality murder poor Morris, stuff his body in this bag, and now you're making me an accessory to the crime by having me carry it down the steps for you?'

Olivia clucked her tongue in reproof. 'Just because Halloween is this weekend – and we all know that it's your favorite day of the year, Summer – doesn't excuse you being macabre.'

'It is my favorite day of the year,' Summer confirmed with a grin.

'We're going to miss you this weekend, Gram,' Hope said as she began to work her way down the remainder of the stairs with the brick-filled suitcase. 'It will be the first Halloween in recent memory that you haven't spent at the brownstone.'

'It will also be the first Halloween,' Summer added, her grin fading, 'that the boutique won't be hosting its annual party.'

Bailey's Boutique – located on the ground floor of the brownstone in the historic district of downtown Asheville, North Carolina – was the sisters' little mystic shop in which Hope read palms and the Tarot and Summer prepared herbal tinctures and teas. Their annual Halloween party – costumes required; spells, potions, and cocktails optional – was a favorite and much-anticipated event for the boutique's loyal clientele, as well as a large circle of friends and neighbors. The attendance was invariably so robust and enthusiastic that the festivities would spill outside to the brownstone's back garden and the adjoining alley, and the merriment would continue until the wee hours of the morning. Except this year the plan had unexpectedly changed.

Olivia clucked her tongue again, this time with concern. 'It's such short notice. The party has become a local tradition. Everyone will show up at the door of the shop on All Hallows' Eve, only to find the place pitch dark and locked tight. There will be a great deal of confusion and disappointment, I'm afraid.'

'We've given as much notice as possible under the circumstances,' Hope told her. 'We've put up signs in the front windows indicating the new location for the party, and we've explained the change to every person who has either called or come into the boutique over the past few days.'

'And every person,' Summer replied, 'has been unhappy about it.'

'That's true,' Hope acknowledged, 'but it can't be helped. Megan asked us to do this for her, and we couldn't very well say no, regardless of the inconveniently short time frame or unhappy customers.'

Next to her sister, Megan Steele was Hope's oldest and closest friend. They had gone to school together and seen each other through countless difficulties over their thirty-two years. As a result, when one of them needed a favor, there was never any deliberation on the matter; the other simply agreed. So when Megan had abruptly – but earnestly – asked Hope less than a week before Halloween to combine the boutique's customary party with the Green Goat's newly scheduled party, Hope had been more than a little surprised by the request, but she had acceded to it, albeit with unspoken questions and considerable reservations.

'I didn't realize that Megan's relationship with Douglas had grown so serious,' Olivia remarked thoughtfully.

'Not Douglas. Daniel,' Summer corrected her. 'Daniel Drexler, restaurateur and co-owner of the Green Goat. But I highly doubt that there's anything serious between him and Megan, at least from her standpoint. For starters, the pair have been dating for only about two months or so. And secondly, when has Megan ever been truly serious about a relationship? She's like the classic tarantula that mates and then merrily eats the male afterwards.'

Visibly restraining a chuckle, Olivia shook her head at her granddaughter. 'You really are in a ghoulish Halloween mood, Summer. Setting Megan's prior commitment issues aside, there are plenty of relationships that become quite serious quite quickly, with very little advance warning. As I recall, you and Gary announced your engagement no more than a month after your first date.'

Summer pursed her lips. 'Now who's being ghoulish? Thank you for that lovely reminder of my failed marriage and miserable ex-husband, Gram.'

'You know I didn't mean it that way, my dear. I was merely pointing out that people can get swept off their feet completely out of the blue, even someone as solidly attached to the singledom terra firma as Megan.'

When Summer responded by pursing her lips harder, Olivia shook her head once more. 'I don't understand why you're upset at my passing mention of Gary when you've got yourself such a nice new beau now. There isn't any question that Nate is much more honest and upstanding than your former husband ever pretended to be.'

With the compliment of Nate, Summer's expression softened.

'My only reservation about Detective Nate,' Olivia went on, somewhat hesitantly, 'is that since you've met him, you've come into contact with a disturbing amount of crime due to the nature of his work. I'm not sure that it's entirely healthy. Morris has expressed his concern on the subject to me, too.'

There was an aggrieved snort from Summer, but Hope cut in before her sister could give voice to her agitation. 'It's sweet of Morris to worry. He's always thinking of our best interests, and we appreciate it. But looking at it from the flip side – which Morris isn't aware of, but you are, Gram – Nate has come into contact with a disturbing amount of otherworldly activity due to the nature of Summer's work, including ghosts in the attic and spirits at séances. One could argue that it isn't entirely healthy for him, either.'

Summer gave a stiff nod in agreement. 'And Nate hasn't yet pointed at me in horror, shouted the word *witch*, and gathered together the villagers with their pitchforks and blazing torches to storm the boutique—'

Hope couldn't help laughing and nearly dropped the brick-filled suitcase on her foot.

'—So I'm not going to stop dating him,' Summer continued crisply, 'just because he's a police detective who handles serious crimes.'

'Of course not,' Olivia replied with a gentle smile. 'No one is suggesting that you should stop dating him. We're all very fond of Nate. The problem is that a point in time will inevitably come when . . .'

Although she let the sentence trail away unfinished, Hope had no difficulty comprehending its conclusion. A point in time would inevitably come when there would be an irreparable conflict between Nate's work and Summer's work, and then serious trouble would arise, most likely for everyone involved. But it was a thorny issue to address with Summer, who was understandably touchy on the subject of relationships after the wretched ending to her marriage. All Hope could do was cross her fingers that their grandmother was wrong, and any future conflict was neither inevitable nor irreparable.

Having at last reached the bottom of the stairway with the brick-filled suitcase, Hope set it down on the parquet flooring with a thud and steered the conversation back to a less fraught topic. 'Seriously, Gram, what do you have in this bag? In both of the bags?' She gestured toward the second suitcase that Summer was carrying down immediately behind her.

'Essentials,' Olivia answered.

'Essentials?' Summer echoed, depositing her bag next to Hope's with a matching thud. 'You're going to Charleston for an extended weekend. Coastal Carolina has gorgeous weather right now. All you need is a pair of lightweight slacks, a few mix-and-match blouses, and a sweater to throw over your shoulders in case there's a chilly breeze in the evening. But you've packed as though you're heading off on a six-month expedition covering the far corners of the globe.'

'I want to be prepared for all eventualities,' Olivia responded. 'I don't know how elegantly or casually the others might be dressed.'

There was a touch of defensiveness – and also anxiety – in her tone, which surprised Hope. Their grandmother was nearly always the calmest and steadiest of the Baileys. Her feathers rarely ruffled, no matter the occasion.

'You're worried about making a good impression on Morris's school chums?' Hope asked her.

Olivia knotted her hands together. 'I've never met any of them before – or their spouses. Some are probably on their third or fourth marriages at this point, including with much younger partners. Don't forget, I'm older than Morris.'

'Only by a couple of years,' Summer said.

'It's still *older*,' Olivia returned with emphasis. 'Plus, there's Constance.'

Hope and Summer exchanged a questioning glance. 'Who is Constance?'

Olivia's hands knotted some more. 'Morris's girlfriend.'

Summer squinted at her. 'What on earth are you talking about, Gram? *You* are Morris's girlfriend. And he's never made any secret of the fact that if it were solely up to him, you would have been his lawful wife a long time ago. Morris would happily marry you this afternoon before getting on the airplane if you agreed to it.'

Ignoring the latter part of Summer's remark, Olivia clarified, 'Constance was Morris's girlfriend in school.'

It was Hope's turn to squint at her. 'It's a fiftieth-year reunion. You can't honestly be concerned about a relationship dating back fifty years.'

'Morris always speaks extremely highly of Constance,' Olivia said. 'He's arranged to have dinner with her this evening in Charleston.'

'Certainly not alone with her,' Hope countered. 'Morris is as loyal and decent as they come. This dinner no doubt includes you, Gram?'

'Well, yes,' she admitted. 'Constance's husband also. His name is Gene, if I heard correctly.'

The sisters exchanged another glance. Their grandmother never fretted about the number of birthdays she'd celebrated or what sort of an impression she might make on new acquaintances, let alone anguishing about a former flame of Morris's from half a century earlier. Something wasn't right.

Summer didn't beat about the bush. 'What's going on, Gram? What aren't you telling us?'

There was a pause. Olivia examined a dry spot of skin on one of her knuckles. 'I think that I should call Morris and cancel with regard to this weekend.'

'Cancel?' Summer exclaimed in astonishment. 'You can't cancel! I've never seen Morris as excited about anything as attending his reunion with you. It's practically the only thing that he's talked about for weeks on end!'

'You can't cancel,' Hope agreed, more calmly. 'Morris will be here any minute to collect you and your bulging suitcases and drive you to the airport.'

'Dylan is driving us, I believe,' Olivia said.

This time it was Hope who paused. Dylan was Morris's son. Although father and son shared the same profession – physician – they did not share the same temperament. Morris Henshaw was earnest and unassuming, tending most often toward the somber. Dylan Henshaw was cocky and confident, tending decidedly toward the rakish. He and Hope had been flirting off and on for several months since they had first met, but she wasn't sure whether it was wise to take the relationship beyond that, mostly because she wasn't sure whether it was wise to trust Dylan. If he hadn't inherited his father's temperament, then it didn't seem likely that he had inherited his father's loyalty.

Olivia continued to study her knuckle. 'I think that I should call and cancel,' she repeated. 'I realize that Morris will be disappointed by my decision. And Dylan will probably be disappointed, too, both because I've let down his dad and because it means that he's driven here for no reason.' She glanced up at Hope. 'Perhaps if you could pay a little extra attention to Dylan when he arrives, then he wouldn't view coming to the brownstone as having been such a waste of his valuable time.'

Hope raised an eyebrow. 'Don't try to use me to appease Dylan – or as a sly distraction from the real issue. We aren't talking about Dylan's possible disappointment; we're talking about your change of heart with regard to this reunion.'

'And it's an abrupt change of heart,' Summer chimed in, no more fooled than her sister by their grandmother's attempt to switch the subject. 'Otherwise you wouldn't have expended so much energy stuffing nearly half of your wardrobe into those two bags. What happened all of a sudden?'

Olivia's gaze returned to her knuckle. 'It wasn't entirely sudden. I've been thinking about it since this morning.'

'What happened this morning?' Summer pressed her.

There was a brief hesitation. 'Hope had that Tarot reading.'

'The Tarot reading?' Hope looked at her grandmother in surprise. 'My only reading this morning was with Gwen Podolski.'

Olivia rubbed the knuckle. 'Yes.'

Hope was perplexed. 'What does Gwen's reading have to do with you attending Morris's reunion?'

The hesitation was longer this time, and Olivia rubbed the knuckle some more.

Summer turned to her sister. 'I spent most of the morning unwrapping and sorting the new shipment of candles that came in – they're really nice, by the way, much better quality than what we used to get from our old supplier – so I didn't hear any of Gwen's reading. What did I miss?'

'Nothing. Gwen's reading today was the same as her reading last week and the week before that. Her readings haven't changed in the last four months. Each time she asks the same question and wants me to draw a single card in answer.'

Summer nodded. 'And it's never the card that she's hoping for.'

'Not so far, at least. Today it was the Seven of Swords. I did my best to make the card seem somewhat positive and optimistic, but it's awfully hard to connect a picture of a thief slinking away holding an armful of swords to a pregnancy. And Gwen desperately wants her niece to be pregnant. She won't accept anything less than the Empress, which she knows is one of the two definitive pregnancy cards.'

'But her niece only got married this past July, and she and her husband are both very young. They're probably still in the blissful honeymoon stage and aren't thinking at all about diapers and midnight feedings.'

'Exactly. I've given Gwen a gentle hint in that direction and tried to encourage her to let her niece move at her own natural pace, but patience doesn't seem to be Gwen's strong suit. She won't be satisfied until the Empress appears.' Hope turned toward their grandmother. 'I think that we can all agree the Empress has no connection to Morris or your trip to Charleston, and I'm struggling to find a connection with the Seven of Swords, either.'

Olivia shifted uneasily. 'The Seven of Swords isn't the problem. The problem is the card that came afterwards.'

Hope frowned. 'I didn't draw a second card.'

'You looked at it, though. I saw you. While I was packing this morning, I came downstairs and went into the boutique, because I was considering taking one of those crystal bracelets from the jewelry display case with me on the trip. They're so colorful and less stuffy than my old, fancier pieces. When Gwen was making that lengthy speech about pram safety, you surreptitiously glanced at the next card in the deck.'

'I did take a quick peek,' Hope admitted, 'in case it was something overwhelmingly positive that I could share with her.'

'But you didn't share it with her, because you realized the card had nothing to do with her. As you lifted the card, I caught a glimpse of it over your shoulder.'

Hope's frown deepened, and she was silent.

'So what was the card?' Summer asked impatiently.

'The Magician,' Olivia told her.

'The Magician?' Summer's brow furrowed. 'But doesn't the Magician almost never appear?'

'It's rare,' Olivia confirmed.

Hope remained silent – and thoughtful. She and her grandmother looked at each other gravely.

'I'm confused,' Summer said. 'Why would a card that Hope didn't actually draw for a reading with Gwen Podolski in relation to her niece stop you from going to the reunion with Morris, Gram?'

Olivia sighed. 'Because it's almost Halloween, my dear, and everything is turned around on Halloween.'

TWO

Taking the handle of the suitcase that was standing nearest to her, Hope headed down the hallway toward the boutique.

'Where are you going?' Summer called after her. 'If Gram isn't flying to Charleston, then don't we have to carry her bags back upstairs?'

Hope didn't respond. With the suitcase rolling noisily beside her, she turned from the living quarters of the brownstone into the shop. The lights were on from earlier in the day, but she and Summer had locked the front door while helping their grandmother prepare for her trip. In the past, the door had routinely stayed open from dawn until dusk, but hard experience had more recently taught the sisters to be increasingly cautious and not leave the boutique accessible to customers while unattended. It was, after all, a mystic shop, which could on occasion attract some strange characters with dubious intentions.

After depositing the suitcase next to the herb-and-tea counter, Hope walked to the row of windows that faced the street. In the far corner – illuminated by a wide band of speckled sunshine – sat the aged, coffee-brown pine table that served double duty for both her palm and Tarot readings. The Tarot deck from Gwen Podolski's reading was still in the same position as it had been that morning, with one card lying face up: the thief from the Seven of Swords slinking away holding an armful of shiny blades.

Hope gazed at the card critically. Although she had interpreted it as encouragingly as possible for Gwen's benefit, the Seven of Swords was in truth far more negative than positive. With little exception, the card meant what it showed: a thief in your camp. It could be a false friend or a back-stabbing colleague. It might be a single harmful lie or an extended scheme of trickery and manipulation against you. If the Seven of Swords had appeared at a reading with a different client, Hope would have immediately drawn additional cards to help clarify who the thief was and how the situation could be successfully resolved, but Gwen wasn't interested in learning about any card other than the Empress.

Slowly, Hope reached for the deck. Her fingers paused as they touched the top card. Should she turn it over? If she didn't look at the card now, then she could pretend that she hadn't looked at it that morning, at least not accurately. Her eyes might have made a mistake earlier. She'd taken only a very quick glance while Gwen had been speaking about prams. Maybe it wasn't the Magician, after all. There were so many other possible cards in the deck. Surely it was one that had some arguable connection to Gwen or her niece.

With lingering reluctance, Hope took a breath and flipped the card. She winced when she saw it. Her eyes – and her grandmother's eyes – hadn't been in error. It was indeed the Magician. He was a master practitioner, and he stared out at her, challengingly.

'Ah, so you decided to check,' Olivia said as she and Summer – with the other suitcase in tow – entered the shop behind Hope. 'And was I wrong?'

'No, you weren't wrong.' Hope regarded the card a moment longer, then she turned from it and the table. 'You weren't wrong about the card. But you are wrong about the reunion, Gram. You should go to Charleston with Morris.'

'You should go with Morris,' Summer echoed her sister, setting the second suitcase beside the first. 'The Magician doesn't mean anything.'

Olivia shook her head. 'I'm afraid that it means plenty, my dear.'

'Maybe for Gwen or her niece, but not for you,' Summer disputed. 'How could it mean something for you? The reading had nothing to do with you. Based on what you said earlier about catching a glimpse of the card over Hope's shoulder, you went into the boutique *after* Gwen had asked her usual question about her niece and Hope had shuffled the deck to get an answer for her. Therefore, it can have no meaning for you.'

She shook her head again. 'If the timing were different and it were almost any other card, then I would agree. But not with the Magician this close to Halloween. Ask your sister. She'll tell you. Her gift with the Tarot is far greater than mine.'

Hope started to object, but her grandmother continued over her protest.

'Ask your sister,' she said once more to Summer. 'That's why Hope came in here just now – to settle all doubt. She tried to ignore the card this morning, but after seeing it again for certain, she knows that we must take it seriously.'

Both Olivia and Summer looked at Hope for a response. She hesitated.

'Well?' Summer pressed her. 'You can't possibly agree with Gram, because you said only a minute ago that she should go to Charleston.'

'I am *not* going to Charleston.' There was a touch of exasperation in Olivia's tone. 'I'm not traveling out of town and leaving you two here alone when the Magician has appeared. It's a warning, and we can't ignore it simply because we don't like it.'

'Our warnings come from the attic,' Summer countered. 'The spirits upstairs always let us know when something bad is afoot, and they've been as quiet as can be. There hasn't been a groan or a moan, a rumble or a thunder from them all day.'

The Baileys collectively fell silent and listened. No sound came from above them. A door didn't creak or slam. Nothing thumped or bumped. There was neither a whisper nor a shudder throughout the brownstone.

'You see?' Summer declared in triumph. 'The spirits are perfectly at ease with your trip, Gram. You can go to the reunion without a care in the world and spend all of your time worrying about such lovely little trivialities as whether you've chosen the correct pair of shoes for each activity.'

Olivia was not amused. 'Don't be flippant, Summer. The occupants of the attic can only warn us about what they are able to see and feel, most usually inside the boutique or directly outside in the garden. They can't warn us about a stranger who they haven't yet encountered. And with Halloween almost upon us, the Magician will be precisely that: a stranger.'

'He might be a good and happy stranger,' Summer proposed.

'If that were the case, then he would have been accompanied by a good and happy card, not the Seven of Swords.'

'But the Seven of Swords was intended for Gwen and her niece.'

Olivia's exasperation grew. 'You're being deliberately obtuse, my dear. The Seven of Swords wasn't intended for them any more than the Magician was. Your sister alluded to it also. She said that it was awfully hard to connect a picture of a thief slinking away holding an armful of swords to a pregnancy.'

Once again, they looked at Hope for a response. As before, she hesitated.

'Avoiding the truth, Hope' – Olivia's exasperation shifted from one granddaughter to the other – 'will not make it disappear.'

Hope sighed. 'All right, then here's the truth: if the Seven of Swords is connected to the Magician, the stranger will not be good. He'll be deceitful and dangerous.'

Summer frowned at her.

'But Magician or not,' she continued, 'I still think that you should go on your trip, Gram. In fact, Charleston is probably the best place for you this weekend. You'll be with Morris, far away from here, and this is where any stranger will appear.'

Now Olivia frowned at her.

'It might end up,' Hope went on quickly before her grandmother could begin to argue, 'that we've interpreted the cards wrong and there won't be a stranger at all. Then you'll have missed the reunion for no reason. How will you explain your absence to Morris? You can't tell him that you don't want to travel out of town and leave Summer and me alone because of a Tarot card whose meaning has been amplified and turned around due to Halloween.'

Summer nodded in agreement. 'There's no excuse that will sound remotely believable to him, Gram. And no excuse is necessary, if you simply get on the airplane and fly to South Carolina. Hope and I can manage on our own without the least difficulty. The brownstone is safe and secure. We'll double-check that all of the windows and doors are locked this weekend. And I'm sure that we can rely on the spirits in the attic to—'

'Yes, the spirits in the attic,' Olivia interjected. 'They would keep an eye out and alert you to any potential trouble, except they can't, because the party won't be here. The spirits aren't able to sense anything at the Green Goat.'

'We don't know for certain that the stranger will even be at the Green Goat,' Summer reminded her.

'And it won't matter if he is,' Hope said. 'We'll have lots of friendly company with us at the restaurant. Half of our clients will be there. Half of our neighbors will be there. Plus, Megan and Daniel—'

'Daniel can't be considered a stranger, can he?' Summer asked abruptly.

The question surprised Hope. 'No. We've met him numerous times over the past two months.'

'And all of those times have been together with Megan elsewhere. He hasn't put one foot in the boutique.'

'He hasn't?' Hope considered for a moment. 'You're right. I don't think that Daniel has even been on this street, let alone inside the brownstone.'

'Exactly. Which means that the spirits in the attic haven't been able to size him up properly and tell us anything about him.'

'That's true, I suppose . . .'

Hope didn't finish the sentence as she watched her grandmother lean against the side of the herb-and-tea counter, listening to the sisters' conversation. There was a weariness in her movement and expression that Hope wasn't used to seeing. It was a clear indication that Olivia Bailey needed a restful and enjoyable weekend in Charleston with Morris Henshaw, not the stress of interpreting ominous Tarot cards with her granddaughters and the potential appearance of a deceitful and dangerous stranger.

'Summer' – Hope gave her sister a meaningful look – 'Gram wanted a crystal bracelet from the jewelry display case to take with her on the trip. Would you pick one out for her that has protective stones?'

'What a good idea!' Summer exclaimed, understanding immediately. 'Smoky quartz. That's the most protective by far. And it has the added bonus of matching beautifully with every outfit.'

'Oh but, my dears,' Olivia objected, 'I haven't agreed to go on the trip.'

Summer paid no attention to her protestations and promptly headed toward the jewelry display case. 'Smoky quartz,' she repeated decisively.

Olivia turned toward Hope. 'I really do think that it would be better if I—'

She was interrupted by the jiggling of the handle on the front door of the boutique. All three of the Baileys were instantly quiet. The handle jiggled again, but it didn't turn because the door was still locked from earlier.

'That isn't?' Summer whispered, her fingers frozen on the latch of the display case. 'It can't be?'

'No, of course not,' Hope answered, although she was wondering the very same thing. Was the warning from the Tarot cards already proving to be true? Had the stranger arrived at the shop?

A moment later, there was a knock on the window of the door. The shadow of a person could be seen standing outside, but with the various signs posted on the glass listing the boutique's business hours and explaining the change of location for the upcoming party, it was difficult to make out anything beyond a vague figure on the sidewalk. The knock repeated itself. The sisters exchanged an apprehensive glance.

'Perhaps we should respond,' Olivia murmured.

None of them moved. The knock came a third time, louder and more insistently.

Finally, Hope forced herself into action. 'We're being ridiculous,' she said. 'Huddling in here like a trio of silly, frightened kittens. It's absolutely ridiculous.' She didn't succeed in convincing herself any more than the others, because her feet weren't quite steady as she walked toward the door and her fingers trembled slightly as she turned the lock.

The door immediately swung open, and the windchimes above it rang out from the accompanying gust of wind. A tall, lean figure with sandy hair that was tousled by the breeze stepped inside. Hope exhaled in relief. It wasn't a stranger; it was Dylan Henshaw.

'Hello, Baileys,' Dylan greeted them amiably. His pale blue eyes traveled to each in turn, reaching Hope last, and his mouth curled with a leisurely smile. 'I just read on your door that you and the Green Goat have teamed up for a party this weekend. Am I invited?'

Before Hope could answer, Olivia rushed toward him. 'Oh, Dylan, I'm so glad that you're here. And I'm so glad that you mentioned the party. You will go, won't you? Please say that you'll go to the party.'

Although he appeared somewhat surprised by the urgency of the request – as were Hope and Summer – Dylan's reply was affable and composed. 'Certainly I'll go to the party, Olivia. I'm already looking forward to it.'

'Thank you.' She grasped hold of his arm with both hands. 'You can't realize how much I appreciate it.'

Dylan's surprise grew, as did the sisters'. Their grandmother was typically neither the nervous nor flirty sort of woman who clutched at men's arms.

'You're very welcome, Olivia.' Dylan looked at her with the scrutinizing gaze of a physician. 'How are you feeling? You look a bit . . . drawn.'

'I feel fine,' she told him. 'Perfectly fine.'

He continued to study her, frowning slightly.

'Perfectly fine,' Olivia reiterated, although she didn't release her hold on him. On the contrary, she seemed to be using his fit frame for support.

Dylan must have had that impression, too, because his gaze moved questioningly to Hope. 'Is everything all right?'

Hope wavered. Dylan was an avowed skeptic who considered the Tarot, palmistry, and all other forms of divination to be nothing more than superstitious nonsense, so she couldn't tell him about the disturbing appearance of the Magician or the Seven of Swords. She also didn't want him to tell his father that Olivia was having reservations about going to the reunion. That left her with no option but to give him an imprecise answer.

'Packing was a little hectic,' she said.

Dylan's frown remained, as though he wasn't entirely satisfied by her response, but he went along with it. 'It took my dad quite a while to get ready, too. He kept asking me to check the weather in Charleston, and I kept telling him that there was no change in the forecast. It's supposed to be sunny and mild the entire weekend all along the coast. But he wasn't willing to trust it, and he ended up packing a raincoat, a wool scarf and mittens, plus a set of galoshes. His suitcase is jammed to capacity.'

Summer laughed. 'It can't be anywhere near as heavy as Gram's. She's got two of them, and they each weigh a ton.' She gestured toward the pair of bags that were sitting next to the herb-and-tea counter. 'Good luck lifting them into your car.'

'I'll do my best,' Dylan replied, chuckling also. He tried to take a step in the direction of the suitcases, but Olivia continued to grip his arm tightly.

'Dylan' – her voice quavered – 'do me a favor, will you?'

'Have no fear, Olivia,' he assured her, 'I will get the bags into the trunk. But we'll need to have them valeted as soon as we reach the airport. My dad will probably argue against it, but there is no way that the two of you can pull this much luggage through the terminal without my dad reinjuring his back and you collapsing in a heap on the—'

'No, no,' Olivia interrupted him, 'it's not about the luggage. It's about the party this weekend—'

Summer interrupted her in turn. 'For goodness' sake, Gram, stop worrying about the party. Nothing bad will happen. There won't be any problems – or a deceitful and dangerous stranger.'

Olivia cast her an admonishing look before continuing to Dylan, 'I realize that it sounds terribly fussy and old-fashioned, and if the party were here at the boutique as it always has been in the past, then I wouldn't be making such a hullabaloo. I haven't discussed it with your father, but if he were apprised of all the relevant facts, I have no doubt that he would second my request. I'd like to ask you, Dylan, if you'll accompany Hope and Summer to the Green Goat on Halloween.'

Hope stared at her. Summer gurgled, stupefied. Never before – even in their most innocent and awkward teenaged years – had their grandmother attempted to arrange a date or a chaperone for them.

Dylan's jaw twitched, as though he was startled, too, but his answer was smooth. 'It would be my pleasure to accompany them to the party, Olivia.'

She gave him a grateful smile. 'You can't imagine how relieved I am, Dylan. You've put my mind at ease.' Releasing his arm, Olivia stood independently, without the need for support. She appeared suddenly hale and hearty, no longer drawn or anxious.

Hope's gaze narrowed. Had the quavering voice and clinging to Dylan been an act? If the spirits in the attic weren't able to keep an eye out and alert them to any potential trouble, was Dylan intended to be some sort of protective substitute?

Dylan must have had a similar suspicion with regard to the acting, because he raised an amused eyebrow at Olivia, but he didn't comment.

Summer gurgled again, this time with patent annoyance. 'Hope and I do not need an escort for the party, Gram.'

'It never hurts to appear at an event – especially one hosted in part by the boutique – accompanied by a dashing and handsome man,' Olivia told her. 'And you can't say that Dylan isn't dashing and handsome. We've all seen how he turns the ladies' heads wherever he goes. Rosemarie Potter, for example. She practically melts into a puddle when Dylan merely glances in her direction.'

Although Dylan laughed, he didn't contest the compliment.

There was more annoyed gurgling from Summer. 'I will already be accompanied by a dashing and handsome man: Nate. I don't know when exactly he'll arrive at the party. It depends on what's happening at his job – Halloween is always a busy night for the police – but Nate has promised that he'll come to the Green Goat as soon as he can manage.'

'I'm glad to hear it,' Dylan said. 'I like Nate. He's got excellent taste in liquor.'

'A large group of friends will be nice,' Olivia remarked. 'The more, the merrier. It's comforting to me in case there's a problem.'

Dylan looked at her curiously. 'That's the second time one of you has mentioned a potential problem. Is there something that I should know about this party?'

There was a pause. It lasted no more than a second or two, but Hope feared that it was long enough for Dylan to perceive that there was indeed some cause for concern.

Olivia responded cheerfully, 'The one thing that you should know, Dylan—' She broke off and turned to Summer. 'And I hope that you've mentioned this to Nate, my dear. He's never been to the boutique's Halloween party before, so he might not be aware.' She turned back to Dylan. 'Costumes are required.'

'Costumes are required, eh?' He cocked his head at Hope. 'Will you and your sister be dressed as witches?'

She cocked her head back at him. 'If we dressed as witches, would that be considered a costume?'

Dylan grinned. 'Touché. So no white coat and stethoscope for me, and no policeman's uniform for Nate. Do you have any suggestions for our costumes?'

'Anything but a magician,' Hope said.

THREE

'Why not a magician?' Dylan asked. 'Do you have something against magicians?'

Hope was spared from having to conjure a response by the sharp sound of a car horn on the street outside the boutique. The subject of suitable costumes for the party was temporarily set aside in favor of the more pressing issue before them: Morris and Olivia's trip to Charleston.

'Morris must be wondering about the delay,' Summer said.

Dylan checked his watch. 'The time is starting to get a little tight. There's no need to panic yet, but we had better set off soon. The traffic to the airport is typically heavy at this hour of the day, and you never know how long it will take to pass through security, Olivia. You don't want to have to run to the gate with my dad, afraid that the flight will leave without the two of you.'

Olivia's expression was contemplative, as though she was still considering whether to go to the airport and get on the flight at all.

'If you're trying to decide whether you've forgotten anything, Gram' – Hope chose her words carefully so that Dylan would think that she was referring to normal travel preparations rather than lingering concerns about the Tarot cards and the potential appearance of a stranger – 'there's no reason to be worried. Summer and I have it all under control. Everything here will be absolutely fine.'

'Absolutely fine,' Summer concurred. Having unlatched the jewelry display case, she withdrew a bracelet comprised of glittering, brownish gray crystals. 'This is the bracelet that we discussed earlier, Gram. Smoky quartz.'

Olivia made no move toward Summer's outstretched hand. 'I don't need it, my dear. You should keep it and use it instead. The protective stones will be of much greater benefit to you and your sister than to me.'

Dylan looked at the bracelet quizzically.

'Take it. Wear it. And stop dawdling in the shop, Gram.' Summer's voice was firm, as was her arm as she continued to hold the bracelet toward her grandmother.

Dylan's quizzical gaze now moved to Olivia. Hope could see that he was beginning to wonder why she hadn't yet left the boutique and joined Morris in the waiting vehicle.

'I'll get one of the suitcases,' Hope said, trying to propel her grandmother in the correct direction. 'Summer can get the other. And if you'll take care of Gram, Dylan, and prop open the door—'

She was interrupted by a repetition of the car horn in the street. It was a loud, protracted noise, which this time seemed to be less of a friendly reminder and more of an imperious pronouncement.

Olivia frowned. 'That's unlike Morris. He's never so brash and impatient.'

'He's probably anxious about what's taking so long,' Hope responded, 'and whether you'll end up missing your flight as a result.' She took the handle of the nearest suitcase and started to pull it across the floor of the shop.

The horn blared again. As Hope got closer to the door, she realized that instead of being immediately outside as she had initially thought, the sound seemed to be coming from the left. 'Did you park down the street, Dylan?'

'No, I parked directly in front of the boutique,' he told her. 'I didn't want Olivia to have to walk far.'

'We don't want to have to pull these bags far, either,' Summer remarked, depositing the bracelet in her grandmother's reluctant palm and then following her sister with the second heavy suitcase.

Now the horn began to blast at regular intervals.

Olivia gave an agitated sigh. 'If Morris keeps that up, one of the neighbors is going to call the police to complain that he's disturbing the peace.'

'You're almost outside, Hope,' Summer said. 'Wave to Morris so that he knows we're coming and stops honking.'

With the suitcase rolling behind her, Hope stepped through the doorway and on to the sidewalk. As Dylan had indicated, his car was parked directly in front of the shop. It wasn't his car, however, that was making the noise. As she had supposed, the honking was coming from the left. A short distance behind

Dylan's car and in front of the neighboring brownstone, two vehicles were parked along the curb. The first was a large black pickup truck that was towing an even larger, gleaming silver Airstream. The second was a small camper van that was three-quarters covered with thick splatters of mud; only the white roof was clean. Hope could see the outline of a person sitting in the driver's seat of the van, their arm moving up and down in conjunction with the sound of the horn.

'Did you signal to him?' Summer called to her. 'Why isn't he stopping?'

'Because Morris isn't the one doing the honking,' she answered.

'He isn't? Then who is?'

'A stranger.'

Hope knew the instant she said it that she probably shouldn't have. She and Summer were on the verge of convincing their grandmother to go to Morris's reunion as originally planned, and at the mention of a stranger, Olivia would balk and begin worrying about the Magician and the Seven of Swords again. But at the same time, it was the truth. Hope had never seen the muddy camper van before, so the person sitting behind the steering wheel was in fact a stranger.

Olivia stopped dragging her heels in the boutique and hurried outside to look at the person in question. Summer and Dylan crowded on to the sidewalk also. To the group's collective relief, the honking abruptly ceased. It was replaced almost immediately by yelling inside the camper van. The van's windows and doors were all closed, so the individual words weren't decipherable, but it was amply clear that two people were involved in a heated argument. One voice was noticeably higher in pitch than the other, giving the impression that the dispute was between a woman and a man, although neither person was more than a blurry shadow through the front windshield.

As the yelling continued, the door on the driver's side of the black pickup truck opened, and a man proceeded to climb out. He stretched his shoulders and back, which were apparently stiff from a long drive. The man was in his mid-thirties with dark wavy hair and several days' worth of dark stubble on his jaw. He wore rugged, earthen brown pants and an olive-green T-shirt that had a faded logo printed on it. His arms and face were deeply tanned, with a pale stripe of skin visible at the edge of the sleeves and along the neckline.

'That man,' Olivia mused, 'isn't a stranger.'

'He's not?' Summer replied in surprise. 'I don't know him. Do you, Hope?'

'No, I—'

'Yes, you do,' Olivia corrected her. 'You both do.'

They took a closer look at the man.

'I definitely don't know him,' Dylan said.

'That's to be expected,' Olivia responded. 'If I recall my dates correctly from Morris, you were living in California with your grandparents, Dylan, when Hope and Summer were skinny-dipping with' – she gestured toward the man from the truck – 'him.'

'Hope and I did *what*?' Summer exclaimed.

Olivia chuckled. 'Don't act so shocked, my dear. It was only once or twice, and you were still young and innocent.'

Dylan grinned. 'Any time you want to go skinny-dipping, Hope, just let me know. I'm game.'

'I bet you are,' she remarked dryly. In the same dry tone, she said to her grandmother, 'I'm pretty sure that Summer and I would remember if we had . . .'

When the sentence trailed away unfinished, Olivia chuckled again. 'You're beginning to remember now, aren't you?'

Hope squinted at the man. 'That isn't . . . He can't be . . .'

'I believe he is,' Olivia told her. 'I didn't recognize him immediately, either. But I did recognize the travel trailer. You don't see those big Airstreams every day – especially in the heart of the city – and that one looks exactly the way Martin's used to, with the same spit and polish that makes the aluminum shine brighter than a mirror.'

'Martin?' Summer questioned. 'The only Martin that I know is from ages ago: Martin Deering.'

'Precisely. Which means that he' – Hope nodded toward the man – 'is . . .'

Summer's hazel eyes stretched wide. 'Good Lord, it's Lucas Deering!'

Lucas Deering smiled at them. It was a crooked smile with one side slightly higher than the other. 'I figured that I should give you a minute or two to piece it together and recover from the shock of my unexpected arrival.'

Hope and Summer were still sufficiently shocked to be momentarily silent.

Olivia greeted him warmly. 'It's wonderful to see you, Lucas. Your arrival may be unexpected, but it's very welcome.'

The smile tilted some more. 'I have to admit that I'm relieved to hear you say that. I was a little nervous. It's been a long time since we've seen each other.'

'A long time indeed,' Olivia confirmed. 'And your father? How is Martin?' Her own smile faded. 'It just occurred to me that if Martin isn't with you, then perhaps he . . .' She broke off awkwardly.

Lucas shook his head. 'No worries on that score. My dad is doing well. He'll probably outlive me by a dozen years at least! He simply doesn't want to travel anymore. One day – after nearly half a lifetime and tens of thousands of miles on the road – he decided that he'd had enough of moving from place to place. And it wasn't just idle talk. He bought a cabin in northern Maine, and he's stayed put there. He doesn't drive or own a motorized vehicle of any sort. All he has is a bicycle – and not even an e-bike; pedals only. It's a little problematic in winter after a snowstorm, but aside from that, he's as happy as a clam.'

'Martin did always have a remarkable way of being happy wherever he found himself,' Olivia said. There was a marked wistfulness in her tone, and her gaze was soft and faraway.

Hope looked at her with interest. Had her grandmother and Martin Deering been in a more intimate relationship than she was previously aware? Martin and Lucas had traveled to Asheville on numerous occasions, all about two decades ago when she and Summer were in their early teens. But now that Hope was older and viewed it from a different perspective, it occurred to her that only in the beginning had the Deerings used the Airstream during their visits. Later on, they had stayed in the brownstone. Lucas had slept on the pull-out sofa in the study. Had Martin overnighted in a guest room – or Olivia's bedroom?

Dylan must have noticed Olivia's wistful tone and faraway gaze, too, because he also looked at her inquisitively. Similar to Hope, he seemed to have an inkling that there had been some degree of closeness between her and Martin, because he cleared his throat and reminded Olivia of her current relationship.

'I dislike being the one to interrupt pleasant reminiscences,' Dylan said, 'but if you and my father want to catch your flight to his reunion, Olivia, then I'm afraid that you'll have to cut this reunion short.'

It wasn't clear if Morris heard his son's words or was simply tired of sitting alone while everyone else was gabbing on the sidewalk next to him, because he opened the car door and began to turn in his seat in preparation for exiting the vehicle. It was an unusually slow and laborious process, because Morris had undergone back surgery earlier that year. Although the surgery had been a success, and Morris was working again nearly full-time and could engage in almost all of his previous activities, there were still a few physical movements that caused him problems. Twisting in the seat of a vehicle and then climbing out was one of them. It was why he had remained in the car while Dylan had gone into the boutique to collect Olivia and her luggage. If Morris had known from the outset that he would be forced to wait for as long as he had, he probably would have suffered through the pain and difficulty of climbing out much sooner.

Perceiving his struggles, Olivia awoke from her haze. 'Oh goodness, no, Morris. Don't get out, dear. Stay where you are. Dylan and I will be there in a moment.'

Morris paused. Hope could guess that he was debating with himself whether or not to continue. Morris prided himself on his excellent manners, and if Olivia had encountered an old acquaintance, then he wanted to be courteous and introduce himself to that person. But at the same time, he didn't want to risk reinjuring his back when he shortly had to get on an airplane and meet old acquaintances himself.

Lucas's crooked smile drooped. 'You're going away, then? When I saw the suitcases, I feared as much. Evidently my timing is rotten.'

'No, your timing is marvelous,' Olivia told him. 'Only Morris' – she pointed at Morris, who had remained in the car – 'and I are going away – and only for the weekend. Hope and Summer are staying here. The boutique's party is this weekend, so you couldn't have chosen a better occasion for your visit.'

The smile reappeared. 'I've heard about the boutique's Halloween party, and truth be told, I've always wanted to attend.'

'You're familiar with the boutique?' Dylan asked him.

Hope thought that she detected a hint of frostiness in Dylan's voice.

'Of course. Everybody in my circle is familiar with the boutique,' Lucas said.

'Your circle?' Dylan questioned, the frostiness slightly more pronounced.

Lucas didn't answer directly. 'I invariably keep an ear open for stories about the boutique as I travel around. I have to know how the inimitable Baileys are faring. And I can see that they're all doing splendidly. Olivia hasn't aged a day since we were last together . . .'

Olivia laughed heartily.

'Summer,' Lucas went on, 'has grown – as I always suspected that she would – into a ravishing beauty . . .'

Summer laughed also – and blushed.

'And Hope still has the ability to stop my breath. For years, I've dreamt of her haunting green eyes. I would wake up in the middle of the night wondering if they were real or my mind had invented them. But now I know that they weren't a product of a faulty memory and a boy's wild imagination. Those emerald cat's eyes of yours, Hope, have the power to bring a man to his knees.'

Summer leaned toward Dylan. 'If you haven't guessed already, in their younger years, Lucas was quite keen on Hope.'

Hope shot her sister a sharp look. Thankfully, Summer's voice had been too low, and Lucas was too far away to have heard her.

Olivia laughed some more. 'Lucas, you should have gone into politics or become an investment banker. You are a smooth talker, my dear.'

It was his turn to laugh.

'What is your line of work?' Dylan inquired, the frostiness now unmistakable.

Summer was the first to reply. 'If he's traveling around with that Airstream, then he's the same as his dad used to be: a conspiracy theorist.'

'I prefer *seeker of truth*,' Lucas said.

'*Seeker of truth?*' There was a derisive snort from Dylan. 'What does that mean? Are you trying to work out if the Mafia was behind the Kennedy assassination and whether the CIA set up Lee Harvey Oswald as the patsy?'

Lucas spread his hands ruefully. 'I don't touch anything dealing with Kennedy. Not even slightly. People who dispute the official story and the lone gunman theory have a funny way of disappearing.'

For a moment, no one spoke.

'My research is focused on a somewhat less perilous subject,' Lucas informed them. 'Cryptozoology.'

There was another snort from Dylan.

'I'm not entirely sure what that is,' Olivia said.

'Cryptozoology is the science—' Lucas began.

'*Pseudo*science,' Dylan interjected.

Lucas cast him an irritated glance before continuing to Olivia, 'It's the study of animals – cryptids, as we in the field call them – whose existence is disputed or unsubstantiated.'

'They're disputed and unsubstantiated,' Dylan responded, 'for one very simple reason: they don't exist.'

The irritated glance repeated itself. 'I'm convinced that they do exist, and I'm searching for the evidence to prove it.'

'Then you'll be searching for a damn long time,' Dylan said, 'because no cryptids are real. They're nothing more than rumor and folklore.'

'That's where you're in error,' Lucas countered. 'Just because something is folklore doesn't mean that it isn't real. Quite the opposite, in fact. All folklore has a kernel of truth at its core. Every custom and legend and belief – no matter how ancient or seemingly far-fetched – is based upon an actual event – or, in this case, creature.'

'What sort of creatures are we talking about?' Olivia asked.

'The Loch Ness Monster and Sasquatch,' Summer said.

'Those are two examples,' Lucas confirmed. 'My current area of interest is the chupacabra.' In reply to Olivia's puzzled expression, he explained, 'The physical description of the chupacabra varies based on region, but it always attacks livestock. It was first reported in Puerto Rico, and there have been numerous subsequent sightings in Mexico and the southwestern United

States. I just came from the border between Texas and Arkansas where an entire flock of chickens had been drained of their blood.'

'Drained of their blood?' Olivia echoed. 'You mean like a vampire would do?'

'Yes, exactly. That's actually where the name chupacabra comes from. It literally translates to *sucker of goats*.'

Olivia grimaced.

Dylan rolled his eyes. 'Don't listen to him or trust a word that comes out of his mouth, Olivia. It's rot.'

'It is *not* rot—' Lucas rejoined indignantly.

'Do you have a medical degree?' Dylan cut him off. 'Do you have a relevant degree of any kind? I graduated from medical school. I have two doctorates. I've worked in a university hospital for nearly a decade. And I can assure you – along with all of your fellow *seekers of truth* – that there are no goat-sucking vampires walking on this earth, waiting to be miraculously discovered. There are, however, coyotes and feral dogs with mange that will on occasion attack livestock, which is why dead chickens or lambs are intermittently found with a set of canine teeth marks on their neck. End of story.'

'That is *not* the end of the—'

This time Lucas stopped himself, apparently coming to the realization that arguing further with Dylan about the existence of the chupacabra – or, for that matter, all other cryptids – would be a fruitless and frustrating endeavor. He changed tactics.

'You're a skeptic and a cynic, aren't you?' he said to Dylan. 'Anything mystical or spiritual is make-believe and fanciful to you, isn't it? But what about the boutique? Do you think that what Hope and Summer do at the boutique is make-believe and fanciful, too?'

It was a thorny string of questions, no doubt intended to irritate Dylan in turn and cause him to say something that the sisters would not take kindly. Dylan, however, was too clever to rise to the bait.

'I think,' he replied evenly, 'that if Hope and Summer are in possession of any magical hocus-pocus, then they should use it now to cause a minor disruption at the airport and delay the flight to Charleston. Otherwise, their grandmother and my dad will sadly be left behind.'

Olivia gave a dismayed yelp. 'We're late! The plane will depart without us!'

Any lingering hesitancy or misgiving about whether she should attend the reunion with Morris that weekend or remain in Asheville with her granddaughters vanished as Olivia hurried toward the car.

'Will you get the luggage, Dylan?' she cried.

Dylan had already finished loading the pair of suitcases into the trunk by the time Olivia settled herself into the vehicle.

'Goodbye, my dears! Goodbye!' The smoky quartz bracelet glittered on her wrist as she waved and called to Hope and Summer through the open window. 'I'll give you updates! I'll send you photos!'

The sisters waved in return. Just as he was about to climb into the driver's seat, Dylan paused and looked at the group remaining on the sidewalk.

'Summer,' he said, 'when Nate shows up here in a little while – which he undoubtedly will after the police station gets half a dozen complaints by the neighbors about the honking and non-stop yelling from inside that camper van – tell him that I have an idea for our costumes for the party.'

'What's the idea?' Summer asked with evident reluctance.

Dylan chortled. 'Nessie and Bigfoot.'

FOUR

As he watched the car containing Dylan, Olivia, and Morris pull away from the curb, Lucas's face twisted with anger and resentment. Hope watched the car pull away, too, but she was considerably less aggrieved and more anxious. Had she and Summer made a mistake by encouraging their grandmother to go on the trip with Morris? If the warning from the Tarot cards was true, would Olivia be safer in South Carolina or at the brownstone?

'I feel as though I should be suddenly worried,' Summer said, scraping at a loose bit of concrete from the curb with the heel of her sneaker. 'Except I'm not sure if I should be worried about Gram or us. On the one hand, maybe we were wrong, and we should have urged Gram to stay instead of leave.'

'I was thinking the same thing,' Hope told her. 'But the more I consider it, the more I realize that it isn't logical. Of course Gram is better off there than here. Yes, she'll encounter a whole group of strangers at the reunion, but how deceitful and dangerous could Morris's old school chums be? They'll merely drink too much wine or Scotch during dinner and spend the remainder of the evening exaggerating how smart and successful their kids and grandkids are, as all people at such events tend to do.'

'Good point.' Summer went on scraping. 'So we should be worried about us rather than Gram. Which means that she was right, and you and I are the ones in need of protection, not her. Unfortunately, we don't have any more bracelets with smoky quartz.'

'Who needs a protective bracelet when we have Dylan as our escort for the party?' Hope responded drolly.

Summer stopped scraping and looked at her. 'You don't think that he was serious about the Nessie and Bigfoot costumes, do you?'

At the mention of the cryptids, Hope glanced quickly at Lucas. To her relief, he didn't appear to be listening to her and Summer's conversation. He was still glaring down the block, wholly absorbed in his own – patently unhappy – thoughts.

'No, I don't think that Dylan was serious. Or at least, I hope that he wasn't.' Although she kept her voice low to reduce the risk of further agitating Lucas, Hope couldn't help chuckling. 'Can you imagine Dylan dressed as a giant sea monster and Nate wearing some sort of modified hairy gorilla suit?'

Summer laughed with her. 'That settles it. We should rush to the airport and check if they have any empty seats left on the flight to Charleston. Gram definitely has less to worry about there than we do here, so we should go to South Carolina, too. We could spend the weekend lounging on the beach with a cocktail. Imagine how lovely that would be. Then we wouldn't have to think about costumes or strangers at all.'

'If we weren't obligated to attend the party on behalf of the boutique, it would be a splendid idea, especially considering that between the party and' – Hope lowered her voice further – 'our unexpected visitors, we will be encountering a large number of strangers over the next couple of days.'

It was Summer's turn to glance at Lucas. Her words were barely above a whisper. 'He wouldn't be considered a stranger, would he?'

Hope hesitated for a moment before shaking her head. 'I suppose he falls into the same camp as Daniel. We've met both of them before, so technically neither one is a stranger to us. But at the same time, we don't really know much about either.'

'We've known him' – Summer motioned toward Lucas – 'a lot longer than we have Daniel.'

'That's true, except all of our interactions with him were ages ago. I'm not sure that horsing around on the tree swing in the garden and toasting marshmallows over a firepit counts toward knowing what a person's character will end up being in later years.'

'What about playing spin the bottle? Does that count?' Summer grinned. 'Because I recall you and Lucas doing that on more than one occasion.'

'Good Lord, that brings back the memories.' Hope smiled with a touch of wistfulness, then she shook her head again. 'In any event, when I said that our unexpected visitors were strangers, I wasn't referring to Lucas. I was referring to them.' She turned toward the camper van.

Summer turned with her, and they listened to the shouting still going on inside. The argument between the two people hadn't waned. On the contrary, it seemed to have gotten louder and even more heated.

'I hate to admit it,' Summer said, 'but Dylan is most likely right about the police. We have more than a few neighbors with watchful eyes – and ears. They're pretty fussy about noise, and after this much yelling – joined with the earlier honking – somebody has probably called to lodge a complaint by now.'

Hope nodded in agreement. 'It's hard to believe that at least one of those people in the van hasn't grown tired or hoarse after so much hollering.'

'Not Amber,' Lucas said. 'And she's the one making most of the din.'

The sisters looked at him. No longer glowering down the street, Lucas was standing beside them, likewise facing the van. His expression was genial, the anger and resentment completely gone as though they had never been there at all.

'Amber doesn't ever lose her voice,' Lucas told them. 'No matter how long she talks – or, in this case, bellows. And trust me when I say that she bellows frequently. It isn't a problem for me; I simply ignore her and go into the Airstream when she starts thundering like an elephant. It isn't much of a problem for Erik, either. He just wanders away. Erik can wander for hours at a time, lost in his own little world. Plus, he almost never sleeps in the van, only when there's a torrential downpour or the temperature drops well below freezing. Otherwise, he prefers a tarp and a sleeping bag on the ground. Erik is down-to-earth, in every sense of the phrase.'

Summer gave her sister a slight nudge with her elbow. Hope knew what she was thinking, because she was thinking it, too: outdoorsman aside, how down-to-earth could Erik be if he was traveling in a convoy of conspiracy theorists?

'The one who really bears the brunt of Amber's bad temper is Collin,' Lucas went on. 'I would call him Amber's boyfriend, but they eschew such terms. You would naturally think that means they have an open relationship, except they don't, at least not from Amber's viewpoint. She gets roaring mad if she imagines that Collin is standing a little too close or talking a little too long to another woman. And it doesn't matter if the woman is married or single, sixteen or ninety-six. Amber has a wicked jealous streak in her.'

'So you're warning us that when Hope and I meet Collin, we shouldn't purr in his ear and drape ourselves on his shoulder?' Summer joked.

'Probably best to avoid it,' Lucas agreed. 'But Hope can purr in my ear and drape herself on my shoulder whenever she wants.'

Summer nudged her sister again. Hope pretended not to notice. And she was saved from having to figure out to what degree Lucas was joking in return, because a moment later, the yelling in the van stopped. It had been going on for so long that the abrupt stillness was almost unnerving.

'Should we assume that they're all right in there?' Hope asked Lucas.

'I was wondering that, too,' Summer said. 'The silence doesn't mean that Amber throttled Collin – or Erik, as collateral damage?'

'There's no need to worry about Erik, because he isn't in the van,' Lucas responded. 'Erik isn't good at sitting in a confined place for a prolonged period, so the instant that we pulled up at the curb, I saw him dart outside. I didn't catch which direction he headed in exactly, but it's a safe bet that he's meandering through your back alley right about now.'

Summer groaned. 'Then in addition to the shouting and the honking, the neighbors will call the police about a prowler skulking behind the houses.'

Lucas grimaced. 'You've got nervous neighbors, eh?'

'We've got nosy neighbors,' Summer clarified.

'But we love them nonetheless,' Hope reminded her sister.

'Yes. As I've remarked on more than one occasion, they haven't yet gathered together with their pitchforks and blazing torches to storm the boutique, so all is well.'

Hope expected Lucas to laugh at Summer's comment, but he didn't.

'Are your neighbors hostile and threatening because of the boutique?' he inquired earnestly. 'Or are they merely ignorant of the truths of this world, like that man who was driving Olivia to the airport?'

'Dylan isn't ignorant,' Hope corrected him. 'On the contrary, he's often far too smart for his own good.'

'You're right about that,' Summer muttered.

Lucas's expression was doubtful. 'Dylan is woefully blinkered. Frankly, I'm amazed that you aren't spitting mad at him for his reference to your *hocus-pocus* and—'

He was interrupted by a loud crash from inside the camper van.

Summer jumped, startled. 'What was that?'

'A plate, I think,' Lucas answered. 'Or possibly a cereal bowl.'

There was a second crash, followed in swift succession by a third.

'That sounded like a cup and saucer set,' he observed.

'You mean Amber is throwing dishes?' Hope said.

Lucas nodded. 'Throwing, smashing, generally chucking them about. As I told you, she has a bad temper.'

Several more pieces shattered inside the van with considerable noise and evident force. When Lucas gave no indication of intending to intervene, Hope and Summer looked at him questioningly.

He shrugged. 'They aren't my dishes, and I don't have to clean up the mess afterwards. That's why I live in the Airstream, and they live in the camper van.'

'But isn't there a risk that Collin – or Amber herself – could be seriously injured?' Summer said.

Lucas shrugged again. 'It's unlikely. Amber hurls mugs, not kitchen knives. And as far as I'm aware, she doesn't own a gun—'

'Whoa. Wait. What?' interjected a new voice.

The sisters and Lucas spun toward the person in surprise. They had been so involved in their discussion of Amber and the shattering tableware that they hadn't noticed the arrival of Detective Nate Phillips behind them.

'Nate!' Summer exclaimed cheerfully.

She took a step forward to welcome him with a kiss, but then visibly checked herself. Nate was dressed in his customary work attire consisting of tan slacks and a white button-down shirt, which indicated – as Dylan had predicted – that he had come on business.

'Do you have a standing instruction at your station that when there's a noise complaint or some other trouble on our street, you're automatically notified?' Hope asked Nate with a smile. 'If that's the case' – she winked at her sister – 'it's awfully sweet.'

Summer – who was prone to blushing – turned a little pink.

Nate brushed the pleasantry aside. 'What firearm were you talking about just now and who has possession of it?'

'No, no,' Summer explained quickly. 'There is no gun. It isn't a serious situation like that. It's just a lovers' tiff with loud voices and a few broken plates, no broken arms or heads. Isn't that right, Lucas?'

When Lucas's reply was limited to giving Nate a dubious look and Nate responded in kind, Summer introduced the pair in an effort to break the ice.

Nate's manner remained formal and stiff. 'Is Summer correct that there is no gun?' he questioned Lucas. 'I distinctly heard you mention a firearm before.'

'Then you didn't bother to actually listen,' Lucas rejoined, 'because I said that Amber *doesn't* own a gun. But that's typical of the police, isn't it? You're always overreaching and overreacting and trying to stitch up innocent people to conceal your continual failures and abysmal performance.'

Hope and Summer exchanged an uneasy glance. Clearly Lucas – similar to most conspiracy theorists they had met over the years – was not a fan of the government generally and law enforcement specifically.

Summer attempted to smooth the situation. 'We know Nate very well,' she told Lucas, 'and he's not at all as you describe. He doesn't fabricate evidence, or try to stitch anybody up, or—'

'I don't need you to defend me, Summer,' Nate cut her off.

Nate and Lucas looked at each other with wary, mistrustful eyes. Their mutual dislike was undisguised. Hope found herself somewhat relieved that Dylan had departed for the airport, because if he were still there with them, he would have certainly sided with Nate against Lucas, and the situation might have escalated unpleasantly. She tried to think of something innocuous to say to break the tension.

'Dude, what has Amber done now?' a man asked.

In unison, the group's gaze snapped toward the man, who

was approaching them from the far corner of the brownstone. He was in his mid-to-late twenties, dressed in worn jeans that had been roughly cut into shorts and an old college sweatshirt. Although clean, his hair hung limply and unevenly to his shoulders, imparting the impression that similar to the jeans, the man had given himself a rough haircut. Based on his meandering gait and down-to-earth appearance, Hope assumed that he was Erik.

Erik blinked at Nate. 'Dude, is that your unmarked police car parked up the street? You look like the law, and if you're here, then Amber's being a nuisance again, isn't she?'

He was answered by the sound of shattering glass from inside the van and then a piercing caterwaul.

'I've been hit!' a voice wailed. 'I've been hit!'

Nate rushed toward the van and the wailing voice. Lucas followed after him, although at a less hurried pace. Hope and Summer were about to follow, too, when Erik stepped directly in front of them.

'Dude, are you the Baileys with the boutique?'

'We are, dude,' Summer confirmed.

Hope had to bite her lip not to laugh. For his part, Erik didn't appear to notice Summer's wryness.

'When I was walking around, I saw a little patch of open grass between the shrubbery,' Erik said, waving toward the side of the brownstone. 'It's just big enough for my tarp. Do you mind if I roll out my sleeping bag there for a couple of nights?'

'We don't mind in the least,' Hope told him. 'Right, Summer?'

To Hope's surprise, Summer hesitated.

'I won't make a mess,' Erik promised. 'No trash or anything foul left behind.'

'Oh, I wasn't concerned about that . . .' Summer hesitated again.

Hope wondered if her sister was worried about Nate's reaction. If they allowed one of the visitors to camp on their property, would Nate be offended and think that she and Summer implicitly agreed with Lucas's critical view of the government and police?

'It's our neighbors,' Summer said after a moment. 'They get anxious when they see *strangers* who they don't know.'

With her emphasis on the word, Hope understood. The problem

wasn't Nate. The problem was the warning from the Tarot cards. Erik might be down-to-earth, but he was definitely a stranger.

'The neighbors shouldn't fret.' Hope gave her sister a meaningful look. 'It's a tarp and a sleeping bag on the lawn. How dangerous could that be?'

Summer nodded at her. Then she nodded at Erik. 'The patch of grass is yours for camping.'

'Dude, I appreciate it.' He appeared genuinely grateful. 'Being outdoors is good. There's way too much drama in that van.'

Collectively, they turned toward the van. Both Nate and Lucas had disappeared inside, leaving the sliding door ajar, which made the continued caterwauling even more shrill.

'Amber loves drama,' Erik told them. 'But don't be fooled by Collin. He may seem docile, but it's deceptive.'

Hope and Summer shifted uncomfortably. They weren't eager to hear about deceptive strangers.

'How long are you and Lucas and the others planning on remaining in the area?' Summer asked, with a distinct note of hopefulness that their intended residency would not be of an extended duration.

Erik shook his head. 'I don't know. It wasn't my idea to come to this place. But I wouldn't mind staying here for a while, because there have been several reported crossings in the region recently.'

'Crossings?' Summer echoed. 'You mean like animal or bird migrations?'

This time there was even more hopefulness in her voice, and Hope knew why: if Erik was a biologist or ornithologist who tracked migratory patterns on a professional basis, then he was in all likelihood neither a dangerous stranger nor a fervent conspiracy theorist who could potentially cause trouble between Summer and Nate.

Erik shook his head again. 'Not migrations. Interdimensional crossings.'

'Huh?'

He moved a step closer to the sisters and spoke in a low tone, as though sharing a grave secret with them. 'That's the reason Yeti and Mothman and the other cryptids only appear sporadically. It isn't that they're hiding from us or that there are just a few of them in existence. I believe that they have huge populations, possibly even greater than humans presently do. But the difference is that the cryptids live in another dimension. When we see them here, they've traveled through space and time to reach us.'

Hope and Summer didn't say a word.

'I haven't yet determined,' Erik went on, 'if their travel is accidental or intentional. Do they choose to come – like on a vacation or an exploration – or is their journey a mistake? Did they pass through a looking glass or fall down a rabbit hole in error? And then the next question is: can they get back to their own home? Are they forced to linger and eventually die in our world because of disease or incompatible nutrition? Or are they able to jump back and forth whenever they decide to do so?'

The sisters still didn't speak.

'Because if they can move at will or by creating the correct conditions to enable travel, then I might learn how to travel along with them,' Erik concluded excitedly. 'Imagine how marvelous that would be! And then other forms of time travel would similarly be possible. We could go back through the millennia and watch the dinosaurs, or see the construction of the Sphinx, or—'

As Erik proceeded to enumerate a lengthy list of historical events that he was eager to witness, Summer leaned toward her sister.

'If Dylan thinks that the Tarot and palmistry are hocus-pocus,' she whispered, 'what would he say about *this*?'

Hope forced a slight smile in reply, but her mind wasn't on Dylan at that moment. It was on the bloody figure that stumbled out of the camper van.

FIVE

The blood was smeared across her left temple and cheek. It ran in a thin rivulet down her arm and hand, and dripped from the tip of one finger, leaving a trail of bright crimson dots first along the edge of the van and then over the sidewalk. The color was so vivid and the blood created such a delicate spider's web pattern on the woman's face that it looked almost as though it had been intentionally painted on as part of a decorative Halloween costume.

'You need to apply pressure to the wound, or it won't stop bleeding,' Nate told the woman as he climbed out of the van after her. There was more than a hint of exasperation in his tone, giving the impression that he had repeated the instruction several times already.

'For criminy sake, Amber,' Lucas said – exiting the van next – 'hold the towel on the cut. You're making a mess.'

Amber dabbed at her temple with a green-checkered dishcloth.

'I was expecting someone . . . different,' Summer murmured.

Hope was thinking the same thing. Amber could apparently bellow and thunder like an elephant – to use Lucas's description of her – but that was where the woman's resemblance to a pachyderm ended. Amber was no more than five feet tall and was so small-boned that she appeared as though she might tumble over if a puff of wind hit her unexpectedly. Hope wasn't sure whether the color had been bestowed by nature, but Amber's hair matched her name. It was a peculiar shade of honey yellow with a touch of orange in it. She was around thirty and had quick, darting eyes.

As Amber continued to dab with the dishcloth, Hope saw that although the cut wasn't alarmingly deep, it was large enough to possibly require a surgical suture or two. At the very least, the wound needed a thorough cleaning.

'There's an urgent care center only a few blocks away,' she told Amber. 'My sister' – she motioned toward Summer – 'or I would be happy to drive you there, or give you directions, if you prefer.'

The quick eyes darted to her. They appraised Hope briefly, then Amber responded, 'No hospitals.'

'It isn't a hospital,' Hope clarified, 'so you won't have the long wait or the high cost of an emergency room visit. It's a neighborhood clinic. They treat flus and colds, scrapes and sprains – those sorts of things. They're usually pretty quick and affordable even if you don't have any insurance.'

'No hospitals,' Amber repeated, her voice rising a notch.

'I don't pretend to be a medical expert,' Summer said, 'but I really do think that you should have someone examine that cut. It's already starting to look a little angry, which means that it could—'

The voice rose further. 'No hospitals!'

'All right, no hospitals.' Summer shrugged. 'It's your head, not mine.'

Hope frowned. She agreed with her sister that the wound was starting to look a little angry. She wished that Dylan was there, because he could have quickly checked it over and determined whether Amber needed more serious care.

'You go in, but you don't come out,' Amber said.

'Do you mean out of the hospital?' Hope asked her.

'Of course I mean out of the hospital!' she exclaimed, just shy of a bellow.

'Huh?' Summer squinted at her, not understanding the remark any more than her sister.

'If you go into the hospital,' Amber explained to them, 'you'll never come back out. They'll kill you in there – deliberately. If you're young and reasonably healthy, it will be to harvest your organs so that they can sell them for transplants to the rich and powerful. And if you're old and ill, it will be to cut costs so that the doctors and nurses and drug companies and insurance providers don't lose money on your care.'

That answered one of Hope's questions: Amber was definitely a conspiracy theorist. Hope took back her wish from a minute earlier. Thank heaven Dylan wasn't there. He might have laughed aloud at the preposterousness of Amber's accusations, but at the same time, he would have been highly offended by them.

Nate may not have been offended, but he visibly wasn't amused, either. He pulled a small black notepad from his pocket in preparation for jotting down information. 'Now would you kindly explain to me how you were injured?' he questioned Amber.

'It was an accident,' said a man.

He was the final person to emerge from the camper van. Similarly to Amber, the man was around thirty, but it took Hope a moment to determine his age because, at first glance, he appeared substantially older due to the fact that he was graying prematurely. It wasn't limited to a few streaks of white along the edge of his brow; the man's hair was a true salt-and-pepper. Also similarly to Amber, he had a slim build and was about half a foot taller than her.

'We didn't intend for it to happen—' he began.

'Are you blaming me?' Amber cut him off sharply. 'How typical of you, Collin. You're always blaming me for everything when in actuality *you* are the one who—'

'For criminy sake, Amber,' Lucas cut her off in turn, 'let Collin speak.'

Amber harrumphed discontentedly, but she was otherwise silent, dabbing some more at her temple with the dishcloth.

Hope noted with interest that it was the second time Amber had heeded a directive from Lucas. Nate must have noticed it, too, because he studied the pair for a moment before turning his attention to Collin.

'You were saying something about an accident?' Nate prompted him. 'What exactly do you mean by that?'

'Well, Amber and I were having a little disagreement, and she started yelling and throwing stuff—' There was another disgruntled harrumph from Amber, and Collin amended himself. 'Both of us were upset and shouting, and one thing led to another . . .'

As he continued his narrative about how the tableware began flying around the inside of the van and an errant shard from a juice glass ricocheted off the corner of the microwave and scratched the side of Amber's face, Collin surveyed the group standing before him. Unlike Amber's darting eyes, his moved leisurely from one person to the next until they reached Summer. At her, they paused. It was clear that they liked what they saw, because they brightened perceptibly, and an admiring smile passed across Collin's lips.

Amber apparently observed the reaction as well, because the wicked jealous streak that Lucas had warned the sisters about earlier flared.

'Why are you looking at her?' Amber demanded.

'Hmm?' Collin responded, his gaze remaining on Summer.

'Don't pretend that you don't understand what I'm talking about!' Amber's voice started to rise once more. 'We can all see that you're staring at her! We can all see what you have in mind!'

Balling up the dishcloth, she hurled it at Collin in anger. The cloth was far too soft to injure him, but it left a streak of dark blood on his blue T-shirt before dropping down to the sidewalk.

'You're imagining things,' Collin told her calmly. Then he addressed the group. 'Amber imagines things – lots of things, all of the time. But I doubt that comes as much of a surprise to any of you after hearing her ravings a minute ago about the supposed evils of hospitals and their secret organ transplant schemes.'

Hope looked at him curiously. It didn't sound as though Collin was a conspiracy theorist like the others. But if he wasn't, then why was he traveling around the country with them? Considering his undisguised appreciation of Summer and the extended fight with Amber in the van, it didn't seem that his and Amber's relationship was strong enough to be the sole reason for sharing a life on the road.

'Dude, you're wrong,' Erik objected to Collin. 'They aren't ravings in the least. Everything Amber said is true.'

Although the words were spoken quietly, there was enough emotion trembling beneath the surface that Hope began to suspect Erik of having feelings for Amber. It explained not only his quick defense of her, but also his desire to camp outdoors with a tarp and a sleeping bag rather than spend the nights in the van together with her *and* Collin. Hope now also better understood Erik's earlier criticism of Collin. From his even tone and easy demeanor, Collin might give the impression of being docile, but there was something deceptive about it. He was *too* tranquil and easy-going, as though it was part of a well-crafted act.

Based on his narrow gaze, Nate also appeared to be rather skeptical of Collin, most likely because he was as unhappy as Amber about the way Collin was admiring Summer. To his credit, however, Nate remained professional.

'Am I correct in concluding that no one here intends on making a formal complaint against anyone else?' he inquired.

'I have no complaint,' Collin answered casually. 'No harm, no foul.'

Nate turned questioningly to Amber. Although the wound on her head was no longer dripping blood, it was indisputably a harm.

'No complaint,' Amber echoed stiffly. She glared first at Collin and then proceeded to glare even more angrily at Summer.

Summer responded with an annoyed exhalation, which Hope seconded. After all, it wasn't Summer's fault that Collin ostensibly found her attractive. She hadn't spoken a single syllable to the man, let alone reciprocated his attention. But it was becoming increasingly apparent that Collin's interest in Summer – regardless of whether it was genuine or merely another well-crafted affectation – was going to cause her trouble, not only with Amber, but also potentially with Nate.

Closing his notepad, Nate returned it to his pocket. 'The original noise complaint came from an anonymous telephone call to the station, so unless that person contacts us again, we will simply let the matter go. And while we're on the subject of going, when do you anticipate moving that trio?' He motioned toward the camper van, pickup truck, and Airstream.

'No time soon,' Lucas said.

'They'll have to be removed before this evening,' Nate informed him.

'It's a public street,' Lucas countered.

'Yes, it's a public street, but public parking in the historic district of the city is only allowed during daytime hours. Overnight, parking is strictly limited to residents holding permits.'

'Is that true?' Lucas asked Hope. 'Or is it just another typical police lie?'

Before she could reply, Erik said to Nate, 'Dude, I have permission to be here overnight. The Baileys with the boutique told me that I could camp on the open patch of grass at their place.'

Although he concealed it reasonably well, it was nevertheless clear that Erik's announcement surprised Nate. He glanced at Summer, frowning heavily.

Hope sighed. The troubles were already starting – with Nate and his job, with Amber's jealousy, with Collin's roving eye, with Lucas's dislike of the government, and even with Erik's camping. She found herself exceedingly envious of her grandmother at that moment. Charleston, South Carolina, with no Halloween party and no visiting conspiracy theorists seemed like a wonderful place to be that weekend.

Summer frowned back at Nate. 'There isn't a law or ordinance forbidding Hope and me from allowing someone to use our side lawn for a couple of nights, is there?'

Lucas spoke first. 'Of course there isn't! The government can't prohibit any of your actions on private property.' He cast Nate a challenging look.

Summer's frown turned to Lucas. 'I'm pretty sure that isn't entirely accurate. I mean, the government can obviously stop a person from building a nuclear power plant or an airport in the middle of their backyard.'

'Those are two overly naïve and unrealistic examples,' Lucas rejoined. 'We aren't talking about industrial slaughterhouses or ballistic missile silos, either. We're discussing whether or not the government can stick its big nose into your personal affairs and interfere with who you choose to allow on your land.'

Erik blinked at Hope and Summer, befuddled by the direction of the conversation. 'Dude, you haven't changed your mind, have you? I'm still allowed to camp on that patch of grass, aren't I?'

'You can still camp on the patch of grass,' Hope confirmed.

Nate cleared his throat gruffly. 'Then you should expect additional problems with your neighbors. If they were willing to call the station with noise complaints from the street this afternoon, I have little doubt that they'll contact us again – with heightened concern, in all likelihood – when they see tents popping up in your garden at night.'

'There won't be any tents popping up,' Summer corrected him. 'Only a tarp and a sleeping bag. Isn't that right, Erik?'

Erik nodded.

'And the side lawn where Erik will be,' Summer continued,

'isn't visible from the street in any case. The only neighbors who could potentially see it are the Larsons – except they don't live there anymore. Their place is empty.'

It was Nate's turn to nod. 'Dylan mentioned that the property had recently come on the market.'

The sisters exchanged a startled look.

'The Larsons' brownstone is for sale?' Summer said.

'But how does Dylan know that?' Hope questioned. 'There aren't any real estate signs out front.'

'I have no idea how he heard about it,' Nate answered, 'but I know that he had a viewing of the place last week – or maybe it was earlier this week. I don't remember the exact date.'

The sisters' startled look repeated itself.

'Dylan is thinking of buying the property?'

'He might become our new neighbor?'

Hope wasn't at all sure how she felt about the possibility of having Dylan move in next door to them and the boutique.

'Which house and neighbor are we talking about?' Lucas asked her.

'That one.' Hope pointed toward the brownstone nearest to her and Summer's. 'Your truck is parked in front of it.'

Lucas studied the property for a moment. 'It's a nice house. Maybe I should schedule a viewing and put in an offer on it, too.'

Summer gave a little laugh.

'I wasn't joking,' Lucas said.

'You're serious?' Summer squinted at him. 'You're actually considering buying the place?'

'Why not?' he replied. 'Asheville is a good city in a good climate in a good part of the country.' Lucas's crooked smile surfaced. 'And the proximity to the Baileys is an undeniable bonus.'

Nate's expression darkened with displeasure.

Summer quickly tried to dissuade Lucas. 'I don't know what the asking price is, but it must be quite high. It's a double lot, and the brownstone itself has been renovated several times over the years, so the interior is relatively modern.'

'The price isn't an issue,' Lucas told her.

'It isn't? Really?'

Lucas must have been somewhat offended by Summer's misgivings regarding the state of his finances, because he responded coldly, 'You didn't question Dylan's ability to purchase the place.'

Hope and Summer didn't question it, because they knew that Dylan could afford to buy whatever property he liked. Dylan was very well employed and also had a considerable amount of family money at his disposal. But they certainly couldn't say that to Lucas for fear of offending him further.

In an evident effort to lighten the mood, Summer gave another little laugh. 'The conspiracy theory business must be lucrative.'

Lucas did not laugh with her, and his answer was brusque. 'It's lucrative enough.'

There was an awkward silence, and Hope switched to a previous subject to avoid continuing with the current subject.

'I have an idea with regard to the parking issue,' she said. Almost as soon as she had spoken, she wished that she had remained quiet, realizing that her proposed solution might cause more problems than it solved.

Everyone turned their attention toward her, forcing her to go on.

'Considering that the Larsons' brownstone is currently empty and up for sale, and the Airstream and truck and camper van are all parked directly in front of it, couldn't we consider the vehicles as temporarily belonging to the non-existent residents of the property for permit purposes?'

'That's an excellent idea,' Summer concurred, giving her sister a grateful look.

In contrast, Nate's look was distinctly irritated. 'That's a clear violation of the local ordinance.'

'Yes, but it doesn't harm anyone,' Summer replied, using her sweetest tone. 'And none of the neighbors will object, because then all of the vehicles will remain where they are rather than moving repeatedly, making a lot of noise and commotion each time.'

Nate couldn't dispute that point. 'All right,' he agreed reluctantly. 'Except it really must be temporary – no more than a night, two at the absolute maximum.'

Lucas began to argue the time limit, but Collin cut him off.

'Two nights won't be a problem,' Collin said. 'We weren't intending on staying any longer than that regardless.'

While Nate was visibly relieved by the news that the group expected to depart in only a couple of days, Hope looked at Collin quizzically. Erik had specifically told her and Summer earlier that he didn't know how long they planned on remaining in the area, because it wasn't his idea to come there. She had naturally assumed that it had been Lucas's idea to go to Asheville since he was familiar with the boutique. But now it sounded as though it might have been Collin's idea, instead.

'We'll be gone as soon as our business here is concluded,' Collin went on. 'To that end' – he turned toward Summer with a repetition of his admiring gaze – 'I hope that you can steer me in the proper direction.'

Amber scowled. Nate grumbled under his breath.

Summer's response was hesitant. 'What direction are you interested in?'

'Yours – and the Green Goat's.'

SIX

'Dude, I'm thirsty.'

'That makes two of us, dude,' Hope said.

She and Erik were sitting at a tiny, black-lacquered table in the far back corner of the Green Goat. They had been lucky to get their seats. Friday afternoon was turning into evening, and it appeared as though every person in downtown Asheville had flocked to the establishment, which was prominently located along one end of the main square in the historic district. Based on their attire, some of the customers were local office workers, others were visiting tourists, and a few were early Halloween revelers, who had evidently decided to give their costumes a tryout a day in advance.

Although the Green Goat had been in business for nearly six months, it still seemed unable to make up its mind whether it wanted to be primarily a bar or a restaurant. The interior was divided almost equally in half, with a chic dining area decorated in a glass-and-chrome motif occupying the left side of the place and a slightly more casual bar decorated in a black-and-white motif occupying the right side. Both sides were currently filled to capacity, with a considerable line having additionally formed outside, waiting for admittance to obtain some combination of food and drink.

'Your friend will come back, won't she?' Erik asked, anxiously craning his neck to spot Megan through the crowd. 'With beverages?'

Hope restrained a laugh. Ever since Megan had disappeared into the throng, promising to return with liquid refreshment, Erik had been rubbing his dry lips together as though he were a parched camel having trekked all day through the blistering Sahara sun.

'Yes, she'll come back,' Hope told him, 'and I have every confidence that it will be with beverages. Megan is the Director of Activities at Amethyst, the luxury hotel and spa that we passed on our way here. As part of her myriad duties, she frequently handles their four o'clock wine-and-cheeses, which means that she can navigate a rapacious group of drinkers and diners with ease while at the same time juggling an armful of carafes and platters.'

Their present seats – on black-lacquered chairs in the same diminutive style as the table – were due entirely to Megan. When Collin had asked Summer to accompany him to the Green Goat, Hope's first thought had been of Megan. It had been partly because Megan's current beau – Daniel Drexler – was co-owner of the place, and partly because it had been immediately apparent that Summer needed assistance in extricating herself from a thorny situation. Amber's eyes had shot daggers at her. Collin's gaze had bordered on simpering. And Nate's expression had been filled with a mixture of concern and agitation.

Summer's response had been to hem and haw in an effort to delicately decline Collin's invitation. But when Collin had made it clear that he wasn't going to easily accept her polite refusal, Hope had taken the opposite tack from her sister and promptly declared that his idea of going to the Green Goat was brilliant. It was so brilliant, in fact, that why didn't the entire group accompany the pair? Furthermore, she and Summer had a dear friend, Megan Steele, who was connected with the Green Goat and one of its owners, and wouldn't it be jolly to invite her along, as well?

It had been impossible to determine whether Summer or Nate had been more pleased by Hope's proposal. They had both looked at her with immense relief. Amber had also appeared relieved and had quickly voiced her support for the plan, no doubt because then she could keep a close watch on her precious Collin. Lucas and Erik had likewise indicated their enthusiasm for imbibing a beverage or two. Collin had been the only equivocal member of the party. Hope couldn't tell if he was disappointed at not being alone with Summer or annoyed at being together with one or more of the others. He did live in very close quarters with Amber, and he continually saw Erik and Lucas, so it wasn't difficult to imagine that he might have wanted some time and space away from his travel partners.

'Here I am, my darlings!'

Like a parting of the sea, the Green Goat's multitude swept apart, and Megan appeared out of their midst. Nearly every man – and most of the women, as well – looked at her as she passed by them. It came as no surprise to Hope. Megan had always been exceptionally attractive. She had the long, sinewy legs and untamable air of a colt, a bob of baby fine blond hair, and a pert nose.

'Not a single drop spilt, I'm proud to report.' Megan deposited a tray of brimming glasses on the table, completely covering its round top.

'Excellent job,' Hope commended her.

Erik was equally impressed. 'Dude, I wouldn't have made it five paces in that mob before falling down and dropping everything in a monstrous crash.' He leaned eagerly toward the tray. 'Is one of those pints for me?'

Megan handed him a beer, then she offered Hope a cocktail.

'Martini, darling?'

'Oh yes, please.'

Also selecting a martini, Megan settled herself into an empty chair next to Hope. After saluting each other with their glasses, they both took a sip.

'That tastes a little bit like heaven,' Megan said, promptly taking another more generous drink.

'My thoughts exactly,' Hope agreed. 'And exactly what I needed this evening. Next time you talk to Daniel, tell him that this is one of the best martinis I've ever had.'

'Beer's good, too,' Erik chimed in.

Megan nodded. 'Regardless of the Green Goat's copious problems, it can be solidly relied upon to serve a fine cocktail.'

Hope looked at her with surprise. 'Copious problems? What sort of problems do you mean?'

'Dude, there can't be a problem with lack of customers, because this place is packed to the gills. It's so full I'm almost starting to get claustrophobic. The beer helps, though.' Erik took a soothing swig. 'I'm glad that I get to sleep by you tonight. It'll be quiet there.'

It was Megan's turn to express surprise. 'Sleep by you?' she echoed to Hope.

'Not by me personally,' Hope explained. 'Or by Summer, either. With his tarp and sleeping bag, Erik is going to camp on the side lawn of the brownstone for a couple of days. He's fond of being outdoors.'

A wry smile crept across Megan's lips. 'Does Dylan know about this camping arrangement?'

'No.'

'Uh-oh. He isn't going to like it when he finds out.'

'That is Dylan's problem, not mine,' Hope replied, a touch defensively. 'And I don't see why he would care one way or the other.'

'He'll care because he's crazy about you. A man who is crazy about a woman does not like it when another man sleeps within shouting distance of that woman, including on the side lawn of their brownstone.'

Hope took a large swallow of her martini.

Megan's smile grew. 'Admit it, you're secretly pleased that I said Dylan is crazy about you.'

'You are a rotten and irritating friend,' Hope said.

'I am your absolute best friend,' Megan rejoined. 'I supply you with superb cocktails. When you inform me that you and Summer are bringing a group to the Green Goat on short notice, I reserve a table for you so that you don't have to wait outside with the rabble. And I always tell you the unvarnished truth, including that you and Dylan Henshaw are a pair of obstinate mountain goats who foolishly insist on butting heads rather than more enjoyably nuzzling necks.'

Holding her index fingers up by her ears as though they were a set of horns, Megan made a butting motion with her head. Hope tried to pretend to be offended, but she ended up laughing instead.

Megan laughed as well, drained her glass, and reached for a second martini from the tray. 'I brought cocktails for the entire group, but everybody appears to have vanished into thin air, so one of their cocktails will now vanish, too.'

'Dude, can I have another one also?' Erik asked, likewise draining his beer.

'Be my guest.' Megan gestured toward the tray – from which Erik promptly removed a new beer – then she turned toward Hope. 'So where did they all go? In addition to Summer, I thought that I counted five people who came in with you.'

'Four,' Hope corrected her. 'Erik, plus three more: Lucas, Amber, and Collin.'

'And who are they exactly?'

As she spoke, Megan lowered her voice to keep Erik from overhearing. Such a precaution wasn't necessary, however. Megan was seated much closer to Hope than to Erik, and there was so much noise in the place that it was impossible to understand any word that wasn't directed specifically at a person.

Hope told Megan about the unexpected arrival of Lucas and the others outside the boutique earlier that day. For a long minute, Megan remained silent, sipping her martini contemplatively. She glanced at Erik, who had rapidly finished his second beer and was now slumped in his chair with his chin resting on his chest and his eyes closed. It wasn't clear if he had actually managed to fall asleep in all of the surrounding din, but in any case, they didn't have to worry about him listening to their conversation.

'Poor Nate,' Megan mused. 'He finally convinced Summer to give him a chance after that horrid marriage of hers ended, and now some bizarre stranger shows up out of the blue and immediately makes a move on her. But why didn't Nate come here with you and Summer to ensure that Collin couldn't inveigle himself with her further?'

'Nate didn't have a choice in the matter. He was still on duty, so after resolving the noise complaint, he had to go back to the station.'

'Ah, that explains it.' Megan added after a moment, 'And it means Dylan will probably appear before too long.'

'What makes you think that?'

'It's only logical. If Nate is worried about Collin's intentions and he can't keep an eye out himself, then he'll ask Dylan to check that Summer is all right.'

Hope nodded, somewhat absently.

'At the same time,' Megan continued, 'it also gives Dylan a perfect excuse and opportunity to check on you.'

The absent nod repeated itself.

'And for once you'll decide not to be an obstinate goat, so you'll leap straight into Dylan's arms, and he'll carry you off to bed.'

'Hmm?'

'Hope!' Megan gave her a sharp poke in the shoulder.

Startled, she jumped in her seat and almost spilled her drink in the process. 'What? What's wrong?'

Megan rolled her eyes with exasperation. 'Nothing is wrong other than you clearly haven't been paying any attention to what I've been saying.'

'Oh, I'm sorry. My mind wandered. I was thinking about Collin.'

The eyes stretched wide. 'You aren't interested in him, are you? Granted, I haven't met the man, but I find it difficult to believe that you would choose a weird conspiracy theorist who travels around the countryside sharing a camper van with other weird conspiracy theorists' – she inclined her head toward Erik, who was still slumped in his chair, eyes closed – 'over rich and hunky Dylan, who lives in five-star hotels.'

It was Hope's turn to roll her eyes. 'No, of course I'm not interested in Collin. It's his interest in Summer that I was wondering about.'

'But his interest in her isn't really surprising, is it?' Megan responded. 'With her peaches-and-cream complexion, Summer is awfully pretty, and even though it isn't at all accurate, she does give off that lost-lamb-in-need-of-a-sturdy-shepherd-to-guide-and-protect-her vibe that many men are irresistibly drawn to like the proverbial moths to the flame.'

'Summer has always had plenty of admirers,' Hope agreed, 'including on occasion, instant veneration from complete strangers. Except there's something different with Collin. I had an odd feeling from the outset that his interest in Summer wasn't genuine – or at least, not entirely genuine. It seemed more like an act or affectation to me.'

'Maybe he was deliberately trying to provoke his girlfriend,' Megan suggested. 'You said that Amber has a wicked jealous streak. It certainly wouldn't be the first time in history that a man has flirted with one woman for the sole purpose of provoking another woman.'

'That's true. And I might have it all wrong. Erik warned Summer and me just before we met Collin that he was deceptive, so I could be simply imagining that Collin's behavior is off based on that.'

Megan shook her head. 'You don't usually imagine those sorts of things. Your instincts tend to be pretty accurate when it comes to fishy men.'

Hope replied with a sardonic laugh. 'On that score, my instincts aren't nearly accurate enough. If they were, I wouldn't still be single.'

'Both you and I are still single precisely because we have been able to identify and keep away from fishy men,' Megan returned.

Although not nearly as confident as Megan on that point, Hope saw no purpose in debating it further. After taking a consoling drink from her martini, she said, 'Well, in this case, what really struck me as peculiar about Collin was that he asked Summer to come here.'

Megan frowned. 'Why is that peculiar? I mean, it's a bar and a restaurant. People usually get to know each other and have dates at bars and restaurants.'

'Yes, but Collin specifically wanted to go to the Green Goat. He said the name before anyone else had mentioned it. How does a guy who's driving from coast to coast and state to state in a camper van filled with conspiracy theorists – and I'm not convinced, by the way, that Collin actually is a conspiracy theorist like the others, which then raises another set of issues – know about the Green Goat?'

The frown deepened. 'That's a good question. It certainly isn't a famed destination like Maxim's in Paris or Café Du Monde in New Orleans. The Green Goat hasn't even been in business long enough to be listed in restaurant and tour guides.'

'Exactly. So where did Collin learn about it? He only arrived in Asheville today, this very afternoon, so he couldn't have stumbled across the place while on a tour of the city, or by getting a local recommendation, or from accidentally . . .'

Hope left the sentence unfinished as Megan's gaze and frown abruptly moved toward someone in the crowd.

'Hope,' Megan said, 'take a look over there. Almost directly ahead of us, just past that pair of big tables.'

She turned in the direction that Megan indicated.

'Do you see those two men standing at the near side of the bar?'

There were a lot of people standing at the near side of the bar. Hope shifted in her chair for a better view.

'The man in the blue T-shirt. Do you know who he is?' Megan asked.

Hope shifted again until she was able to find a man in a blue T-shirt. She immediately recognized his prematurely graying hair and slim build, and there was no possibility of mistaking the dark streak of blood on his shirt.

'That's Collin,' Hope told her.

'You're positive?'

'Definitely. Amber threw a dishcloth at him that she had been using to staunch the cut on her head, and he got her blood on his shirt from it. The blood is still there.'

Collin and another man were engaged in what appeared to be a grave conversation. Both men had tense expressions, and their body language was not warm and friendly.

'I think,' Megan said slowly, 'that you're right, Hope. And I think that Erik is right, too. Collin is deceptive.'

Hope looked at her questioningly.

'I'm not sure if Collin is honestly interested in Summer. And I'm not sure if Collin is honestly a conspiracy theorist. But I am sure that Collin was aware of the Green Goat before today, before coming to Asheville.'

'How can you be certain of that?'

'Because I know the man that Collin is talking to, and in my experience, he never mixes and mingles with strangers. He only talks to people that he's already familiar with, and he only talks about business.'

'Who is he?' Hope asked.

'Nelson Hatch. He's the other owner of the Green Goat.'

SEVEN

Hope immediately turned back to the near side of the bar to take a better look at Daniel's business partner, but it was too late. The crowd in the Green Goat had swelled and undulated like a gigantic wave, and Nelson Hatch had been swallowed into it. Collin was no longer visible, either.

'Did you see where they went?' she asked Megan.

'No. I blinked, and they were gone. My guess is that they headed to the office at the rear to get away from the noise.'

'I wouldn't mind getting away from the noise, too,' Hope murmured, more to herself than to Megan. Her ears were beginning to ring a bit. In a louder voice, she said, 'Whatever Collin and Nelson were discussing, it seemed to be pretty serious.'

Megan nodded in agreement. 'That was my impression, too. I've only met Nelson on a couple of occasions – always here and always with Daniel – but I wasn't exaggerating when I said before that his sole topic of conversation is business. Each time that we've crossed paths while having dinner, Daniel has introduced us, Nelson has given me a perfunctory greeting, and then the pair have excused themselves to discuss Green Goat affairs in the office while I was left to finish my meal alone.' She added dryly, 'At least I always had a good bottle of wine to keep me company.'

Although Hope responded with a smile, her mind remained on Collin. 'Earlier this afternoon, Collin told Nate that he and the others would stay in Asheville for no more than a couple of days until their business here was concluded. Based on what we just saw, it appears that business is with the Green Goat. And I'm inclined to think that it's primarily Collin's business, not the others – or at least, not all of the others.'

As she spoke, both she and Megan looked at Erik, who sagged limply in his chair like a rag doll. He was definitely sleeping now. His mouth had flopped open, with distinct wheezing sounds emanating from it.

'How did he manage to do that?' Megan said in amazement. 'To be able to fall asleep in this racket and commotion must rank as some sort of a natural wonder.'

Hope's smile reappeared. 'Or it's the result of great study. According to Erik, his area of expertise is interdimensional crossings, so it might be that he's not actually sleeping at all. Instead, he's traveled through time and space to a quiet, peaceful location. He told Summer and me that he wanted to go back through the millennia and watch the dinosaurs. Maybe in his mind, he's currently sitting at some ancient spring, serenely gazing at primordial ooze.'

Megan laughed. 'If that's the case, then when he wakes up and returns to our present day and age, I'll have to beg him to teach me how to time travel, too. I can't count the number of times that I've wanted to escape to another dimension at the hotel when some snotty, spoiled guest has spent half an hour haranguing me about a ridiculous triviality such as the lavender fragrance of the bath soap not lingering in the air sufficiently for their liking, to give you an example from earlier this week.'

'If Summer were sitting with us right now, she would be nodding wildly. We had a lavender complainer this week also, except this one was the opposite of yours. For ours, the lavender fragrance of a candle supposedly grew too strong the longer that it burned, and even though we had already offered the woman a full refund, she insisted on burning the entire remainder of the candle in front of us in the shop in attempt to prove her point. You wouldn't believe how many problems we have with scented candles.'

'Oh, I can well believe it. I'm firmly convinced that there are some people in this world who make it their mission in life to complain about *everything* and turn it into a problem. I've seen it at the hotel. You and Summer have seen it at the boutique. And Daniel has certainly seen his share of it here.'

Remembering Megan's previous remark about the Green Goat's copious problems, Hope asked, 'Is that what you meant before about this place's problems? Too many of the customers are complainers?'

Megan shook her head. 'There are a lot of complainers, but the bigger problem is not enough customers.'

Hope wondered whether the ringing in her ears had gotten worse without her realizing it. 'I must have heard you wrong,' she said. 'Not enough customers?'

'Not enough customers,' Megan confirmed.

It was Hope's turn to shake her head. 'I don't understand. How can there be not enough customers? There isn't any room for more customers. The only reason that we aren't getting squashed like sardines right now' – she gestured toward the mob surrounding them – 'is because you got us this wonderful little table and chairs in the corner. Erik said it best: the place is packed to the gills. And if Nate were here, he'd probably say that it's packed far beyond official fire and safety limits.'

'Tonight, yes,' Megan concurred. 'But last night, no. The night before that, no. And the night before that, also no. It may be like squashed sardines packed to the gills this evening, but most of the time, it's a few sad and lonely herrings in a vast ocean.'

'I don't understand,' Hope said again. 'When the Green Goat initially opened, it was tremendously busy and nearly impossible to get a reservation. I know that Gram and Morris ate here several times with other couples – as I recall, Morris particularly enjoyed the fried oysters – and they considered it somewhat of a coup.'

'That's exactly it. New restaurants and bars are always all the rage, because everybody wants to be the first one to try them and then tell everybody else about it. But before long, what was fresh and shiny grows old and tired. The bloom quickly comes off the rose, so to speak, and the place loses its appeal, supplanted by fresher and shinier places. That's what has happened to the Green Goat.'

'I had no idea. Can anything be done to fix it?'

'Daniel is trying. Do you remember when he went to that restaurateur convention in Atlanta a month or so ago?'

Hope nodded.

'Well, he was there primarily because they had a number of seminars and speakers on regaining appeal and making a place fresh and shiny again. Some of the suggestions included switching to different forms of advertising, finding new investors, changing menus, offering promotions and theme nights, and—'

Megan broke off, shifting uncomfortably in her seat.

'And?' Hope prompted her.

She shifted once more and then said in a hurried breath, 'And that's the reason Daniel wanted to combine the boutique's Halloween party with the Green Goat's Halloween party. He had heard how popular your party was, and he was hoping to direct some of that popularity toward this place. So he asked me, and I asked you, and I've been feeling terribly guilty about it ever since.'

'But why would you feel guilty about trying to help Daniel's business?'

'Because after I'd had a proper chance to think about it, I realized that helping his business might end up hurting your and Summer's business, which is the absolute last thing that I want to do.' Megan looked at her anxiously. 'You aren't angry, are you?'

'Of course I'm not angry,' Hope said.

Now in addition to anxious, Megan also looked doubtful.

'I'm *not* angry,' she repeated with emphasis. 'Honestly not. The combined party won't hurt the boutique's business to any significant degree. Admittedly, some of our clients are disappointed and even a little miffed about the unexpected change of location, but that's only because most of them don't like change of any type. Once they've had a good grouse about it, they'll still go to the party here, and they'll still come to the boutique for their readings with me and Summer's tinctures and teas.'

Megan's expression relaxed somewhat.

'And I'm quite certain,' Hope went on, 'that more than a few of our neighbors will be secretly pleased about the move. They won't admit it aloud, because they enthusiastically attend the party every year, so they can't really complain too much. But at the same time, they'll be happy that the noise and hubbub will occur elsewhere rather than so close to them.'

'I can't tell you how relieved I am.' Megan took a substantial drink from one of the unclaimed martinis on the tray.

Hope took a drink also. 'I just wish that you would have told Summer and me about the Green Goat's problems earlier so that we could have helped sooner. If Daniel gives us some advertising signs, we can put them up in the boutique's windows. Plus, there are always tourists who wander into the shop to ask for restaurant recommendations within walking distance, and from now on, we'll direct them here.'

'Daniel will really appreciate it, Hope.'

'He should appreciate *you*. Not every girlfriend is willing to expend substantial energy for the benefit of her boyfriend's business—'

She stopped abruptly.

'What is it?' Megan asked her.

'It just occurred to me,' Hope mused, 'that your boyfriend's business could be Collin's business.'

'Huh?'

'You said a minute ago that one of the suggestions from the restaurateur convention for making a place fresh and shiny again was to find new investors.'

Megan nodded.

'What if Collin is a new investor – or a potential new investor – in the Green Goat? It would explain his coming to Asheville, his knowledge of the Green Goat, and also why he was speaking with Nelson so earnestly a minute ago, before we lost sight of them.'

'It would explain a lot,' Megan agreed. She hesitated. 'Except Daniel hasn't mentioned anything to me about a new investor.'

'Is it likely that he would have mentioned it?' Hope questioned.

She hesitated again. 'Yes, I think so. Daniel told me about the Green Goat's loss of customers, and his reason for going to the convention, and the purpose behind combining the two Halloween parties, so he hasn't been cagey or secretive about what's happening with the place. Why would he keep mum about a new investor?'

Hope considered for a moment. 'Maybe Daniel isn't aware of it.'

Megan's brow furrowed. 'What do you mean?'

'Well, I don't know how Nelson and Daniel's business relationship is structured, but it's possible that Nelson is negotiating with a new investor and hasn't told his old partner.'

The furrow deepened.

'And perhaps I shouldn't say it,' Hope went on with some reluctance, 'but it's also possible that—'

'The new investor is replacing the old partner,' Megan concluded for her, grimly.

Hope nodded. 'We don't have any proof of that, obviously. At this point, it's no more than speculation . . .'

'But what about money?' Megan interjected.

Now Hope's brow furrowed. 'Isn't money the whole purpose of a new investor?'

'Yes, of course, from Nelson and Daniel's perspective. But how is Collin getting the money? He's currently living in a small camper van with two other people, and although he isn't dressed in rags, his appearance isn't exactly exuding riches, either. So where would he find the money to become an investor in a business?'

'I don't know,' Hope answered. 'But Summer made a similar assumption about Lucas's finances this afternoon, and she was resoundingly corrected.'

Megan looked at her in surprise. 'Summer thought that Lucas might also become an investor in the Green Goat?'

'No. It had nothing to do with the Green Goat. It had to do with the sale of the Larsons' brownstone next door.' When Megan's surprise visibly grew, Hope shook her head. 'That's another story for another time, preferably one that doesn't involve us shouting to be heard. Suffice it to say, Lucas is apparently much wealthier than one would guess for a conspiracy theorist. Granted, his pickup truck and Airstream are worth considerably more than a communal interest in an aging camper van, but even setting that aside, Lucas evidently has plenty of money to his name. So maybe Collin has plenty of money, too.'

There was a brief pause, then Megan sprang to her feet. 'Let's go and find out!' she exclaimed.

Not eager to give up her chair in the crowd without a thoroughly compelling reason, Hope remained seated. 'Find out what?' she asked.

'Whether Collin actually has plenty of money, and if he intends on using it to invest in the Green Goat!'

'How are we going to find that out?'

'The easiest way possible: we follow Nelson and Collin to the office and eavesdrop on them there.'

Hope still didn't rise. 'Are you sure that's such a good idea?'

'Why wouldn't it be?' Megan returned, a touch indignantly. 'Daniel has worked terribly hard to keep this place afloat. He deserves to know if Nelson is planning on adding a new investor, and he should certainly be informed if that new investor is replacing him as Nelson's business partner.'

'I can't argue with you on that,' Hope said, 'but Nelson and Collin might not still be in the office, and even if they are, it seems unlikely that we would be able to eavesdrop with any degree of success in this cacophony.'

'The office is at the rear.'

'You mentioned that earlier.'

'At the rear, *downstairs*,' Megan clarified.

'This place has a lower level?'

Megan nodded. 'Wine cellar, a supply room, and the office. They'll all be much, much quieter than up here – and we could grab ourselves a bottle or two of something nice to take along at the same time. Daniel is always telling me that I should, but I never do, so by this point, I more or less have a case on account.'

Although Hope wasn't the least convinced about the eavesdropping scheme, she could see that Megan was determined enough to continue debating the point indefinitely.

'Oh, all right,' she agreed. 'But we'll lose our seats and this table, and if there's no one in the office – as I suspect – it will have been for naught.'

Megan shrugged. 'Do you honestly care about losing the chairs and the table? I don't. My head is starting to hurt, so I couldn't have stayed in this place a lot longer anyway.'

'Same for me,' Hope told her. 'My ears are ringing like cathedral bells. The only question is: what do we do about him?' She motioned toward Erik, who hadn't moved an inch during nearly their entire conversation. 'It's kind of weird that he's still asleep, isn't it? If it weren't for the fact that I can see his chest rise and fall, I'd be worried that he had stopped breathing somewhere along the way.'

Megan shrugged again, this time with amusement. 'Maybe he really can time travel. Take a look at his face. There's a sort of a smug grin on it, isn't there? Instead of going back through the millennia to watch dinosaurs and primordial ooze, Erik might be viewing ancient Egyptian belly dancers.'

That made Hope laugh.

'But you're wrong about one thing,' Megan went on, laughing

also. 'There's a second question: what do we do about the leftover cocktails?'

'Take them downstairs with us, of course!'

They laughed harder and each reached for a new martini from the tray.

Suddenly, Hope grew serious. 'Actually, there is a third question, and it's the most important of all: what do we do about Summer? Leaving Erik to fend for himself in this scrum is very different from leaving Summer, wherever she might be at the moment.'

'That's true—' Megan began.

A bellowing voice cut her off.

'I can tell you where Summer is at this moment. She's with Collin. And when I next see the two of them, I'm going to kill them both.'

EIGHT

Amber's words startled Megan considerably more than they did Hope, but that was because Hope was already familiar with her wicked jealous streak. Amber's face was flushed with such intense anger and resentment that Hope turned to the first thing that she could think of which might defuse the situation.

'Would you like a cocktail, Amber?' she asked, gesturing toward the one remaining martini on the tray. 'Or there's beer, if you prefer.'

'What I would prefer is for you to keep your sister and her grubby hands away from Collin,' Amber snarled.

Hope took a long, slow drink from her glass to keep her own anger and resentment in check. 'My sister isn't with Collin.'

'That's a lie!' Amber shouted. 'I heard you say just a minute ago that you don't know where she is.'

A sharp retort bubbled on Hope's tongue, but it was preempted by Erik, who chose that moment to either wake up or return to the present from his ancient Egyptian belly dancers. His eyes popped open, and his chin lifted from his chest.

'Oh hey, dude,' he said.

Although ambiguous, the greeting appeared to be addressed primarily to Amber, which Hope took as further confirmation of Erik's warm feelings for her.

Amber barked a question in reply. 'Have you seen Collin?'

Erik stretched in his chair and surveyed the tray on the table. 'Dude, do you want that last beer?'

This time his remark was clearly directed toward Amber. She didn't respond to it any more than she had to his greeting.

'I want to know if you've seen Collin!' she hollered.

Stretching again, Erik took possession of the beer and enjoyed a leisurely swig. 'So much drama, dude. Always so much drama.'

Perhaps because she was still seated, Hope had no difficulty understanding Erik, but Amber – who was standing on the opposite side of the table from him – either didn't hear his words or didn't like the portion that she did catch.

'What did you say?' she snapped.

Erik took another swig of the beer. 'When I last saw Collin, he was over there.'

They all turned in the direction that he indicated.

'Where over there?' Amber demanded. 'Be more specific.'

'Straight ahead,' Erik told her. 'Past those two big tables, standing with some other guy by the bar.'

Hope and Megan exchanged a glance. If Erik had seen Collin – together with Nelson – in the same place that they had, did that mean he had merely been pretending to be asleep? How much of their conversation had Erik listened to?

'What other guy?' Amber asked. 'Do you mean Lucas?'

Erik shook his head. 'No, not Lucas.'

'So where did Collin and the guy go?' she pressed him.

He shook his head again. 'I don't know.'

Amber's nostrils flared. 'Where did Collin go!'

'Dude, I *don't* know.'

Although slight, it was the first time that Erik's voice had betrayed any hint of annoyance. No matter how down-to-earth he was and how deep or sincere his feelings for Amber might be, apparently even his patience for her drama had its limits.

Amber scowled and folded her arms across her chest. 'Well, somebody must know. Collin couldn't have magically disappeared. He has to be somewhere!'

From out of the corner of his eye, Erik looked at Hope and Megan. It was so subtle that Amber didn't appear to notice, but Hope did, and she knew what it meant. Erik wasn't being entirely honest with Amber. Although he didn't know exactly where Collin had gone, he had an inkling on the subject, either because he'd had a better view than Hope and Megan of Collin and Nelson's subsequent movements, or because he had heard Hope and Megan discuss the office downstairs. But Erik seemed to have no intention of sharing that inkling with Amber, most likely for the very simple reason that if she wasn't with Collin, then Erik could spend time with her instead.

'You're absolutely right, Amber,' Hope said.

The group turned to her in collective surprise.

'Collin has to be somewhere,' she continued, 'and Megan and I will go find him.'

'I'm going with you,' Amber replied.

There was no mistaking the disappointment in Erik's drooping expression. Clearly Hope's guess had been correct: Erik wanted to spend time with Amber, minus Collin. For her part, Hope didn't care who Amber spent time with, as long as it wasn't her and Megan. They didn't have the slightest chance of learning anything about Collin's business dealings with Nelson, Daniel, and the Green Goat if Amber was tagging along. Amber wouldn't passively eavesdrop on a conversation to gather information; she would burst into the office and demand to know why Collin hadn't given her a detailed itinerary of his movements.

Megan must have come to a similar conclusion, because she attempted to dissuade Amber from joining them by using a modified version of Hope's earlier argument against the eavesdropping scheme. 'But you two *must* remain here,' she told Erik and Amber jointly. 'Otherwise, we'll lose our wonderful table and chairs – and who wants to be left in this melee without a seat?'

Erik was quick on the uptake, and his expression brightened. 'Dude, that's so true.' He turned to Amber. 'They'll go, while we stay.'

Amber ignored him. She looked at Megan dubiously. 'You're friends with Summer, right? Then you're on her side, and you want to find her and Collin before I do so that I don't see them together and kill them as promised.'

Megan rolled her eyes. 'That is ridiculously dramatic – and it's also rubbish. I can assure you that Summer and Collin aren't together, because Summer isn't interested in being with your boyfriend. She has her own boyfriend.'

'You met Summer's boyfriend this afternoon,' Hope added. 'He's the police detective who helped you in the camper van after you cut your head during the fight with Collin.'

'Collin and I weren't fighting!' Amber disputed. 'What happened in the van was an accident; Collin told the detective that.'

It took Hope some effort not to roll her own eyes at the claim that the tableware in the camper van had *accidentally* taken flight, but at the same time, she realized that there was no purpose in arguing the matter further. How Collin and Amber chose to work out their relationship problems wasn't really any of her concern. Neither one had wanted to file a complaint against the other with the police, and after Amber had cleaned the blood from her face, the wound on her temple was almost invisible in the Green Goat's dim lighting.

'Well, now that we've agreed on everything,' Megan announced in a brisk, cheerful tone, even though they hadn't in actuality agreed on anything, 'Hope and I will set off on our search. It shouldn't take us too long, so stay here and guard our places until we return.'

'We'll guard them,' Erik responded with equal cheerfulness, no doubt because he could at last be alone with Amber. Turning toward her, he patted the seat next to him. 'Dude, sit down. Relax.'

Megan was so quick in grabbing hold of Hope's arm and pulling her away from the chairs that she didn't see whether Amber accepted the proffered seat. Hope couldn't help thinking, however, that Erik might have a bit more success with Amber if he stopped referring to her – and everyone else, for that matter – as *dude*. It sounded as though Amber yelled something after them, but in less than two steps, they were enveloped by the crowd, and Amber and her bellows were left behind.

'Head toward the bar, and then turn right. Go all the way to the end.' Megan mouthed the directions rather than shouting them. 'If we get separated, wait at the mirrored door.'

'Mirrored door,' Hope echoed in confirmation.

They were separated almost instantly. It was nearly impossible not to get separated as the mass of people pitched first in one direction, and then a moment later, without warning, lurched in the opposite direction. Hope was grateful that with her hurried departure, her martini had remained on the table. It was difficult enough to stay on her feet and not get jostled too severely without at the same time attempting to hold a cocktail glass and keep it from spilling, most likely on herself.

Hope moved as best as she could toward the bar, albeit slowly. She had more success slipping between little gaps in the mob at an angle rather than pushing straight ahead. As instructed, at the bar she turned to the right. Once or twice, she thought that she heard her name being called, but when she stopped and raised herself up on her toes to look around, she saw neither Megan nor anyone else that she knew. The faces that she passed were all unrecognizable to her. They were blurry and indistinct, as were the fragments of conversation that she caught. Oddly enough, it seemed easier to hear a whisper than a scream in the clamor, perhaps because her ears were ringing so hard. She had been surrounded by too much noise and too many people for too long, and not for the first time that day, Hope wished that she were in Charleston at the beach that weekend instead of in Asheville at the Green Goat.

Megan had told her to go all the way to the end, but Hope couldn't see an end. There was simply an interminable throng that felt as though it was continually tightening around her. With considerable effort and an uncomfortable amount of squeezing, she wriggled through a particularly dense portion of the swarm, and when she popped out the other side, she found a wall in front of her. She didn't know if it was the correct end, but at least it was an end of some sort. It also explained why the crowd kept compressing: blocked by the wall, there was no place left for it to go.

In adherence to the black-and-white motif of the bar, the wall was painted coal black with decorative white splashes added in intermittent intervals. Hope tried again to raise herself up on her toes to look around, but there wasn't sufficient space to maneuver. It was a good thing that Erik wasn't there with her. If the comparatively roomy table and chairs had been bordering on claustrophobic for him, then he would have had serious problems squashed against the wall. Not able to look from above, Hope bent down as far as she could manage to see what was visible from below. To the right, the black wall appeared to continue uninterrupted. To the left, after a few feet, the black began to glitter.

Straightening back up, Hope immediately started to edge along the wall toward the glitter, figuring that it could be light reflecting off a mirror and she was supposed to wait for Megan at a mirrored door. As she drew nearer, the glitter brightened, and when her leading hand moved from the roughly textured wall to cool, smooth glass, Hope exhaled with relief. It was indeed a mirror – or, more accurately now that she was standing directly before it, a dozen or so mirrors pieced together. They created a shimmering geometric effect that was both visually attractive and lightened an otherwise murky back corner. The mirrors also served a more functional purpose: they disguised a door.

The door wasn't truly hidden, but it also wasn't detectible enough that anyone who didn't already know about its existence would easily discover it. The reason behind the concealment wasn't difficult to comprehend. An obvious door would have been used by half of the Green Goat's customers, whether in search of a fresh beverage, a water closet, an exit, or simply out of curiosity. That was especially true now with such a large, compacted crowd, some of whom were no doubt as eager to get away from the tumult as Hope.

There was no sign of Megan. Hope was reasonably certain that she was at the correct location. She found it hard to imagine that there could be another mirrored door. She also found it hard to imagine that Megan hadn't reached the door before her, considering that Megan had known where it was from the beginning, while she had needed to search for it. So where was Megan now? In all likelihood on the other side of the door, waiting in the peace and quiet, which was where Hope planned on being in a short minute.

As inconspicuously as possible, she ran her fingers along the edge of the mirrors until she found the recessed handle of the door. Hope glanced once around to check if somebody happened to be looking in her direction. Happily, no one seemed to have taken any notice of her or the door. She took a preparatory breath, and then in one swift movement, she turned the handle, opened the door the narrowest of gaps, and slipped through it.

The door creaked as it shut behind her. The sound surprised Hope, mostly because she was surprised to be able to hear it. She had become so accustomed to the overwhelming din that the abrupt stillness by which it had been replaced was almost startling. All that remained of the racket that she had left behind was a muffled murmur on the other side of the door – and some residual ringing in her ears.

Her eyes didn't need nearly as long to adjust as her ears, because the lighting was only slightly brighter than it had been in the bar. There was a dull yellow glow on the wall beside her and also along a short corridor in front of her. She could see the outline of more lights above, but she didn't see a switch to turn them on, and even if she had, she probably wouldn't have used it. She felt out of place somehow, almost as though she were trespassing. There had been no lock on the door, and there was no sign specifically designating it as a private or restricted area, and yet, Hope had the impression that she shouldn't be there.

'Hello?' she whispered. 'Megan?'

There was no answer.

Hope took a few tentative steps down the corridor. 'Megan, are you here?'

Again, no response. Where could Megan have gone? She was usually so reliable. Why hadn't she waited at the mirrored door – on either side – as they had agreed?

After a few more steps down the corridor, Hope came to a room without any door at all. It was filled from floor to ceiling with mops, buckets, brooms, leaning towers of paper towels, and rows upon rows of rusty metal shelving crammed with giant plastic jugs and tubs. This was clearly the supply room that Megan had mentioned earlier.

'Megan?' Hope whispered once more.

This time, she didn't expect a reply. It seemed unlikely that Megan would be loitering with the Green Goat's jugs of sanitizing bleach and oversized tubs of dishwashing soap. But the supply room reminded Hope of another room that Megan had mentioned: the wine cellar. Megan had talked about grabbing a bottle or two of something nice to take along after their proposed visit to the office. Maybe she was in the wine cellar now, collecting part of the case that she had on account.

Shortly after the supply room, the corridor ended with a long, steel staircase. Hope peered down it. There was a shadowy grayness at its base, illuminated by the same dull yellow glow as the corridor in which she was standing. Part of her doubted that Megan – or anyone else, for that matter – was below, otherwise they would have turned on more lights. Or perhaps they didn't need more lights, because they were familiar enough with the path to the office and the wine cellar and whatever else was located on the lower level.

Hope hesitated, debating whether to try the staircase or go back through the corridor and the mirrored door. She wasn't eager to return to the bar. Even though she still felt as though she was trespassing, at least here she was away from the crowd and the noise. Megan had certainly been correct about this area being far quieter. If anyone had been carrying on a conversation, eavesdropping would have been easy.

With lingering trepidation, Hope started down the steps. She no longer had much expectation of finding Megan. Now she was more interested in finding a way out of the place. The front entrance to the Green Goat was on the main square. She figured that there must also be a back entrance – and thereby exit – albeit not for public use and mostly likely on the alley. Deliveries for the business had to occur somewhere, as did trash collection. And there was a good chance that Daniel and Nelson were entering privately, as well, heading directly to their office rather than marching through the restaurant and bar each time.

The staircase was sturdy, and the individual steps weren't overly narrow or slippery, so Hope was able to descend without difficulty, even in the limited light. At one point – about halfway down – there was a loud creak, and she halted. She couldn't tell whether the sound had come from the metal steps beneath her own feet or the mirrored door to the bar opening and closing above her. She waited for a moment, and when there was no subsequent noise, she continued swiftly to the bottom.

The corridor that stretched out from the base of the stairway was longer – and darker – than the upper corridor from which she had come. Hope squinted into the gloom. There appeared to be three rooms on the right, all with their doors tightly closed. She assumed that one was the office, or possibly Daniel and Nelson each had their own office. On the left, there was a single room without any door at all, similar to the supply room above, although from the distance and her angle, Hope couldn't see any supplies.

There was another creak. It definitely wasn't her feet this time. But she didn't know if it was someone else's feet on the stairs or the mirrored door opening and closing once more. Could she have been mistaken about Megan? Maybe Megan had been slower to reach the mirrored door, after all, and she had waited there as they had agreed, only to depart after Hope didn't appear. Hope listened carefully. There was no voice calling her name – nor were there any additional creaks.

Without further delay, she hurried along the corridor. She was growing increasingly uncomfortable. It might have been no more than the weak light or the uncertain nature of the creaks, but she was beginning to feel that she wasn't alone. She glanced at the closed doors on the right as she passed them. None were marked, which Hope found somewhat odd. But perhaps there were so few visitors to the office that signs weren't necessary.

When she reached the room on the left without the door, Hope stopped to look inside. It wasn't another supply room; it was the wine cellar. There were stacked cases of wine, colossal wine refrigerators with blinking temperature controls, gleaming wine racks filled to capacity, and an entire wall of locked wooden wine cabinets with wire fronts to display the especially rare and expensive bottles, of which there were too many to count. The Green Goat apparently did a brisk business in wine. Their business in beer and spirits must also have been good, because another wall was lined with varying sizes of kegs and more stacked cases ranging from rum to vodka. Either one of the kegs or the cases was leaking, because Hope saw the shimmer of liquid on the concrete floor in the far corner.

There was no indication that Megan had been there recently selecting any bottles, and Hope was about to proceed further down the corridor when she suddenly caught the sound of footsteps behind her. Instinctively, she darted into the cellar. She paused next to one of the locked cabinets, wondering if her ears might have deceived her. They hadn't. The footsteps continued. Although it was impossible to tell exactly who they belonged to, Hope was reasonably sure that they weren't Megan's. Hope's own footsteps had been nearly inaudible in the corridor, and Megan was similar in both height and weight, so her footsteps wouldn't have been much different. These steps were distinctly heavier, almost certainly belonging to a man.

The footsteps came closer, confirming that they were headed toward her rather than away from her. Hope hurriedly debated her options. Should she grab the nearest bottle as a prop and come out smiling and confident, as though she belonged there?

If the person were Daniel, she could tell him that Megan had sent her. If the person were Nelson, it would be more difficult, because she hadn't previously met him. In either case, it would be an awkward situation, and it would probably cause Megan problems, too. Hope decided that the best solution was to remain silent and out of sight until the person passed by. In all likelihood, they were going to the office or exiting the building. If she just waited patiently for a few minutes, she could probably exit herself without ever being detected.

Hope moved closer to the wine cabinet, tucking herself next to it and the concrete wall. Although she had to turn her back to the corridor – which prohibited her from being able to look out – she was almost completely concealed in the shadows. Unless the person was specifically coming to the cellar, they wouldn't be able to spot her. And even if they did enter to take a case of dry gin or Riesling back to the bar, they still might not notice her. She simply had to keep still and hope for the best.

As the footsteps neared the cellar, Hope pressed herself even more tightly into the shadows. Would the person continue down the corridor, or stop? She waited and listened. The footsteps slowed. When they paused, Hope winced in apprehension. After a moment, there were two or three steps, then they paused again. Was the person looking into the cellar? They couldn't possibly see her, could they? Hope held her breath and stood perfectly motionless. She couldn't tell whether the person moved. They were quiet, too.

For a long minute, there was no sound. Hope almost began to relax. Was the person gone? Although she hadn't heard them walk away or take anything from the cellar, they surely must have left by now. There was no reason for them to be lingering in silence.

An instant later, she felt two strong hands on her shoulders, spinning her around.

NINE

As the hands spun Hope around, they pulled her from her hiding place in the shadows of the wine cellar. It happened with such speed and so unexpectedly that she couldn't immediately react. Arms were encircling her, and her chin was being lifted. For a split second, she had the instinctive urge to struggle and wrench herself free. Then a pair of lips touched hers, and all resistance failed her.

She knew the lips. She had felt them before. They were warm and confident, and tonight, they had the fiery taste of whiskey. Hope met them with equal warmth. The kisses intensified in response, and she melted into them.

'Dylan.' She sighed as his lips began to work their way slowly down her neck. 'I'm so glad that it's you.'

He chuckled. 'I'm glad that it's you, too, Hope.'

Abruptly the kisses stopped, and this time when Dylan spoke, there was no laughter in his voice.

'You thought I might be someone else?' he said.

'No one else,' she murmured, pressing against him, eager for his mouth to return to her neck.

Dylan's mouth did not oblige.

'You were expecting a different person?' he asked stiffly.

There was a slight hesitation on Hope's part, which Dylan clearly did not interpret in her favor. His arms released her.

'Who?' he questioned.

'Dylan . . .' Hope leaned toward him. It was partly because she wanted him to take her in his arms again, and partly because she needed his body for support. His unanticipated appearance in the cellar and the electric effect of his touch on her skin had left her somewhat unsteady on her feet.

Dylan took a step away from her. 'I'm not Nate, who's willing to fall for Summer's teasing little caresses and manipulative smiles after she's deliberately done something that she knows he won't like.'

The harshness of his tone – combined with the undue criticism of her sister – instantly cooled Hope's feelings toward him.

'So don't imagine,' Dylan continued sharply, 'that you can blink those emerald cat's eyes of yours at me, and I'll be wondrously brought to my knees. They may have that power over certain other men, but they don't with me.'

It took Hope a moment to realize that he was paraphrasing Lucas's description of her from earlier that day outside the boutique – except in Lucas's case, it had been meant as a compliment.

'I suppose that he's the one you were waiting for?' With a grim expression, Dylan took another step away from her. 'You arranged to meet him down here, and I unfortunately got in your way?'

Hope looked at him with a mixture of confusion and irritation. She didn't know what he was talking about, or how he could switch from kissing her with such ardor one minute to glaring at her with such vehemence the next minute.

'Well, I'll get out of your way now,' Dylan said, 'and then the two of you will have this place all to yourselves to reminisce and rekindle and' – he gave a derisive snort – 'confer over Sasquatch and vampires.'

Finally, Hope understood. 'Oh, you think I was expecting Lucas.'

'Weren't you?' Dylan snapped.

'As a matter of fact, I wasn't,' she snapped back at him. 'I didn't arrange to meet Lucas – or anyone else – down here.'

Dylan didn't appear to believe her, which only annoyed Hope more.

'Not that it's any of your business,' she informed him tetchily, 'but I was looking for Megan. We got separated upstairs in the bar.'

'If you were looking for Megan,' Dylan rejoined, apparently still unconvinced, 'then why were you hiding?'

'Because I heard footsteps, and I didn't know who they belonged to. I was worried that it might be Daniel or Nelson, and I didn't want to cause problems for Megan if they consider this to be a restricted area of sorts and she wasn't supposed to tell me about it.'

There was a brief pause.

'Who is Nelson?' Dylan asked.

'He's the co-owner of the Green Goat and Daniel's business partner.'

There was another pause, and it was Hope's turn for a question.

'Speaking of restricted areas,' she said, 'what are *you* doing down here?'

'I followed you,' Dylan answered. 'Those were my footsteps that you heard.'

Hope frowned at him. 'You could have announced your presence. You didn't have to skulk around in the dark, frightening me half to death.'

He raised an amused eyebrow. 'You didn't seem frightened when you realized that it was me. On the contrary, you seemed quite . . . enthusiastic.'

She felt her cheeks flush. Thankfully, the light in the cellar was too weak for Dylan to see the rosy hue – or at least, he couldn't see it to its full degree.

'And while we're on the subject of skulking around in the dark' – he reversed directions and now took a step toward her – 'I can think of a few other things that you and I can do in the dark.'

His meaning was obvious, and Hope's cheeks flushed even more. In an attempt to conceal it, her response was dry.

'I can think of something, too,' she said. 'I can leave, as I was planning on doing before you arrived.'

Dylan took another step toward her, and his voice softened. 'Don't be mad at me, Hope. You don't really want to leave, do you?'

He was near enough to her again that her unsteadiness returned. But rather than lean against him for support, she leaned against the wall beside her.

'You want to stay here.' Dylan's voice softened further. 'You want to stay with me.'

Counter to her better judgment, Hope met his gaze. In the shadows of the cellar, his eyes were a deep midnight blue. They drew her closer to him.

'Be with me, Hope.' Dylan reached out his hand and ran a long, caressing finger down her cheek.

Her breath caught in her throat. She was tempted – sorely tempted – to fall into his arms and stay there for as long as she could.

Dylan's lips curled with a smile. It was a knowing smile. He knew the effect that he had on her – and, truth be told, on most women he encountered. He was well aware of how difficult it was to resist his charms. And that was where the problem lay for Hope. Dylan's charms ran so hot and cold. First he kissed her rapturously, then he turned frosty and aloof when he thought that she had planned a romantic rendezvous with Lucas, and when he realized that he had been in error about the rendezvous, Dylan became sweet and seductive once more. Only a few minutes earlier, he had criticized Summer for utilizing the exact same techniques with Nate that he was employing himself.

In response, Hope gave a slightly bitter laugh. 'Now who's using teasing little caresses and manipulative smiles?'

If she had expected her remark to anger him, and thereby chill his further advances, she had calculated wrongly. Dylan's smile grew, and his hand traveled slowly across her cheek into her hair.

'I'm not teasing in the least,' he replied, his magnetic gaze holding hers, 'and I promise you that none of my caresses will be little.'

His fingers stroked the back of her neck. Hope's pulse raced, and her limbs weakened until it took nearly all of her effort to remain standing.

'Hope' – Dylan purred her name – 'don't tease me in turn . . .'

Almost involuntarily, she was drifting toward him when an unexpected voice broke in and burst the spell.

'There you are, Hope! I thought for certain that I had lost you. What a chaos it was upstairs by the door! I couldn't see where you had gone, or whether you had . . .'

As the sentence trailed away unfinished, both Hope and Dylan turned toward the entrance to the wine cellar. Megan was standing at the edge of the corridor, with Daniel Drexler close by her side. Megan's astute eye didn't have any difficulty comprehending what she had walked in on.

'My apologies,' she said, with a distinct hint of laughter in her tone. 'I appear to have interrupted . . . something.'

'You have indeed,' Dylan confirmed.

There was a hint of laughter in his tone, too. But when Hope looked at him, he wasn't smiling. She couldn't tell whether he was in fact amused, or instead displeased, or wholly unaffected by the sudden arrival of Megan and Daniel. Dylan's expression was impossible to read. For her part, Hope wasn't sure if she was more regretful or relieved at the pair's timing.

Megan's pert nose twitched, and she murmured in Hope's direction, 'An amorous assignation in the wine cellar?'

Hope shot her a sharp look, and Megan promptly switched the subject.

'My prediction was correct, wasn't it, Hope? I said that Dylan would appear in the Green Goat before too long.' She turned to him. 'Nate called you, told you about Collin making a move on Summer, and asked you to come here and check on her for him?'

'He did,' Dylan replied.

Megan's pert nose twitched again, and she gave Hope a sideways glance. 'I believe that there was also a second part to my prediction . . .'

Hope's sharp look repeated itself. The second part to Megan's prediction had been that Dylan would use the request from Nate as an opportunity to check on Hope, which he had obviously done.

This time Megan only slightly switched the subject. 'I don't know how you managed to find Hope, Dylan. As I said before, I was certain that I had lost her. There are simply too many people jumbled together upstairs.'

'There are a lot of people,' Dylan agreed, 'but for me, Hope is impossible to miss, regardless of whether she's surrounded by a crowd or secreted in a cellar.'

Megan grinned at him, then she grinned at Hope. Hope pretended not to have heard the remark.

'And Summer?' Megan asked him. 'You didn't by any chance happen to find her, as well?'

Dylan nodded. 'Briefly.'

'You did?' Hope looked at him with interest, eager to both have news of Summer and steer the conversation further away from herself. 'When was this – and where?'

'I saw her when I first arrived, in the alley at the back.'

'In the alley at the back?' Hope echoed in surprise.

He nodded again. 'She was on the phone, attempting to reach your grandmother. Apparently the signal was too weak inside, and Summer was walking around the building in search of a better connection.'

It was Megan's turn to nod. 'I can almost never get a signal in this place, so I don't even bother trying to use my phone here anymore.'

'I've been told that the girders are the problem,' Daniel said.

Collectively, they turned toward him. It was the first time that he had spoken since his arrival with Megan. Daniel Drexler was in his early forties, with a tall forehead, a heavily pointed chin, and a sharply straight nose, all of which gave him a rather austere appearance. But according to Megan, Daniel wasn't austere in the least. He was popular with the Green Goat's employees, forbearing with difficult customers, and generous in his gifts to her, sending beautiful bouquets of flowers and numerous thoughtful trinkets. Megan's only complaint was that Daniel could on occasion be too splashy on their dates, as though he was gratuitously trying to show off. In Hope's limited experience with Daniel, however, he was far too reserved to be considered ostentatious.

'The steel in the girders interferes with the cell signals,' Daniel explained.

They waited for him to continue, but he didn't.

'So Summer was in the alley, attempting to reach Gram?' Hope prompted Dylan after a moment. 'Do you know whether she—' She stopped herself, suddenly remembering that Dylan had been the one to drive her grandmother and Morris to the airport. 'Did Gram and Morris make their flight to Charleston?'

'They did,' he told her. 'The traffic ended up being lighter than expected; we succeeded in having their absurd amount of luggage valeted; and then Olivia and my dad somehow managed to wriggle through security in record speed.' Dylan added with a little chuckle, 'Whatever magical hocus-pocus you and your sister used to make things go their way, it evidently worked.'

Hope did not chuckle with him.

'And after the alley?' Megan asked Dylan. 'Where did Summer go?'

'I have no idea,' he answered. 'I came through the alley from Amethyst. There are never any parking spaces available around the square, so whenever I have to go to this area, I automatically park at the hotel and walk the couple of blocks.'

'I park at Amethyst, too,' Daniel said. 'So does Nelson. There is no other option. In my opinion, it's one of the reasons that our business has been declining. The lack of nearby parking discourages people, especially with regard to dining in the restaurant.'

'But business is terrific tonight,' Megan countered encouragingly.

Daniel didn't appear encouraged. 'One night of good receipts doesn't compensate for many weeks of poor receipts.'

There was a short pause, and then Megan said, 'Maybe a new investor would improve the situation?'

Hope was impressed with how casually Megan had inserted the remark, as though it was nothing more than a general, helpful musing, when in truth, she was cleverly inquiring whether Daniel knew that Nelson and Collin had been talking together by the bar and whether Collin was in fact being added as an investor or business partner in the Green Goat.

'A new investor might be the solution,' Daniel mused in return, 'or perhaps not.'

Hope and Megan exchanged a glance. His reply was so vague and noncommittal that it gave them no information at all.

Megan tried again. 'Have you spoken to Nelson about it? Has he expressed an opinion on a possible new investor?'

'Nelson?' Daniel echoed absently, even though he had mentioned Nelson himself only a minute earlier. 'He's been here this evening.'

This time Hope and Megan exchanged a frown. That response from Daniel was even less useful than the previous one. They already knew that Nelson had been there that evening; they had seen him speaking with Collin.

Megan made one last attempt. 'Is Nelson in the office? If so, I'd like to stop by and say hello.'

The question didn't come across quite as nonchalantly as its predecessors. There was a slightly meddlesome edge to it.

Daniel frowned now, too. 'He might be there. We can check on our way out if that's what you want to do.'

He spoke with such flatness that Hope couldn't tell if he was uninterested in seeing Nelson, or annoyed with Megan's string of inquiries, or simply fatigued from a long day with too many problems on his plate.

Megan didn't seem sure how to interpret his words, either. With some hesitation, she put her arm through Daniel's and said lightly, 'Perhaps it's time for us to leave?'

Daniel neither leaned into nor away from her. He also didn't immediately reply. As before, he appeared preoccupied.

'Time for all of us to leave,' Dylan said decisively after a moment.

Hope gave him a grateful look. At the outset, the stillness and seclusion of the Green Goat's lower level had been a welcome relief from the overwhelming noise and throng upstairs in the bar. But over time, the atmosphere had changed somehow, becoming increasingly uncomfortable and disquieting. The dim lighting and the dampness in the wine cellar were beginning to feel almost oppressive.

Dylan started to walk toward the corridor. 'When we get outside, we'll check the alley and circle once around the building to find Summer.'

Although he couldn't see it, because Hope was following behind him, her grateful look repeated itself. 'Summer doesn't do well in crowds, especially for long periods. When she left our group in the bar, it was to get a little air and elbow room. But the place only got busier afterward, so I can't imagine that she ever came back inside.'

'Probably not,' Megan agreed. 'And even if she did, Summer certainly wouldn't stay long at the table with Erik and Amber as company. Considering Amber's extreme jealousy, it would probably take her less than a minute before she started accusing Summer of stealing Collin from her and threatening to kill them both again.'

'What!' Dylan halted abruptly. 'Who was threatening to kill Summer? Has Nate been told about this?'

'It wasn't a real threat,' Hope explained to him. 'It was overwrought histrionics. Nate doesn't know about it, but he does know about Amber. Do you remember the honking and yelling in the camper van by the boutique this afternoon? That was Amber – arguing at full volume with Collin.'

'For such a small person,' Megan said, 'Amber is extraordinarily loud. Erik is right about how dramatic she is.' She added with a chortle, 'Wouldn't it be funny if when we found Summer, she was actually with Collin?'

Hope looked at her in surprise.

'Not that Summer would be with Collin in a romantic way,' Megan quickly clarified. 'I meant that they might be sitting together on a bench in the square: Summer exchanging messages with Olivia, and Collin debating whether to become' – she watched Daniel's face – 'an investor in the Green Goat.'

There was no visible change in Daniel's expression. It wasn't clear if he had even heard the remark. His thoughts were obviously elsewhere, probably – Hope surmised – on some combination of business concerns relating to the receipts from that evening, the unresolved parking difficulties, and whether the Halloween party tomorrow evening would improve the receipts further.

When she reached the corridor, Hope paused and turned toward Daniel. Although she wasn't eager to burden him more, she felt obligated to mention the problem that she had observed earlier.

'I hate to add to your list of worries,' she said to him, 'and hopefully it isn't really a worry at all, but I noticed some leakage in the corner of the wine cellar.'

'Leakage?' Daniel's gaze snapped in her direction. 'Leakage!'

'Leakage,' Hope confirmed somewhat reluctantly, startled by the force of his reaction. Daniel had been distant and distracted for nearly the entire time that he and Megan had been standing in the corridor, but suddenly he was giving Hope his full attention.

'What sort of leakage?' he demanded.

'Well, I'm not certain,' she answered, 'but it looked to me like a keg or a case might be leaking.'

'The kegs don't leak unless someone has tampered with them,' Daniel rejoined sharply. 'And the cases don't leak unless someone has either carelessly or intentionally broken one of the bottles.'

Hope was taken aback. There was an unmistakable accusation in his tone as though *she* was responsible for the leakage.

Megan appeared equally astonished. 'It isn't Hope's fault if a bottle has cracked, or a keg has malfunctioned, or—'

Daniel unceremoniously cut her off. 'No? Who else's fault is it then? If she was the one who noticed it, then the odds are that she was the one who caused it.'

'What an absolutely absurd thing to say!' Megan pulled her arm away from his and glared at him. 'And how would I know who else's fault it might be? I've been with you down here, and before that, I was with Hope upstairs. I haven't been monitoring the condition of your stupid cases and kegs in the wine cellar.'

'Stupid?' Daniel retorted. 'You didn't think the cases and kegs were stupid when I offered to give you a . . .'

Hope didn't hear the conclusion of the sentence, because Dylan moved next to her and said in an undertone, 'Are you grievously offended by his allegations? Should I jump in to defend your honor?'

She gave a little laugh. 'While I appreciate the gallant offer, I assure you that my dignity is unharmed.' After considering for a moment, she added more earnestly, 'It's a bit of an overreaction from Daniel, isn't it? We should probably feel sorry for him. Megan told me earlier that he's been working terribly hard to keep this place afloat. I guess hearing about a leak was one problem too many for him to handle at this time of night.'

Dylan nodded. 'That was my impression, too. With any luck, it will end up being a problem that's quick and easy to fix. Where did you say the leak was?'

'In the far corner.' Hope pointed toward the spot. 'You can't see it very well from this angle.'

'We'd better take a closer look.'

Dylan turned and headed into the cellar once more. Hope walked with him. Megan and Daniel remained squabbling in the corridor.

'Could you have been mistaken about the leak?' Dylan asked her as they weaved their way around tall stacks of Cognac and Canadian rye.

Hope shook her head. 'I don't think so. It's pretty hard to mistake shimmering liquid on a concrete floor.'

'It might not be from a case or a keg at all,' he suggested. 'One of the refrigerators may be in need of repair. Or there could be a plumbing issue upstairs, and thanks to gravity, it's trickling down here.'

They approached the back of the cellar.

'This corner?' Dylan said.

'Yes. There's the shimmering liquid that I was talking about, and—'

Hope's words and feet stopped simultaneously as she stared at the floor before her. When she had first noticed the liquid, she'd been too far away and had too little time to do anything more than give it a cursory glance. But now that she was closer, she saw that both she and Dylan were wrong about the leakage. The problem wasn't quick and easy to fix, and it wasn't due to a malfunctioning keg, a cracked bottle, a broken refrigerator, or a plumbing issue upstairs. The shimmering liquid wasn't beer, or liquor, or water. It was blood.

TEN

The blood on the floor of the wine cellar bore no resemblance to the delicate, bright crimson spider's web that had been on Amber's cheek and temple when she had emerged from the camper van outside the boutique. This blood was heavy and patternless. It lay in a thick, dark pool that shimmered along the edges with a magenta sheen. Also unlike Amber's face, a dishcloth was insufficient to absorb the blood. There was far too much of it. It hadn't come from a small cut or another equally minor wound. This was from something more – something grievously worse.

Hope's dazed gaze traveled slowly across the length of the pool to its origin. In the narrow space between one of the locked wine cabinets and the side wall of the cellar lay the prone body of a man.

'Dylan,' she said, almost inaudibly, 'do you see . . .'

'Yes, I see him.'

With swift strides, Dylan moved past her, stepping agilely around the pool toward the man. Hope started to follow him.

'Stay back,' he warned her.

His voice didn't rise, but his tone was sufficiently stern that she halted. She watched as he bent down next to the man to check for signs of life and determine the extent of the injuries. When she heard Dylan give a low exhalation, Hope knew for certain what she had already fearfully supposed: there had been too much blood loss for the man to still be alive.

Dylan examined the man for a minute longer, then with another exhalation, he returned to his feet. 'I'll contact Nate. He needs to be informed as soon as possible. Megan mentioned an office earlier. Do you know whether it has a landline if I can't get a signal down here on my phone?'

Hope didn't answer. She barely heard his words. Her mind and eyes were frozen on the lifeless man in front of her. She had seen only the indistinct outline of his body before, and when

Dylan had leaned over him after they had moved nearer, her view had been blocked entirely. But now that Dylan had straightened back up, the man was lying unobstructed, and to her horror, Hope realized that she recognized him.

'I don't understand,' she whispered.

'There's a deep gash behind his right ear,' Dylan told her.

'But how can . . . I don't understand,' she said again.

'This obviously isn't the time or the place for a detailed medical exposition, but in plain terms, that sort of a head wound can bleed heavily,' Dylan explained.

Hope gave a slight shake of her own head. It wasn't the injury that she was struggling to comprehend and come to terms with; it was the identity of the person who had been injured – and was now dead.

Taking his phone from his pocket, Dylan began to check for a signal.

'I just saw him upstairs,' Hope murmured.

Dylan's gaze snapped toward her. 'You saw him upstairs?'

'We both saw him upstairs.'

'You both saw him? You and Megan?'

The squabbling between Megan and Daniel had apparently ended, because Megan caught the mention of her name by Dylan and promptly turned her attention to him and Hope.

'Is that the spot of the leakage?' she asked, walking toward them from the corridor. 'Have you been able to figure out the cause?'

Disregarding her, Dylan kept his focus on Hope. 'When you say that you saw him upstairs, does that mean you know who he is?'

Before Hope could respond, Megan was halfway across the wine cellar.

'I can see the leak – or at least, part of it,' she reported to Daniel, who had remained in the corridor. 'The good news is that it appears to be a puddle, not a lake.'

'A puddle of blood is not good news,' Dylan said tersely.

'A puddle of *what*?' Megan exclaimed.

She answered her own question a moment later as she reached Hope and followed the direction of her troubled gaze.

'Good God, that really is blood.' Megan gasped. 'And there's a man's body lying next to it! Is he . . . He isn't . . .'

'He's dead,' Dylan confirmed.

'Did you say a man is *dead*?' Daniel echoed in disbelief. He received no reply.

'How . . .' Megan stammered. 'Why . . .'

Her feet were even shakier than her words, and Megan began to sway. Worried that she might tumble over on to the concrete, Hope hurriedly took a step toward her and put a steadying hand on her arm.

Dylan must have had the same concern, because he also took an alert step toward Megan. 'Do you have a hold on her?' he asked Hope.

'Yes. She won't fall.'

'I won't fall,' Megan told them weakly. After a few seconds, her legs firmed, as did her voice. 'I won't fall,' she repeated with greater confidence.

Hope waited a few more seconds before withdrawing her hand to make certain that Megan was stable.

'I'm all right,' Megan assured both her and Dylan. 'It was the shock of the man's body being there on the floor.' She took a closer look at the man. 'I saw him only briefly and from a distance upstairs, but that's Collin, isn't it, Hope?'

She nodded. 'I'm afraid so. It was his salt-and-pepper hair that I recognized first, followed by the blue T-shirt.'

'There was a lot less blood on the T-shirt before, only the streak from the fight with Amber. Now it's sodden.'

Hope grimaced. Although Megan was correct about the change in the condition of the shirt, it was a morbid comparison.

'So he's Collin,' Dylan mused, gazing contemplatively at the deceased.

'But it doesn't make any sense,' Megan said. 'Collin was alive and well, walking and talking in the bar just a short while ago. How can he suddenly be dead?'

'That's what I've been struggling to understand, too,' Hope replied.

'Granted, Collin left the bar earlier than we did, so that at least explains how he got downstairs before us.'

'Except we don't know when exactly he left the bar,' Hope reminded her. 'We couldn't see him any longer, but we didn't see where he went, either. He was simply gone.'

'That's true. I had assumed that Collin headed to the office with Nelson, because it was quieter there and—' Megan broke off abruptly, her eyes stretching wide. 'Nelson! I forgot all about him. You don't think that he might also be . . .'

Although she left the sentence unfinished, Hope had no difficulty comprehending its conclusion: Nelson might also be lying in a pool of blood.

For a moment, Hope and Megan stared at each other in alarm, then they began to dash around the interior of the wine cellar, scanning the shadowy floor and checking in between cases and kegs.

'This corner is clear,' Hope called.

'Empty over here, too,' Megan reported.

'Nothing but electrical cords behind the refrigerators.'

'Nothing but dust bunnies behind the wine racks.'

They returned to their starting position next to Dylan and shared a sigh of relief.

'Well, that's a blessing, at least,' Hope said.

Megan nodded. 'One dead body is enough.'

Dylan – who hadn't joined in their search – raised an eyebrow. 'Were you expecting a second dead body?'

'Nelson,' Hope explained to him. 'When Megan and I last saw Collin by the bar, he was speaking with Nelson. So we thought – or feared – that the same thing which happened to Collin might also have happened to Nelson.'

The eyebrow remained elevated. 'If you last saw Collin with Nelson, then there's a good chance that Nelson is what happened to Collin.'

Hope was startled. 'That never occurred to me.'

'It never occurred to you that Collin's death wasn't accidental?' Dylan questioned.

There was a mixture of incredulity and something bordering on amusement in his tone, which instantly put Hope on the defensive.

'I didn't consider it one way or the other,' she answered curtly.

'I didn't consider it, either,' Megan said.

'And even if I had considered it,' Hope continued to Dylan, 'my natural instinct would not have been to automatically assume that somebody could have done something so terrible to another person.'

Dylan responded with a slight smile. 'For a woman who spends her days listening to the woes of Asheville's citizenry and then telling their fortunes based on those woes, you have a remarkably optimistic view of human behavior.'

Uncertain whether it was intended as a compliment, Hope didn't reply.

'Although I suppose we should have considered it,' Megan remarked reflectively after a moment. 'I mean, a man doesn't end up lying in a pool of his own blood by sheer happenstance, does he?'

'Not in my professional experience,' Dylan told her. 'Of course, there's always the argument of suicide—'

'Suicide?' Hope interjected. 'But didn't you say there was a deep gash behind his right ear?'

Dylan nodded in confirmation.

'Then how would it be suicide? Collin couldn't have reached around and cut the back of his own head.'

'Although technically not impossible, it's highly improbable,' Dylan agreed. 'Theoretically, a person can cause all sorts of injuries to himself, but based on the way that Collin has fallen, as well as the length and shape of the laceration, the chance of it being self-inflicted is extremely low.'

'Do you know what it was inflicted with?' Megan asked him.

'The lighting in here is poor, and I didn't want to move the body in any way that would interfere with the police's investigation, so I can only hazard an educated guess. The medical examiner will be able to make a definitive determination, but in my estimation, the most likely culprit is a box cutter.'

There was a pause.

'Such as that box cutter?' Hope said, pointing to the floor a few feet away from them. 'You can see the end of the plastic orange handle sticking out from underneath the last refrigerator in the row.'

Both Dylan and Megan moved toward the refrigerator for a better look.

'Again, the lighting is poor,' Dylan observed, bending over the box cutter and studying it, 'but from what I can discern, there appears to be blood on the handle as well as the blade.' He straightened back up and turned to Hope. 'Congratulations, I believe that you've located the murder weapon.'

Hope frowned. Although no doubt beneficial for the police's investigation, she wasn't sure that finding a murder weapon was something to be proud of. She also had an uncomfortable feeling that it might cause her trouble later on.

'You have a sharp eye,' Dylan commended her. 'When did you first notice the box cutter down there?'

'Only a minute or so ago, when I was checking that Nelson wasn't lying behind the refrigerators.'

'How well do you know Nelson?' he asked.

'I don't know him at all. I've never met him. I've only seen him once: this evening, upstairs by the bar, speaking with Collin. Megan was the one who identified him to me and—' Interrupting herself, she said to Megan, 'Be careful not to touch it. You don't want the police lab to find your fingerprints on it.'

Megan – who had knelt down next to the box cutter and was reaching to pull it clear of the refrigerator – quickly drew back her hand.

'As it is,' Hope added, 'when the police learn that we were the ones who discovered Collin's body, we'll be considered persons of interest. An errant set of fingerprints could easily move us to the list of suspects.'

Dylan gave a little chuckle. 'Perhaps I spoke too soon about your remarkably optimistic view of human behavior.'

Hope's frown resurfaced.

'Don't listen to him, Hope.' Megan rose to her feet. 'You're right that we should be cautious. Too much attention from law enforcement is never good.'

Dylan chuckled some more. 'You're starting to sound like a conspiracy theorist. They must be rubbing off on you.'

'I'm not a conspiracy theorist,' Megan rejoined, a touch haughtily, 'but if I were, I would much prefer to be a happily alive one than a dead pretender.'

'A dead pretender?' Dylan said, not understanding the reference.

Hope responded to Megan, 'We don't know whether Collin was a pretender or a true conspiracy theorist.'

'And it doesn't really matter now either way,' she concurred.

They gazed at Collin's lifeless body on the concrete and heaved a mournful sigh.

'Except,' Megan mused after a moment, 'maybe it does matter.'

'How so?' Hope asked in surprise.

'Well, maybe someone didn't like the fact that Collin was a conspiracy theorist, or maybe a true conspiracy theorist didn't like the fact that Collin was pretending to be one of them.'

Hope's surprise grew. 'And that would be enough for someone to want to kill him?'

Megan spread her hands ruefully. 'By their inherent nature, conspiracies evoke strong emotions. Maybe Collin trod too heavily on someone's toes, or maybe he made light of an issue that was too dear to someone's heart. With such intense feelings, that may have been more than sufficient to trigger a fierce reaction.'

'That's a lot of maybes,' Dylan said.

It was Megan's turn to frown at him. 'I don't hear you offering any brilliant alternative theories.'

'I didn't know Collin,' he replied, 'and I know very little about him, so I'm disinclined to vaguely speculate on the potential reasons behind his murder. And that's precisely what you're doing: vaguely speculating.'

Her frown deepened. 'Here's something that isn't speculation: now that Collin is dead, he can't be an investor or partner in the Green Goat.'

As soon as she had said it, Megan must have realized what her words meant in relation to Daniel, because she drew a sharp breath.

'Daniel would never hurt someone to stop them from being a new investor or business partner,' she clarified hastily.

When neither Hope nor Dylan responded, Megan grew increasingly defensive.

'Daniel was with me,' she contended, 'so he couldn't have had anything to do with what happened to Collin.'

Hope shifted uneasily.

Megan looked at her, aghast. 'You can't seriously believe that Daniel would kill Collin!'

'No, of course not,' Hope assured her. 'I was just thinking – and the police will no doubt think it, too – that there's a gap in time between when we saw Collin upstairs and when we found him down here. Daniel was with you for only a portion of that time.'

'But we never saw Daniel with Collin at any point,' Megan argued. 'Unlike Nelson.' She turned to Dylan. 'You're the one who said that if we last saw Collin with Nelson, then there's a good chance that Nelson is what happened to Collin.'

'A good chance, yes,' Dylan answered. 'But certainly not convincing evidence that Nelson, or, for that matter, Daniel—' He paused, his brow furrowing. 'Speaking of which, where is Daniel?'

'Where is he?' Megan echoed, as though it was an inane question. 'He's in the corridor, waiting for us.'

'No, he isn't,' Dylan said. 'At least not in any part of the corridor that's visible to me.'

'Then you should have your eyes examined. Of course he's there.' With an impatient cluck of her tongue, Megan turned toward the corridor.

Hope turned with her, likewise expecting to see Daniel standing at the edge of the wine cellar. But the edge of the wine cellar was empty, as was the corridor. Dylan was correct. Daniel Drexler had disappeared.

ELEVEN

'I'm dating a murderer.'

Megan spoke the words calmly, without any agitation or other indication of sentiment. She might as well have been announcing the daily weather forecast.

Hope shook her head. 'That's quite a leap, isn't it?'

'No, I don't think so,' she replied. 'Daniel was in the corridor with me; you and Dylan discovered Collin's body on the floor in here; I came in here, too, and we talked about the death, and Nelson, and the box cutter. During all that time, Daniel didn't join us. He didn't race – or even stroll – over to look at Collin. He didn't participate in our search for Nelson. He didn't make any comment on whether the box cutter was regularly used in the wine cellar or whose fingerprints might ordinarily be found on it. Instead, Daniel left – or, more accurately, he hightailed it. Why would he run off without giving us any notice or explanation if he didn't have something to hide? Conclusion: I'm dating a murderer.'

Although Megan was dispassionate by nature, and she had never been prone to undue hysterics or dramatic flourishes, Hope was still somewhat surprised by the degree of her placidity under the circumstances.

'It makes an interesting addition to the list,' Megan said.

'There's a list?' Dylan inquired.

Hope looked at him. His expression was as phlegmatic as Megan's. If Dylan was in any way concerned about Daniel's disappearance, he didn't show it.

'Of course there's a list,' Megan responded. 'I'm over thirty and have never been married or engaged for any substantial period, so by this point, my list of past relationships is no longer short. It may also be a little more extensive than some others.'

'A little more extensive?' Hope chortled. 'Your list is a veritable encyclopedia compared to the rest of us.'

Megan grinned. 'I've dated a varied cast of characters over the years.'

'Varied, indeed. There are few people who can claim to have dated a trapeze artist, a coal miner, *and* an alligator wrestler.'

Dylan was dubious. 'An alligator wrestler?'

'It's true,' Hope told him. 'Megan dated a professional alligator wrestler from the Gulf Coast of Alabama. He was a strapping fellow.'

'The relationship didn't last long, though,' Megan confessed.

'Should I ask why not?' Dylan said.

'Because I was always rooting for the alligators to win.'

Dylan burst out laughing.

'They're fascinating reptiles,' Megan continued. 'Do you know that they can survive for months without—'

She was interrupted by a reproving cough.

'Is this really an appropriate time for jokes and anecdotes?'

Startled, they collectively turned toward the unexpected voice, which came from a short distance behind them in the wine cellar.

'Daniel!' Megan exclaimed.

In addition to the obvious surprise, Hope also noted a hint of anxiety in Megan's tone. She understood why, because she shared the concern: how long had Daniel been in the wine cellar with them, and how much of their conversation – particularly the portion relating to him potentially being a murderer – had he overheard?

Either Daniel hadn't heard much, or he chose to ignore whatever snippets he had caught, because he didn't express any anger at Megan's accusation or march out of the cellar in outrage. On the contrary, he came over to the group and stood by Megan's side.

'I don't mean to sound harsh,' he said apologetically, 'but given the situation, humorous stories can come across as unseemly.'

Megan hesitated for a moment, as though debating with herself whether or not to continue dating a possible murderer. She decided either in the affirmative, or – more likely – that she had misinterpreted Daniel's temporary disappearance, because she moved closer to him and replied, 'You're right. My only excuse is stress and fatigue.'

Daniel wrapped a supportive arm around her shoulders. 'Of course you're tired.' He gave a nod in greeting to Hope and Dylan. 'You must all be tired.'

Dylan returned the nod, slightly. He also took a slight step backward.

Hope wondered about his cool response. Dylan was usually much less reserved than Daniel. Did his reaction mean that he didn't think Megan had misinterpreted Daniel's disappearance?

'Where did you go?' Megan asked Daniel. 'One minute you were in the corridor, and the next minute you had vanished.'

'I went to the office and called the police.'

Megan blinked at him. 'You called the police?'

'Yes. Dylan said that a man was dead. It took me a moment to process the words, and then I realized that I had better report the matter to the proper authorities.' A crease formed in Daniel's brow. 'Now I'm worried that I misunderstood and made a false report.'

'You didn't misunderstand,' Megan told him. 'But I wish that you had, even if it meant that you made a false report, because then it would also mean that he wasn't dead.' She motioned toward Collin lying on the floor.

As Daniel turned in the direction that she indicated, Dylan took another small step backward. This time Hope realized why he was moving away. Dylan was observing Daniel, watching his reaction to the surroundings – and to seeing Collin's body. Hope watched him, too. Daniel looked at Collin, and a barely perceptible flicker passed across his face. Was it a flicker of recognition?

Dylan must have had the same question, because he said to Daniel, 'I had intended to call the police also. If I had spoken to them, I wouldn't have been able to identify the man without Hope and Megan's assistance. Were you able to provide the police with sufficient information about him?'

Hope was impressed. It was an ingenious way to ask if – and how well – Daniel knew Collin.

There was a pause. A crease now appeared in Megan's brow. Hope could guess its cause, because she was similarly troubled. Why didn't Daniel answer immediately? Was he calculating his response? But if he had nothing to do with Collin's death, why would he need to calculate a response?

After a long moment, Daniel said, 'I'm not sure if I did the right thing when I spoke to the police.'

The crease in Megan's brow deepened. 'How do you mean?'

'I asked them to relay the information to that detective – Nate Phillips – I've met a couple of times with Summer. But it occurred to me afterward that I haven't seen Nate and Summer together recently, so if they're no longer dating, then I may have created a somewhat awkward situation.'

'No more awkward than having a dead body discovered in your wine cellar,' Dylan remarked.

He spoke the words sufficiently under his breath so that only Hope – who was nearest to him – heard them. She gave Dylan a sideways glance. She also noted that Daniel hadn't actually answered Dylan's question as to whether he knew Collin. Had it been a deliberate omission, or merely an oversight?

'Nate and Summer are still dating,' Megan told Daniel. 'Do you know if Nate was given the information by his station, or whether he—' Breaking off abruptly, she turned to Hope. 'We forgot about Summer.'

'Huh?'

'We forgot about Summer,' Megan repeated, her voice rising a notch. 'And we forgot about Amber.'

'Amber?' Hope shook her head, not understanding. 'The last time that we saw Amber, she was upstairs at the table with Erik.'

'But what was she doing before then?'

'I have no idea. Probably wandering around the bar trying to find a drink, or trying to find a seat, or . . .' Hope stopped and corrected herself. 'She was trying to find Collin.'

'Exactly! Now we know that poor Collin was lying down here.' Megan pointed toward the floor.

'Yes, and?' Hope shook her head again, still not understanding the connection.

Megan gave an exasperated sigh. 'And it might have been an act! All of Amber's bellowing and griping and accusations. What if it was only make-believe?'

Hope frowned. 'You think that she was pretending? But why?'

'To throw us off the scent, of course! If she was desperately searching – or *pretending* to be desperately searching – for Collin in the bar, then we wouldn't suspect that she had already killed him in the wine cellar.'

'*Killed* him?' Daniel exclaimed.

Disregarding him, Megan went on, 'It's a brilliant plan, albeit a despicable one. If everybody imagines that you're madly in love with Collin, then nobody would ever imagine that you'd murder Collin.'

As she listened to Megan, Hope looked at Daniel. He was gaping at Megan to such an extent that his pointy chin almost reached down to his chest. If his shock at her words was make-believe, then his acting abilities were superb, because Daniel appeared – at least in Hope's view – to be genuinely staggered at the idea that Collin's death had been anything other than tragic misadventure.

'The more I think about it,' Megan said, 'the more it fits together. Amber was far too dramatic with us. Even Erik talked about there being too much drama. Why would Amber be so ridiculously frenetic if it wasn't part of a scheme?'

Hope considered for a moment. 'But if she was pretending in the bar this evening, then wouldn't that mean she was also pretending in the camper van this afternoon? Because that seems a stretch to me. There was an awful lot of honking and yelling and hurling of tableware to have been fake. Theoretically anything can be staged, but I doubt that Amber would have cut her face for show.'

'The episode in the camper van could have been real,' Megan suggested, 'while the episode in the bar wasn't. There's no question that Amber has a short fuse.'

Hope nodded. 'Even before Summer and I met her, Lucas told us that she had a bad temper.'

At the mention of Lucas, Dylan's gaze narrowed.

'He was also the one who warned us about her wicked jealous streak,' Hope added.

Megan nodded in return. 'And that wicked jealous streak is what sets off her fuse. Sometimes Amber can check the fuse, but other times, it explodes out of control. This afternoon, for example, she lost control in the camper van. And I think that she lost control with Collin down here tonight, too. That's what I meant before when I said that we forgot about Summer. Amber was so upset at Collin for supposedly flirting with Summer – or possibly some other woman that she believed he was ogling upstairs – that she couldn't rein in her resentment any longer.

They argued; she grabbed the box cutter from the top of one of the cases; the fight escalated; and in her rage, Amber slashed at Collin, mortally wounding him. Stunned by what she had done, Amber dropped the box cutter on the floor, which is how it ended up under the edge of the refrigerator. It also proves that Amber didn't plan on killing Collin, because otherwise she wouldn't have left the box cutter behind with his blood and her possible fingerprints on it. Plus, no one would deliberately choose a box cutter as a murder weapon. You have to get too close to your victim to use it, which would endanger you in the process. That's particularly true of a small woman such as Amber.'

'You seem to have spent a considerable amount of time contemplating the fine art of the box cutter,' Dylan remarked drolly.

Megan looked at him with annoyance. 'No, of course I haven't. But that doesn't make my conclusions any less valid—'

He didn't let her finish. 'I said it before, and I'll say it again: you're vaguely speculating. You have no proof for anything that you've alleged. But I will agree with you in one regard: the perpetrator had to have been close to Collin to use the box cutter, particularly with the location of the wound. It would have been virtually impossible for a stranger to sneak up to within the short distance necessary to cut him behind the ear. Therefore, in all probability, Collin knew his attacker. But it doesn't mean that Collin was fighting with the person. He could just as easily have been on the verge of making love to the person.'

Megan appeared as though she wanted to argue, but she couldn't, because Dylan's point was a good one.

'What do you think?' she asked Hope. 'Do you see what I mean about it all fitting together?'

'It does fit together,' Hope agreed. 'Especially considering that Lucas – who has obviously spent much more time with Collin and Amber than we have and knows them both far better than we do – said that Collin was the one who really bears the brunt of Amber's bad temper.'

'Collin may in fact have borne the brunt of Amber's bad temper,' Dylan responded, 'but I certainly wouldn't rely on Lucas for the accuracy of it. He claims to study cryptids, for criminy sake. He lives in an ignorant fantasy land.'

Hope raised an eyebrow at him. 'That's interesting, because

Lucas said something quite similar about you. If I recall his words correctly, he called you *woefully blinkered* and *ignorant of the truths of this world.*'

Dylan raised an eyebrow back at her. 'I won't pretend to be offended. It's impossible to take anything seriously from a man who believes that Bigfoot is tramping through the Appalachians and might appear on the boutique's doorstep at any moment.'

Megan gave an amused snort. 'Maybe he'd want a palm reading from Hope. She could tell him if there was a Mrs Bigfoot and a Baby Bigfoot in his future!'

Although Hope tried to be indignant, she didn't succeed. The idea of examining the love line on Bigfoot's palm was funny to her, too.

After shaking her head in reproach, she said to Megan, 'Returning to the more important issue at hand, no pun intended—'

There was another snort from Megan.

'—a large amount of what you said before about what might have transpired between Amber and Collin in here makes sense. But Dylan is right, too. It really is no more than speculation on our part. We have no concrete proof of anything. And there are also some considerable uncertainties.'

'Such as?' Megan asked.

'For starters, why were Amber and Collin in the wine cellar?'

'There's no difficulty explaining that. Collin went to the office with Nelson, as we originally supposed. After their meeting ended, Nelson departed, while Collin remained downstairs.'

'And Amber?'

'She must have followed Collin. She easily could have seen him the same as we did, talking to Nelson by the bar. With her extreme jealousy, Amber would have wanted to know exactly who Nelson was and what they were discussing, so she headed after them to investigate. Once Nelson left, she accosted Collin.'

'Assuming that's all correct,' Hope said, 'what about Nelson? Where did he go, why did he leave Collin down here alone after their meeting, and did he hear or see anything that happened between Collin and Amber?'

Megan had no answers for those questions.

Hope turned to Daniel. She was growing impatient with his lack of helpful input – or, for that matter, any input whatsoever.

He simply stood next to Megan, gaping at each member of the group in turn without offering the slightest confirmation or denial regardless of the subject matter.

'Well?' Hope asked him. 'What can you tell us about Nelson?'

He gaped at her without speaking.

'For goodness' sake, Daniel,' Megan snapped, sharing Hope's impatience. 'Pull yourself together! Yes, it's a shock that a man has been killed in your wine cellar. But sadly, we can't turn back the clock and change what happened to Collin. You're a businessman, and right now you have to focus on the future success of your business. The police will no doubt close the Green Goat temporarily while they investigate, so we need to do everything in our power to help the matter be resolved as quickly as possible—'

'What about Summer?' Dylan interrupted.

'Summer?' Megan turned her impatience to him. 'I'm pretty confident that Summer did not attack Collin with a box cutter in a jealous pique.'

'I'm pretty confident in that regard, too,' Dylan replied. 'I'm not so confident, however, that the threat against her wasn't real, as Hope said.'

Hope frowned at him. 'I said that a threat wasn't real?'

A moment later, she realized what he meant. Megan realized it also, and they looked at each other in dismay. During her howling fury in the bar, Amber had threatened to kill both Collin *and* Summer.

TWELVE

Hope was unwilling to wait any longer for the police to arrive. Nate and his colleagues would no doubt be displeased by her departure, but Summer took top priority, and she needed to know as soon as possible what had befallen Collin and to be warned about Amber's threat. When Hope had originally told Dylan that the threat wasn't real, she had meant it. She had honestly considered Amber's menacing words to be nothing more than overwrought histrionics. But that was before Collin had turned up dead. Did she now think that the threat had been real? She wasn't sure. Although Megan had made some compelling arguments in support of Amber's possible guilt, Hope wasn't convinced. Unlike Megan, she didn't have the impression that Amber had been pretending to search for Collin in the bar. On the contrary, Amber had seemed to truly believe that Collin and Summer were secreted away together. She had badgered Erik about Collin's whereabouts, and she had demanded to accompany Hope and Megan on their search for him. Taken as a whole, Amber's behavior had appeared genuine – and genuinely obsessive – to Hope. But if she was wrong, and Megan was correct about it all being make-believe, then Amber was a frighteningly good – and frighteningly dangerous – actress with ice in her veins.

There was one significant point that additionally fell in Amber's favor, but it didn't occur to Hope until after she had left the Green Goat. Her departure was neither as quick nor as simple as she would have liked. To her surprise, it was Daniel who was the most insistent that she stay. He had barely uttered a syllable after Megan had indicated that Collin had been murdered, but now suddenly he was adamant that Hope remained with the group. Daniel said that he had given the police all four of their names, and the police would blame him if one of the four wasn't there when they arrived.

Megan did no more than shrug at his concern. She stood firmly in Hope's camp that Summer's interests took precedence over the police's convenience. If any trouble arose in relation to her and Hope's absence, she was certain that Nate would sort it out for them. Megan was further of the opinion that when Nate learned about Amber's threat, he would rush to the brownstone to check on Summer himself and chastise Hope and her for not having done so sooner.

When Daniel realized that Megan also intended on departing, he looked so consternated and began to object so strenuously that Hope was finally forced to put an end to his protests by announcing definitively that Megan would stay and only she would leave. In addition to quieting Daniel, Hope figured that Megan's continued presence in the wine cellar would serve two valuable purposes. First, she could smooth over any difficulties with the police, and second, she could listen to the medical assessment of Collin that Dylan gave to the authorities. Hope had the distinct impression that Dylan had noticed something of importance, because he kept turning to examine the spot where Collin's body lay. He appeared to be studying the pool of blood on the floor rather than Collin himself, and she was curious to know what he had spotted.

For his part, Dylan seemed almost as eager for Hope to be gone as she was herself. He was in the process of asking Daniel whether there was a rear set of stairs and back door that led out to the alley, so that Hope wouldn't have to go through the bar to exit the building from the front, when the police began to arrive from both directions simultaneously. The information from Daniel's telephone call must have been widely disseminated, because more than a dozen people in varying official capacities appeared all at once. There were shouts about setting up a protective perimeter, shouts about needing more lights, and shouts about closing the Green Goat and removing all of the remaining customers. Daniel looked around bewildered, while Dylan looked once more at the blood on the floor.

Taking advantage of the momentary chaos, Hope gave a hasty parting nod to Megan and slipped quietly out of the wine cellar as everybody else poured noisily into it. She was forced to move against the tide down the corridor, but fortunately, the police weren't yet sufficiently organized and enough of the lights remained off that she managed to pass through unseen. The rear stairs were a jumble of people and equipment, and as Hope weaved her way up them, a pair of uniformed police officers and one man in a corduroy blazer – who she vaguely recognized as a colleague of Nate's – noticed her. She pretended not to hear their inquiries and continued onward until she reached the back door, which had been helpfully propped open by someone carrying a large cardboard box. A minute later, Hope was outside, escaping into the concealing shadows of the alley.

The moon was blanketed by a thick layer of clouds, and the alley behind the Green Goat was only dimly illuminated by a solitary orange security light. Under other circumstances, Hope might have been somewhat ill at ease heading home at the late hour by herself, but she wasn't actually alone. The alley was filled with bustling members of law enforcement, and beyond it, the streets were filled with buoyant pedestrians. The temperature was unseasonably warm for the end of October, and the inhabitants of Asheville were taking full advantage of it, especially on a Friday night. There were romantic couples nuzzling on benches, groups of friends laughing together on corners, elderly companions taking leisurely strolls, and parents pushing prams containing bright-eyed youngsters, who'd apparently had long afternoon naps.

Hope tried ringing Summer's phone, but it went through to voicemail. Anxious to get to the brownstone, Hope's pace started off swift, but it slowed after the first block or two. The air was sultry and had the feeling of an impending thunderstorm. She was glad that she had been indolent in her clothing choices and had worn casual shoes. They were both comfortable on the uneven cobblestone sidewalks and wouldn't get ruined if it began to rain. She wondered if Nate was now in the wine cellar and how much Megan had told him. Depending on how seriously Nate took Amber's threat, he might race to find Summer and reach the brownstone with his car before Hope reached it on foot. But she thought it more likely that Nate would remain in the cellar for a considerable length of time, examining Collin with his colleagues and Dylan. Hope wished that she knew why Dylan had been studying the pool of blood so intently. What had he noticed? And that was when she realized that regardless of any argument from Megan to the contrary – no matter how persuasive – there was little chance that Amber had been the one who killed Collin.

It was the blood – or, more accurately, the lack of blood – that proved it. There had been no blood on Amber when she had joined the group at the table in the bar. Amber's blouse, hands, neck, and face had all been clean. In fact, Hope had specifically noted at the time that once the blood from the incident in the camper van was gone, the cut on Amber's temple was almost invisible. Although she was certainly no expert on stabbings and slashings, Hope had difficulty imagining that someone could attack a person with a box cutter, inflict a gash behind their ear that was deep enough to mortally wound the person, and not get any blood on themselves in the process. Granted, Collin's blood had been in a relatively neat pool on the floor. There had been no ghastly spray or splatter on the nearby walls or refrigerators. Dylan could no doubt explain it satisfactorily from a medical perspective. Hope guessed that it had something to do with the manner in which an artery or vein had – or had not – been cut. But in any event, there had been blood on the handle of the box cutter in addition to its blade, which meant that at least a small amount of Collin's blood had ended up on his attacker. Amber, however, had been spotless in the bar.

In theory, Amber could have washed herself at a sink in the ladies' room after killing Collin and before joining them at the table, but she would have needed to do it perfectly, including removing any stains from her clothing and flecks in her hair, because Hope saw absolutely nothing on her. Plus, there was the issue of time. The gap between when Collin and Nelson had disappeared and Amber had appeared was already extremely tight. Amber would have had only a few short minutes to follow Collin and Nelson downstairs, wait for Nelson to depart, have the deadly encounter with Collin in the wine cellar, and then both clean herself up and return upstairs. It simply didn't work – or, at a minimum, it was highly improbable.

If Amber couldn't have killed Collin due to a lack of time and a lack of blood on her, then who else did that rule out as a suspect for the same reasons? Erik, for starters. After Collin and Nelson had disappeared from the bar, Erik hadn't once risen from his chair. The only way that he could have been Collin's attacker was if he had sprinted ahead of Hope and Megan after they had departed from the table, and he had somehow managed to get downstairs before them. Hope was pretty sure that Erik knew about the lower level of the Green Goat. Considering that he had told Amber about seeing Collin with Nelson, Erik clearly hadn't been asleep during Hope and Megan's conversation, which meant that he had heard Megan talk about the supply room, the office, and the wine cellar. Was it possible for Erik to have reached the wine cellar and killed Collin before Hope arrived in the corridor? It seemed a stretch to her. She did have to acknowledge, however, that Erik had a motive for wanting Collin gone. With his rival out of the way, Erik would have a clear field to pursue a romantic relationship with Amber, and he would be able to exchange his nightly tarp and sleeping bag for the comparative comfort of the camper van. But could down-to-earth Erik with his dreams of time travel to watch the dinosaurs honestly be a cold-blooded murderer?

Hope remembered that Erik had been quite cheerful about her and Megan leaving the table to search for Collin. At the time, she had assumed that it was because he wanted to be alone with Amber, but the real reason could have been that it gave him the opportunity to leave the table, as well. If Erik had indeed attempted to sprint ahead of them downstairs, Amber would have been left on her own at the table. Could Amber then have also attempted to sprint ahead of them? If so, that would change everything, because it would no longer matter that Amber didn't have blood on her in the bar. Any blood from the attack on Collin would have gotten on her later, and Hope would never have had the chance to see it. Which meant that Amber could have killed Collin, after all. Or Erik could have killed Collin. Or the two of them could have killed Collin together.

Halting on the cobblestones, Hope shook her head at herself. She was doing exactly what Dylan had rebuked Megan for doing: vaguely speculating. She had no proof for any of it, and continued speculation without more information would get her nowhere. She barely knew Collin, so she had little knowledge of the possible motives behind his death. It could be love and jealousy, which would involve Amber and Erik. Or it could be money and the

Green Goat, which would involve Nelson and Daniel. And then there was Collin's life on the road as a (potential) conspiracy theorist, which would involve Lucas and – again – Amber and Erik. There were far too many possibilities and far too many unknowns.

She had been musing for so long and with such concentration that when Hope rounded a corner, she was startled to find that she had reached her street. Her gaze went immediately to the camper van parked along the curb in front of the neighboring brownstone. The van was dark inside; no lights were visible through the windows. Either Amber had retired for the night, or she hadn't yet returned from the Green Goat. If she wasn't involved in the attack on Collin, then the news of his death would surely hit her hard. Hope couldn't help thinking that she'd like to see Amber's reaction, because it might give some insight into her true feelings for Collin. On the other hand, if Megan was correct about her acting talents, then Amber would be able to pretend to be shocked and saddened with equal skill.

There was a faint yellow glow through one window on the far side of the Airstream. It was too high off the ground, so Hope couldn't tell whether Lucas was inside. Similar to Amber, he might have retired for the night – and simply left a small light on – or he hadn't yet returned from the Green Goat. Hope had seen almost nothing of him in the bar. Lucas had arrived with the group, but before they had sat down at their table, he had announced that he saw someone he knew and promptly vanished into the crowd. Although Lucas had said that he would be right back, he had never reappeared. If Hope wanted to be credulous, she might think that he hadn't been able to find their table afterward in the throng, or that he had lost track of time chatting with his acquaintance. But if she wanted to be suspicious, she might think it odd that Lucas – who hadn't been in Asheville for many years – would coincidentally run into an acquaintance in that exact location, at that exact moment.

As she had with Amber, Hope wondered how Lucas would react to the news of Collin's death. Unlike Erik – who had called Collin deceptive and warned her and Summer not to be fooled by him – Lucas hadn't made any critical comments about Collin. On the contrary, he had seemed to feel somewhat sorry for him by saying that Collin was the one who bore the brunt of Amber's bad temper. But the sympathy hadn't gone too far, either, because Lucas hadn't expressed any particular concern or anxiety when the tableware had been flying inside the camper van. He had merely shrugged and remarked that Amber hurled mugs, not kitchen knives. What about box cutters?

After passing by the camper van and the Airstream, Hope approached the boutique. Similar to the Airstream, a faint yellow glow was visible through one of the far windows. Although she wasn't completely certain, Hope thought that they had turned off all the lights before closing the shop and heading to the Green Goat. If there was any illumination now, it meant that Summer had returned and was safely inside the brownstone. Hope was just about to unlock the front door and see if her sister was still awake when she thought that she heard a noise a short distance away. She stopped and listened. It sounded like humming. Where was it coming from? Maybe Erik on the side lawn? As Hope turned down the walkway to find out, it occurred to her that if Erik was camping outside with his tarp and sleeping bag as originally planned, then that could be a pretty good indication that he wasn't aware of what had happened to Collin. If Erik knew that Collin was dead, it seemed more probable that he would spend the night in the camper van instead, either because it offered greater protection from any possible rain or to comfort Amber in her grief.

The humming continued. It was definitely nearby and coming from the direction of the side lawn. But as Hope got closer, she realized that the humming was actually two voices talking. One voice was distinctly higher than the other, most likely belonging to a woman and the latter to a man. Was Amber outside with Erik? Hope had no idea how to interpret that in relation to Collin. Suddenly there was laughter – a great joyful burst of merriment. Clearly the pair was not in the throes of deep mourning.

Reaching the corner of the brownstone, Hope paused and listened once more. There was further laughter and talking. The voices had a familiar tone, but they weren't quite loud enough for her to identify or to distinguish the individual words. Although Hope's natural instinct was to step into view and say hello, she found herself hesitating. Ordinarily she wasn't a fan of eavesdropping, but this seemed to be an acceptable moment to do so, considering that one – or both – of the people presently guffawing on her property might be a murderer.

'Hope?' called one of the voices. 'Hope, is that you peeking around the edge of the brick?'

Hope jumped in surprise, neither expecting to be seen nor to be hailed by her sister. 'Summer? I've been trying to reach you on your phone . . .'

She hurried forward but stopped again a moment later in astonishment. Summer was indeed on the brownstone's side lawn. But she wasn't accompanied by Erik – or, for that matter, Amber. She was with Lucas. And instead of Erik's simple tarp and sleeping bag on the open patch of grass, there was a large pop-up gazebo with an aluminum frame and gauzy net curtains that had been tied back at the four corners. A white faux fur rug was spread over the ground beneath the gazebo. The rug was sprinkled with an assortment of plush cushions in bright colors, on which Summer and Lucas were leisurely lounging. Several cozy blankets lay nearby in case someone developed a chill. A trio of hurricane lamps cast a warm, friendly radiance over the space.

'Hello, darling,' Lucas drawled.

Hope's mouth opened, but no sound emerged.

Lucas's own mouth curved with his characteristically crooked smile. 'It's about time that you showed up. We were expecting you earlier. That bar was a zoo.'

'Where . . . why . . .' Hope stammered.

'Where did the gazebo come from?' he said, completing her first question. 'I live in an Airstream and travel through a lot of remote and uninhabited areas. A tent – or, in this case, a gazebo – is a rather advantageous item to possess. I use it frequently.'

Summer nodded with enthusiasm. 'We should get something like this for the back garden, don't you think, Hope? The patio is great most of the year, but in the dog days of August when the mosquitos become really aggressive, bug netting would be nice for protection.' She motioned toward the gazebo's curtains. 'Lucas was going to put them down but realized there are no mosquitos tonight.'

'Which brings us to your second question,' Lucas continued to Hope. 'Why bother setting up the gazebo when Erik would be fully content with his tarp and sleeping bag? Because it felt like a storm might be rolling in, and I didn't want the *dude*' – he chortled – 'to get drenched by a cloudburst.'

In spite of not yet having fully recovered from her surprise at the scene before her, Hope noted that Lucas was still expecting Erik to spend the night outdoors rather than in the camper van, which suggested that he didn't know about what had happened to Collin. That was further corroborated by the fact that both he and Summer were in far too high of spirits to be aware of anyone's death.

Lucas patted a lime cushion lying beside him. 'Sit down, get comfortable, and have a drink, Hope.'

'Yes, sit down and have a drink,' Summer agreed. 'It's a lovely night. The temperature is almost perfect; we're protected from the rain if any comes; there was an owl hooting in the big pecan tree just a little while ago—'

'Two owls,' Lucas corrected her.

Summer giggled. 'Two owls. Lucas says that they were introducing themselves and telling each other about their respective territories. Wouldn't it be neat if next spring there was a nest of baby owls in the old pecan, Hope?' She giggled again.

Giggling about baby owls? How very unlike Summer. Hope took a closer look at her sister. She was reclining on a fuchsia cushion with a stemless martini glass in her hand, except the glass didn't contain a martini or another similarly colorless alcoholic beverage. Instead, it held a dark red liquid. Hope recognized it instantly.

'Summer, is that the punch for the party?'

Her sister responded with another giggle.

'Oh Lord. How much have you had?' Hope shook her head in reproach. 'There's a reason why we only make it for Halloween.'

'It's a *witches' brew*.' Lucas chortled the same way that he had a minute earlier when he had referred to Erik as the *dude*.

Hope saw that Lucas was also holding a glass filled with the Halloween party punch, which explained his chortling and weak attempts at humor.

He took a generous swallow of the red liquid. 'Tasty – extremely tasty. But potent – much too potent for some of the people that I've shared a drink with.'

His remark reminded Hope of his abrupt departure from their group in the Green Goat, and she asked him about it.

'Were you able to catch up with the acquaintance that you spotted in the bar?'

For the first time since her arrival on the side lawn, Lucas's crooked smile drooped slightly. 'We met and talked,' he confirmed.

Although Hope waited for him to provide some additional details, he didn't. Aside from the faint change to his smile, Lucas gave no indication whether the aforementioned meeting and talking had been pleasant or unpleasant. Perhaps it had been a bit of both.

Turning back to Summer, Hope shook her head once more. 'Why on earth did you start the punch? I warned you after Gram and I finished making it that it was a particularly strong batch this year.'

Summer copied Lucas by taking a generous swallow from her glass. 'I was thirsty,' she replied, a touch petulantly. 'And Nate is angry.'

That garnered Hope's full attention. Was Nate angry because she had left the wine cellar? Did that mean Summer and Lucas knew about Collin's death, after all? Perhaps they were drinking the punch to drown their sorrows.

'Nate didn't like it.' Summer took another sizable swallow. 'I know that he didn't like it.'

'What didn't he like?' Hope asked, wincing slightly in anticipation of her sister's response.

It was Summer's turn to shake her head, as though the answer should have been obvious. 'Nate didn't like how Collin looked at me this afternoon. Why did Collin have to ogle me in front of everybody! It was so annoying. And what purpose did it serve? The way that he invited me to go to the Green Goat with him was just as bad. It annoyed Nate and Amber, too. They both blame *me* for his behavior, which is terribly unfair.'

Hope found herself exhaling with relief. So Nate hadn't complained about her departure. But if Nate hadn't told Summer about what had happened to Collin, then she would have to do it, without any further delay.

'I'm afraid that Amber does blame you,' Hope began in explanation, 'but the good news is that Nate doesn't—'

Summer interrupted her. 'You're only saying that about Nate to make me feel better.'

'No, it's the truth. After he left here this afternoon, Nate called Dylan, told him about Collin making a move on you, and asked Dylan to go to the Green Goat to check on you for him. Didn't you see Dylan in the alley there?'

'I saw him, but I didn't really talk to him. I was trying to get an update from Gram and Morris about their trip, except I couldn't get a signal on my phone—' Summer broke off, looking at Hope with a pleased expression. 'Nate asked Dylan to check on me for him? That's awfully sweet. With any luck, Nate will be able to come to the party early tomorrow and won't be forced to work too late because of Halloween—' She broke off again, this time frowning at her sister. 'What's wrong? All of a sudden, your face went funny.'

Hope nodded and sighed. 'Nate will definitely have to work tomorrow, but it won't have any bearing on his attendance at the party, because there won't be a party. The Green Goat will be closed for the murder investigation.'

THIRTEEN

For better or worse, the consumption of the party punch dampened the shock of Collin's death. Lucas said little and was simply grave. Unable to fully wrap her mind around the murder, Summer turned her focus to its effect.

'Maybe the investigation will be concluded by tomorrow,' she suggested hopefully, 'and the Green Goat can reopen in time for the party.'

'That's wishful thinking. If you had seen Collin on the floor of the wine cellar, you wouldn't have any illusions about the possibility of everything being neatly wrapped up by tomorrow evening—' Hope stopped and corrected herself. 'Technically, the party is scheduled for this evening rather than tomorrow evening, because it's now well after midnight. That makes the time even shorter. You can't expect the authorities – including dear Nate – to have the forensic work done, and the body removed, and all the rest of their work completed so quickly.'

There was a pause. Summer took a contemplative drink from her glass. Hope was about to remind her sister that if she consumed much more of the punch, she could expect a whopper of a headache in the morning, but then it occurred to her that if there was no party for them to attend in the evening, a headache in the morning didn't really matter.

Summer must have read her thoughts, because she rose from her fuchsia cushion and took a clean glass from the top of a short metal footstool that functioned as a small table in the near corner of the gazebo. Also on the stool was a clear plastic pitcher brimming with dark red punch. Summer filled the glass and handed it to her sister. Hope promptly took a sip. Considering that she was the one who had made the punch – in accordance with Gram's age-old recipe – she knew that Lucas hadn't exaggerated its tastiness. On the contrary, the punch was perhaps a bit too tasty, concealing its degree of potency from the uninitiated a little too well. Hope took another sip, slightly bigger this time, as

Summer topped off both her own glass and Lucas's, who accepted the refill with an appreciative nod.

After returning the pitcher to the footstool and herself to the fuchsia cushion, Summer said, 'We could move the party back to the boutique.'

Hope shook her head. 'That's even more wishful than the Green Goat being reopened. In the past, it's always taken us at least a week to prepare for the event – and that included Gram's brilliant organizational skills. You know how much planning and work the party requires. For starters, there's the food and the beverages, none of which we have aside from the punch. Then there's the lighting and the decorations. Even if we use what we can from the Green Goat's preparations and skip some of our usual items such as the bubbling cauldron, or the glowing jack-o'-lanterns, or the apple-bobbing tub, we'll still have to pack up all of the merchandise in the shop – plus a large portion of the furniture – and move it into the living quarters of the brownstone for temporary storage. It isn't feasible for us to accomplish even a quarter of that by this evening.'

Summer was undeterred by her arguments. 'Gram and Morris are obviously unavailable, but there are plenty of other people who will cheerfully lend us a hand. Lucas will help, right?' She turned to him expectantly.

Lucas agreed without hesitation. 'Count me in for anything that you need: supplies, labor, an extra driver to run last-minute errands. I told you before that I've always wanted to attend the Bailey Halloween bash. Even if it isn't quite up to its usual standard due to unforeseen events, I'll do what I can to help make it a success.'

After beaming her gratitude at him, Summer turned back to her sister. 'In addition to Lucas, there's Megan – who is almost as brilliant of an organizer as Gram – and Nate . . .' Her brow furrowed. 'No, Nate has the investigation, so he'll be too busy. But there's Dylan, of course. And I'm certain that plenty of our neighbors will want to pitch in, considering that the majority of them attend the party every year. Plus, we can call on some of our clients for assistance. What about Rosemarie Potter? She would rally the troops in support!'

Hope smiled. 'There isn't any question that Rosemarie – bless her kind and generous heart – would show great enthusiasm for the project, but there's also little doubt that she would spend more time worrying that Percy's costume was in good order than actually facilitating party arrangements.'

Summer laughed. 'That's true. I wonder what Percy's costume is this year. Last year, he was a pumpkin, wasn't he?'

'No, the pumpkin was from two years ago. Last year, Percy was a hot dog with pickle relish.'

'A pumpkin and a hot dog with pickle relish?' Lucas raised an eyebrow. 'I wouldn't be overly thrilled if I had a wife giving me those costumes.'

Hope's smile grew. 'Rosemarie has been married – and divorced – twice. I can assure you that she wasn't half as fond of both of her husbands combined as she is of Percy, who is her beloved pug.'

'A pug?' Now Lucas laughed, too. 'That makes a hot dog costume pretty funny!'

'Frankly – no pun intended – I've never been a tremendous fan of pet costumes,' Summer told him. 'Some of them seem rather cruel to me, with the animal wedged into them solely for human entertainment. But Rosemarie does a remarkable job with Percy's costumes. He appears to be genuinely comfortable in them, and they're always really creative.' She looked at Hope. 'That's another reason we can't cancel the party, because then we'll miss out on seeing Percy's costume!'

Although Hope smiled again, she didn't offer any additional response. While Summer's gusto and determination to host the Halloween party was admirable, Hope didn't want to encourage her further. Perhaps it was because she hadn't consumed nearly as much punch, or because she was more affected by Collin's death after having discovered his body in the pool of blood, but in any case, Hope didn't share her sister's quixotic notions that the party could be successfully moved back to the boutique on such short notice.

Summer tried another approach. 'What about our loyal customers?'

Hope answered with a weary sigh. Lucas must have either heard the exhalation or seen the fatigue in her face, because as he had when she first arrived on the side lawn, he patted the lime cushion lying beside him. This time Hope gladly accepted the invitation. It had been a stressful day, and her feet were tired from standing for so long on the concrete cellar floor, followed by the walk home over the uneven cobblestones. Hope was positive that her sister would eventually see sense and realize that her scheme for the party was impractical, but until then, if Summer persisted in her contentions, Hope figured that she might as well sit down and enjoy some festive punch. It was, after all, now Halloween, if one considered Halloween to be the entire day of October 31 and not only All Hallows' Eve.

As she reclined on the lime cushion, Hope sighed again, except this sigh was one of pleasure rather than exhaustion. The plush cushion was wonderfully comfortable, and the faux fur rug beneath it was heavenly soft. With his crooked smile, Lucas raised his glass to her. Hope raised hers in return. And they shared a drink.

'What about our loyal customers?' Summer repeated, with a distinct note of impatience at the delay.

'I believe we discussed that already,' Hope replied mildly. 'Rosemarie won't be of any real help, and we can't seriously start contacting our other clients, inform them that the location of the party has been changed again, and then ask them to come to the boutique early with a gallon-sized beverage and a potluck dish to share with the other guests.'

'A big barbecue is the solution,' Lucas said. 'Pug Percy and his hot dog costume made me think of it. Bratwursts and beer. That's the way to go. It satisfies a crowd but doesn't require a lot of utensils or fussy ingredients. Throw in some bottled water and soda for the teetotalers and some potato chips and vegan sausages for the meat-abstainers. It isn't perfect, but it covers all the basics.'

'It's a marvelous idea,' Hope told him. 'And you're right that it covers all the basics, except . . .'

'Except it's still too much with too little time,' Lucas concluded for her.

She nodded. 'We need chairs, the grills with either charcoal or propane, mustard and buns, plates and napkins. It all has to be purchased or borrowed and then set up. If the entire party was going to be outside, we could potentially manage to pull it together. But that won't work here. There isn't remotely enough space on this side lawn for everyone who normally attends. In the past, there's been some spillover to the back garden and the adjoining alley, but this year, we haven't prepared the patio and garden for the influx of people or spoken to the neighbors about blocking off the alley. Plus, there are still the issues of the lighting, the decorations, and the boutique itself.'

'I agree.' Lucas nodded back at her. 'It would only work if everything could be outside, and that isn't possible here.'

A gust of wind swept through the gazebo. It rustled the net curtains and carried with it the chill dampness of rain nearby. Hope shivered. Lucas reached for one of the blankets and spread it over her legs.

'Thank you,' she said.

'My pleasure,' he replied. 'We can't have you trembling from the cold, can we?'

Hope looked at him. Lucas's dark eyes were warm and steady. There was something indefinably safe and secure about them. They took her back to the happy, simple days that she and Lucas had spent together so many years earlier.

Summer cleared her throat. 'I didn't mean that we should call our customers and ask them to bring potluck dishes to share.'

'Oh?' Hope murmured, her gaze still fixed on Lucas's.

'I meant' – Summer cleared her throat again, louder this time – 'that if there is no party, then we'll be disappointing our most loyal customers who have supported and encouraged us for such a long time. Not only will we be letting them down, but from a more mercenary standpoint, it will be bad for our business in the future.'

Finally Hope turned to her sister. 'Megan was worried about that, too. She was afraid that our business would suffer with the party moving to the Green Goat.'

'Yes, and this is significantly worse, because it isn't just a different location. It's a complete cancellation. That isn't going to sit well with some of our clients.'

'I think Summer is correct,' Lucas told Hope. 'No matter how devoted they may be to you and the boutique today, your customers can turn fickle and unforgiving tomorrow. You might end up losing a portion of their business as a result.'

Hope took a consoling drink from her glass. 'You're both probably right, and we'll probably have some angry and annoyed clients on our hands. But regardless of how angry and annoyed they are, it doesn't change the unalterable fact that it's no longer feasible for us to have the party at the boutique. And if we lose future business because of it, that can't be changed, either. I would like to believe that most of our clients are also our friends and wouldn't abandon us merely because we didn't provide them with a Halloween party this year.'

Now Summer took a consoling drink, too.

'In any event,' Hope continued, 'the situation is substantially worse for the Green Goat than it is for us. Megan told me that the place is struggling financially. By combining our party with theirs, Daniel was hoping to piggyback on our popularity, but that obviously won't work now. And who knows how long the Green Goat will be forced to remain closed for the investigation? It's going to hit Daniel's business hard.'

'Which makes me glad that I didn't invest in it,' Lucas said.

Hope couldn't conceal her surprise. 'You were thinking about investing in the Green Goat?' She knew better than to voice any misgivings about the state of Lucas's finances after Summer had made the mistake of doing so in connection with his potential purchase of the neighboring brownstone. Instead she asked him, 'How did you hear about the place?'

'From Collin. He was considering investing in it.'

That answered Hope's lingering question as to what Collin and Nelson had been discussing in the bar. She promptly followed with her – and Megan's – related question.

'Did Collin intend on being a silent investor only, or was he also planning on becoming one of the Green Goat's active partners?'

'I don't know. He never shared those details with me. But I have difficulty imagining Collin as an active partner in any sort of business, least of all a restaurant. He's not the type to show up at an office every morning to check over the receipts from the previous evening and figure out the staff's work schedule for the following week. That would be far too mundane for his tastes. I couldn't see him doing that for even one day, let alone on a semi-permanent basis—' Lucas broke off, frowning. 'I keep talking about him as though he's still alive. It doesn't seem to have sunk in for me yet that Collin isn't going to come sauntering down the sidewalk in a couple of minutes, with Amber in hot pursuit, bellowing at him for egregiously flirting with some other woman.'

Hope started to smile at the apt description of Amber, but it faded an instant later. She looked at her sister gravely. 'I forgot to tell you that Amber was bellowing about you to Megan and me in the bar. She threatened you – and Collin. She was convinced that the two of you were secreted away together somewhere, and she said that when she next saw you, she was going to kill you both.'

There was a long, weighty silence as each of them considered Amber's words. Lucas's frown deepened. Summer picked at a row of loose stitching on the fuchsia cushion. Hope adjusted the blanket covering her legs.

At length, Lucas said, 'I don't think that you have to worry about Amber. She wouldn't actually harm you. With her, it's all bluster and very little bite. Admittedly, she was hurling dishes inside the camper van, but I've never seen her do something like that anywhere else – or, for that matter, in connection with anyone else. It's only Collin. Amber's feelings for him get the better of her at times.'

'And you don't think that her feelings for him might have gotten the better of her in the wine cellar?' Hope asked.

Lucas didn't hesitate with his answer. 'No, I honestly don't. I wasn't there, of course, so I can't say what occurred with absolute certainty, but I've known Amber for quite a while. Traveling so closely together gives you the opportunity to see how somebody reacts in all kinds of unexpected situations, both when a person is at their strongest and their weakest. And I can tell you from what I've witnessed that although Amber has a wicked jealous streak, she doesn't have a violent streak. She wouldn't hurt Collin, not only because of her deep feelings for him, but also because she isn't vicious. That's why I'm confident that you have nothing to fear from her.'

Summer's response was limited to taking a generous drink from her glass. Apparently she was going to let the punch soothe any residual concerns that she might have.

'You don't have to worry about Amber,' Lucas reiterated. 'And when she returns to the camper van, I'll speak with her. I'll make sure that she's calm and fully in control of her emotions. She usually listens to me.'

Hope remembered that Amber had indeed listened to Lucas on the sidewalk outside the van. She had heeded his directive to hold the dishcloth to her bleeding face and to let Collin speak uninterrupted.

Lucas looked at her. As before, his dark eyes were warm and steady, and Hope's own lingering anxieties faded away. A gust of wind followed soon thereafter, this one somewhat stronger than its predecessor. It kicked up the corners of the rug and shifted the blanket on Hope's legs. She bent forward to tuck the blanket in more securely. When she leaned back again, Lucas wrapped his arm around her shoulders. It felt so natural – so protective against the dark, uncertain night – that Hope curled up close to him.

FOURTEEN

There was a noise. It sounded like a hollow knock. Hope shifted, only half awake. The knock repeated itself. Was Summer knocking on her bedroom door? She wondered what time it was. Was it still night? No, there was diffuse light around her. It must be morning. A third knock came. She didn't want to get up. The bed was so soft and comfortable. Maybe if she rolled over and kept her eyes closed, she could sleep for a little while longer. As though in answer, there was a fourth knock, louder and harder. Hope grumbled to herself. Why was Summer being so insistent? Couldn't it wait until later? The knocking became a steady drumbeat, impossible to ignore. With another grumble, she started to rise, and that was when she realized she wasn't in her bed – or in her room.

Hope's eyes flew open. She was wrapped in a blanket on the faux fur rug, under the gazebo, on the side lawn of the brownstone. The sun was shining, the birds were singing, and Dylan was standing next to her, looking down at her.

'Dylan!' she exclaimed, hurriedly sitting up and untangling herself from the blanket.

'Good morning,' he responded flatly.

His voice held a distinct note of irritation, and he tapped the toe of his shoe impatiently against the short metal footstool that had functioned as the gazebo's makeshift bar the night before. The tapping created a hollow knocking sound.

'Oh, were you the one making that noise a minute ago?' Hope said. 'I thought that it was Summer knocking on the door.'

'There is no door out here. And your sister isn't doing anything but snoring.' Dylan motioned toward the opposite side of the gazebo.

Hope turned to find Summer a short distance behind her, also lying on the faux fur rug, snuggling her fuchsia cushion. Although she wasn't actually snoring, Summer was breathing deeply, still sound asleep.

'Too much punch.'

Although Hope thought that she had spoken under her breath, Dylan apparently heard it, because he looked at the plastic pitcher that was sitting on the footstool. The pitcher was now about two-thirds empty.

'This punch?' he inquired.

Not waiting for her answer, he picked up an empty glass from the footstool and poured a small amount of the dark red liquid into it.

'It's part of a larger batch that was intended for the party this evening,' Hope told him hastily. 'Unless you've had a big breakfast, you may not want to drink that on an empty stomach, because it—'

Before she could finish her explanation, Dylan downed the contents of his glass in a single swallow.

'Holy hell,' he coughed, 'that is some serious hillbilly moonshine!'

She chuckled. 'I tried to warn you.'

Holding the glass toward the sky, he examined it against the light, as though checking to see if the punch had burned any holes in it.

Hope chuckled some more. 'The pitcher survived intact through the night, so you don't have to be concerned about the punch melting through your insides.'

Dylan poured another small serving into his glass. This time he more prudently took a sip rather than a gulp.

'It's tasty,' he determined. 'Very tasty.'

'That is the consensus,' she said.

He took another sip.

'But potent,' Hope added, gesturing toward her sister, who hadn't yet stirred on the rug.

'Out of curiosity,' Dylan remarked, finishing his second glass and setting it down on the footstool rather than refilling it, 'is the punch legal?'

'I sincerely hope so, because I'm the one who made it.'

His surprise was evident. '*You* made it?'

She gave a nod in confirmation. 'Every year for Halloween in accordance with Gram's recipe.'

Dylan's lips curled with amusement. 'Whenever I think that

I've got you Baileys figured out, you pull another rabbit from your hat.'

'Contrary to popular belief and portrayal,' Hope responded drolly, 'witches don't wear hats. That's only for stage magicians . . .'

She didn't finish the sentence, suddenly remembering the disturbing Tarot cards from the previous morning. The Magician and the Seven of Swords. They had been a warning of a deceitful and dangerous stranger. There was no question that Collin had been deceptive, but he was now dead. Did that mean she and Summer no longer needed to worry about a stranger? Except perhaps the opposite was true instead. A dangerous stranger could have been the one who killed Collin.

'What is it?' Dylan asked her, his amusement fading. 'I can see that something is troubling you.'

Hope hesitated. Although she would have dearly liked to tell him about the Tarot cards, she couldn't. It was for the same reason that she hadn't told him about the cards yesterday in the boutique when Gram had been wavering about the trip to Charleston: Dylan was a skeptic. He put no stock in the mystical world. And this was not the occasion for a grand transcendental debate.

'Strangers,' she replied after a moment. It was a truthful yet inexact answer. 'There seem to be a lot of strangers around right now, and I'm uneasy about some of them.'

'I'm glad that you finally realize the problem,' Dylan said.

There was a snideness in his tone that Hope didn't understand.

'If I had known that you were going to spend the night outdoors,' he continued tersely, 'on a rug, under a wide-open canopy, in the middle of the lawn, I would have agreed with Daniel last night that you remain in the wine cellar with us and wait for the police.'

She frowned, still not understanding his crossness.

'I encouraged you to leave the Green Goat because I thought that it would be substantially safer for you at home in the brownstone. But then I arrive here this morning and find you sleeping in this place.' He waved his arm to indicate the gazebo. 'Anyone could have found you – and Summer – lying here as I did. For

God's sake, any stranger could have strolled right up to the two of you and slit your throats!'

Hope's frown melted away. It wasn't because the idea of her and Summer having their throats slit was jolly. It was because Dylan was worried about them.

'You could be seen from every direction,' he chastised her. 'You were completely unprotected.'

'No, we weren't,' she corrected him. 'For starters, the side lawn isn't visible from the street. And we weren't unprotected. We had—'

She broke off abruptly, realizing that what she was about to say was going to make the situation worse, not better. Her eyes went to the pair of lime cushions that were sitting beside her on the rug. One of the cushions had been hers, and the other had been Lucas's. She didn't know when Lucas had left the gazebo or where he had gone, but it occurred to her that she was lucky – very lucky – that he had departed before Dylan had arrived. Unfortunately, based on the way that the cushions were lying, it was pretty clear that they had been used by two people, in close proximity.

Reluctantly, Hope looked up at Dylan. His gaze was on the cushions, and based on the hardness of his stare, there was little doubt that he grasped the situation. She tried to think of a light-hearted remark to defuse the tension and switch the subject, but Dylan spoke first, remaining pointedly on the subject.

'Was Lucas with you?' he asked, his manner stiff.

'Yes.' In an attempt to offer some explanation that wouldn't make it seem as though Lucas had assembled an amorous meeting spot, she added quickly, 'He set up the gazebo for Erik, to protect him from the rain.'

'There was no rain here last night. The streets and ground are dry.'

'That's true, but there were storms moving through the area. With only his tarp and sleeping bag, Erik would have gotten drenched in a downpour.'

Dylan glanced around the perimeter of the gazebo. 'I don't see a tarp, a sleeping bag, or Erik.'

'Well, I don't know where Erik ended up after Megan and I separated from him and Amber in the Green Goat, but the original plan was for him to stay on the side lawn for a couple of nights instead of inside the van.'

Dylan was silent and thoughtful. Hope heard a rustling sound behind her. Summer was waking up.

'So you've finally decided to regain consciousness and join us,' Hope said, turning to her sister with a smile. 'I warned you when you poured that last glass . . .'

Her words trailed away in surprise as she discovered that it wasn't Summer who had made the rustling sound. On the contrary, Summer was still blissfully slumbering with her fuchsia cushion, wholly oblivious to the dazzling morning sunlight, the traffic noise in the street, or the discussion that had been taking place next to her in the gazebo. Hope wasn't sure whether it was a good sign or not. When her sister ultimately did wake up, she would most likely be at one of two extremes: either she would feel as though she had been run over by a steamroller, or she would rise perky and fully refreshed.

The rustling sound repeated itself, the boxwoods at the corner of the brownstone shook, and a moment later, Rosemarie Potter – accompanied by pug Percy – came bursting through the shrubbery.

'Greetings and salutations!' Rosemarie cried.

A gregarious woman in her mid-fifties with a deep suntan and scarlet-dyed hair, Rosemarie was one of the boutique's most devoted clients. She came to the shop at least two or three times a week – almost never with a scheduled appointment and nearly always accompanied by Percy – so Hope wasn't startled at their impromptu visit. She was, however, somewhat surprised by Rosemarie and Percy's physical appearance. Even though it was well before noon, they were already outfitted in their Halloween costumes.

'The boutique door was locked,' Rosemarie said. 'At first I was worried that something was wrong, but then I remembered that the shop is always closed on Halloween because of the party. Happy Halloween!'

'Happy Halloween,' Hope replied, albeit with slightly less exuberance.

It was difficult to match Rosemarie's effusiveness in any respect. Her cheery sociability was one of the reasons that she dropped by the boutique so often. In addition to eagerly obtaining a reading from Hope regarding her habitually bumpy love life, Rosemarie enjoyed gossiping with the shop's other costumers. For his part, Percy was keen on receiving a doggie cookie from the sisters, followed by an extended nap beneath the palm-and-Tarot-reading table.

'I suppose we've come somewhat early,' Rosemarie remarked, a note of concern creeping into her tone. 'You aren't in your costumes yet.'

'We've started off a little slowly today.' Hope motioned toward Summer, who had failed to budge an inch even with Rosemarie's vivacious arrival. 'But let me take a good look at you and Percy so that I can admire your costumes to the full extent.'

Rosemarie took several enthusiastic steps forward on the grass and spun in a clockwise circle, lifting her arms wide to both sides to show off her attire. Ordinarily she had a penchant for billowy, flowered dresses in vivid shades, and her Halloween costume matched both in its theme and color. Rosemarie had transformed into a black-and-fluorescent-yellow butterfly with large gilded wings and a headband topped by sparkling antennae.

'Once again, you've outdone yourself, Rosemarie,' Hope told her. 'Your costume is fabulous.'

'You shine with radiance,' Dylan concurred.

It was a sweet, simple compliment, but coming from Dylan it might as well have been a thousand-word poem of praise. Rosemarie's cheeks promptly flushed as scarlet as her hair.

Dylan smiled. 'You'll have to be on your best butterfly guard this evening, because you're going to attract the attention of every voracious bird of prey.'

Now Rosemarie's entire face grew red.

With some effort, Hope restrained a laugh. Gram hadn't been exaggerating the day before when she had said that Rosemarie practically melted into a puddle when Dylan merely glanced in her direction.

'Oh, oh goodness,' Rosemarie stammered. 'You're so kind . . . I don't really know what to say . . . I . . . I . . .'

Hope gently assisted her. 'And now let's have a look at Percy.'

'Yes, Percy!' Rosemarie clapped her hands with excitement and turned to the pug. 'Percy, give Hope and Dylan a twirl.'

To his credit, the pug was not a twirler. Instead, he trotted toward them, vigorously wiggling his rump in anticipation of a doggie cookie. Although he wasn't in the boutique, he clearly recognized Hope and Summer as the ones who bestowed his favorite treats. Percy was dressed in a one-piece fuzzy black-and-fluorescent-yellow suit that had little gilded wings attached on the back and tiny sparkling antennae fastened at the top, near his head.

'I apologize for the lack of treats, Percy, but if it's any consolation, you make an exceedingly handsome bumblebee,' Hope told him. 'And you coordinate perfectly with Rosemarie. A pair of friendly pollinators. Considering her love of native plants for the boutique's tinctures and teas, I have no doubt that Summer will gush over your costumes when she sees them.' She added silently, *If Summer ever chooses to return to the land of the living.*

Rosemarie beamed.

'I'm impressed by your ingenuity,' Dylan said.

She beamed harder.

He smiled again. 'For Percy's sake, we'll hope that the temperature doesn't climb too high today. We don't want the poor chap to overheat in all that fuzz.'

'Your concern is greatly appreciated, but Percy will be fine whatever the weather brings,' Rosemarie assured him earnestly. 'We've tested his costume several times over the past week, both when it was hot and cold. Last night, for instance. There were some strong gusts of wind and a damp chill, but Percy was as cozy as a caterpillar. Speaking of the weather, isn't the sky lovely this morning? I can certainly understand why you're all outdoors, enjoying the sunshine and the fresh air. I'm glad that the chance of rain from yesterday has passed, because it would be such a hassle to need raincoats and umbrellas to go to the party this evening. I can't tell you how many umbrellas I've lost at parties. I try to tuck them away so carefully, and yet, when I'm ready to head home, they invariably seem to have disappeared . . .'

Hope sighed. She had to tell Rosemarie that there wasn't going to be a party that evening, at least not one in connection with the Green Goat and the boutique. Rosemarie had a wide circle of friends and acquaintances, both in the city of Asheville and the surrounding area. With any luck, one of them was hosting an affair that she could attend instead. Rosemarie was going to take it awfully hard if she couldn't show off her and Percy's costumes to an audience larger than the one presently under the gazebo.

'And while we're on the subject of Percy's health and comfort,' Rosemarie continued, 'I always make sure that he's well hydrated wherever we go.' She looked first at Percy – who had settled himself down for a snooze next to Summer – and then at Hope. 'You have such a nice bowl for him in the boutique. Do you think the restaurant tonight will have something that I can use for his water?'

The sigh repeated itself. Hope really didn't want to be the bearer of such unhappy tidings, but it had to be done. 'Rosemarie,' she began, 'I'm afraid that I have some bad news about tonight—'

'On second thought,' Rosemarie interjected, 'maybe I should bring my own supplies instead.' She turned to Dylan. 'You're a doctor, so you know about these things. Would it be more sanitary to use Percy's regular dishes from home rather than the ones the restaurant might give him?'

It was Dylan's turn to sigh, evidently finding Rosemarie's question to be rather silly, but he answered with admirable patience; 'Percy won't come to any harm using the restaurant's dishes.'

Rosemarie nodded. 'That's such a relief. And it's so helpful to have such information. Isn't it helpful information, Hope?'

Once again, she started to tell Rosemarie about the party's cancellation, but as before, Rosemarie was too animated to listen to her.

'When are you going to get into your costumes?' she chattered.

'Not until later,' Dylan responded. When Rosemarie's face sagged in disappointment, he added, 'It's a surprise.'

There was a little squeal from Rosemarie, and she clapped her hands again. 'Oh, a mystery! How thrilling!'

Dylan laughed.

'But can't I have a clue?' Rosemarie begged him. 'One itty-bitty clue?'

'All right. Here's a clue: Detective Nate and I have similar costumes.'

Hope's head snapped toward him, remembering Dylan's previous proposal – or perhaps *threat* was a more fitting description – for their costumes. 'Please tell me that it's not a pair of Nessies or Bigfoots.'

Dylan's reply was acerbic. 'Are you worried that Nate and I will offend your precious Lucas?'

Her gaze narrowed, but she couldn't in all fairness be angry at him. The lime cushions on the rug gave Dylan ample reason to be angry with her.

Rosemarie paid no attention to their exchange. 'I can guess. I can guess!' she cried. 'A pair of astronauts?'

'Nope. You'll have to try again.'

'Let me think.' Rosemarie considered for a moment. 'One of you is a salt shaker and the other is a pepper shaker?'

Dylan raised an eyebrow at the peculiarity of the guess. 'No. And no other spices or foodstuffs, either.'

Rosemarie deliberated some more, and just as she was beginning to ask for another clue, a new voice cut in.

'What about a magician?'

FIFTEEN

Startled by the unexpected interruption, both Dylan and Rosemarie spun around, and Hope – who had still been sitting on the rug beneath the gazebo – hastily rose to her feet. A man was standing on the near side of the shrubbery at the corner of the brownstone. He was dressed as a children's storybook depiction of a magician or wizard. He wore a tall, pointy, shiny silver hat with equally shiny silver stars pasted on it, a matching silver cape decorated with more stars, and an obviously fake long white beard.

Dylan gave Hope a questioning glance. Did she know the man? She answered with a slight shake of her head. Dylan responded in kind, and they were both instantly on their guard. Rosemarie, on the other hand, was a considerably more trusting and less suspicious soul – who wasn't aware that a murder had occurred in the Green Goat the night before – and she greeted the man with the warmth of an old friend.

'Hello there!' she exclaimed. 'You look so fun and festive. I love your magician costume! Don't you love his magician costume, Hope?'

After the appearance of the Magician and the Seven of Swords in the boutique yesterday, Hope couldn't honestly say that she was fond of magicians – particularly magicians who also happened to be strangers – at the moment, but it didn't matter, because Rosemarie went on without waiting for her to reply.

'We're big fans of Halloween. Isn't that right, Percy? Big, big fans. Oh, how horribly rude of me. I'm Rosemarie Potter, and this bumblebee is Percy Potter. Say hello to the handsome gentleman, Percy.'

Percy lifted his head slightly, found no treats awaiting him, and promptly returned to his nap beside Summer.

The man began to open his mouth as though he was going to introduce himself in turn, but Rosemarie didn't give him the chance.

'It's so nice to meet someone who enjoys the holidays as much as Percy and I do. You do enjoy the holidays, don't you? That's important. You look like an intelligent person with a great feeling for adventure . . .'

Handsome gentleman? An intelligent person with a great feeling for adventure? As Rosemarie continued with her gushing speech, Hope took a closer look at her. Rosemarie's cheeks were stained a dark pink, and she was fluttering her eyelashes. In addition to his costume, she must have spotted something in the man that she liked, because she was decidedly flirting with him. It didn't come as much of a shock to Hope. She had seen Rosemarie jump into the deep end of the dating pool without the least hesitation before. Even after two divorces and several other failed relationships, Rosemarie was still an incurable romantic with the unshakable belief that some combination of fate, destiny, and the higher powers would eventually deliver her soulmate to her door – or, perhaps in this instance, to the side lawn of the Baileys' brownstone.

'I enjoy getting into the celebratory spirit first thing in the day,' Rosemarie proclaimed. 'You must agree with me, because you put on your costume early, too!'

The man finally managed to slip in a word. 'Yes, my son is at an age where he adores Halloween.'

At the mention of a son, Rosemarie's face fell. Hope understood why: a son in all likelihood meant a wife, and under no circumstances did Rosemarie ever become entangled with married men.

'It was my week with him,' the man explained. 'His mother and I share custody, so my son and I went straight from our pajamas into our costumes to enjoy a Halloween breakfast together before she whisked him away for her week.'

Rosemarie's expression instantly brightened. 'That's one of the sweetest things I've ever heard.' Clutching her hands together, she turned toward Hope. 'A Halloween breakfast with his son. Isn't that one of the sweetest things you've ever heard?'

There was a muffled chortle next to her. Hope looked at Dylan from out of the corner of her eye. He was struggling not to laugh aloud. Hope was busy biting her bottom lip for the same reason. Reassured by a court-approved custody schedule, Rosemarie had apparently set her sights on the man once more. Thankfully, no response was required from Hope.

'It was an enjoyable breakfast,' the man said. 'But I realize now that I should have taken off my costume before coming here. It's disrespectful under the circumstances. My only excuse is that I was in a hurry to see you.'

'Disrespectful under the circumstances?' A furrow appeared in Rosemarie's brow. 'You were in a hurry to see us?'

The man first unclipped the shiny silver cape and then pulled off the matching hat, which had been secured by an elastic strap under his chin. The long beard proved more difficult to remove, but after a bit of determined tugging, the adhesive tape holding it in place eventually gave way. There was no natural beard underneath the fake one. The man was clean-shaven, with short, peppered hair. He was of an indeterminate age, somewhere between his late forties to early fifties. His demeanor was earnest.

The furrow in Rosemarie's brow eased, and she gave a pleased little murmur. Evidently the man's appearance without his costume was more than satisfactory to her. For Hope, there was something vaguely familiar about the man.

'That's better,' he said, rolling the cape, hat, and beard together in a loose bundle and setting them down on the ground next to the shrubbery. 'Now we can address the situation properly. I've come to offer my condolences.'

'Your condolences?' Rosemarie echoed, the furrow resurfacing.

Hope swallowed a sigh. Rosemarie had a tendency to parrot when she was perplexed.

The perplexed parroting must also have been a signal to the man that Rosemarie was not the person to whom he should be conveying his condolences, because he visibly directed his attention toward Hope and Dylan.

'I know about the terrible tragedy that occurred yesterday evening, of course, and truth be told, I had a difficult time believing it at first . . .'

As the man spoke, he tilted his head in such a distinct manner that Hope suddenly realized why he seemed familiar to her. She had seen him once before: last night in the Green Goat, talking to Collin by the bar.

'You're Nelson Hatch,' she said.

'Yes, I am.' Nelson appeared more puzzled than surprised. 'Have we met? I'm sorry, but I don't seem to remember that.'

Hope hesitated. She didn't know anything about Nelson other than that he was Daniel's business partner, nor did she know whether he had played any role in Collin's death, so she needed to be careful of what she said, especially relating to what she and Megan had witnessed between him and Collin.

'No, we haven't met,' she answered. 'A friend of mine pointed you out to me: Megan Steele.'

Although it lasted only for an instant, there was a definite change in Nelson's expression at the mention of Megan. It couldn't be that he actively disliked Megan, because she had said that they'd met only in passing when she had dined at the Green Goat with Daniel. Perhaps Megan was a reminder to Nelson of Daniel and the Green Goat's financial troubles. Megan had also said that in her experience, Nelson's sole topic of conversation was business. Interestingly, Nelson hadn't yet broached a business subject on the side lawn.

'Then you must be Hope?' he asked. 'Or Summer?'

'I'm Hope. And this is my sister Summer.' She motioned toward the sleeping figure on the rug.

After looking at Summer quizzically, Nelson gave Hope a polite nod in greeting. 'At least now I know for certain that I'm in the right place. I was worried for a moment when there appeared to be some confusion' – he cast a glance at Rosemarie, who was utterly befuddled by the course of their discussion – 'about my wanting to offer condolences.'

Hope wavered as to how to respond. She and Summer weren't Collin's family, and considering the brevity of their acquaintance, they couldn't genuinely be considered friends. Amber was a far more appropriate recipient for condolences – or perhaps Lucas and Erik at a pinch.

Nelson seemed to understand her awkwardness, because he said, 'I wasn't sure who exactly I should speak with, but Collin had told me that he parked his van by your shop, so I figured this was the best place to start.'

'Yes, he did park his van here, as you probably saw when you arrived.' Hope tried to keep her voice light and casual. Nelson had just admitted to talking to Collin, which offered her the unexpected opportunity to do some digging into the extent of their connection. 'Did you know Collin well?'

He shook his head. 'No, I can't honestly say that I did. Our association was professional, not personal. Aside from a couple of telephone calls and one brief meeting, our contact was entirely electronic.'

'So you two were working together?' Hope pursued, trying to encourage him to elaborate on the subject. She noted that the conversation had taken a clear turn to business.

Nelson hesitated. 'Ordinarily I wouldn't discuss a deal before it's been finalized, but now that there's no chance of the deal ever taking place, I don't suppose that it can hurt anyone to talk about it. Collin had decided to invest in the Green Goat.'

Hope would have followed up with the same question that she had asked Lucas as to whether Collin had intended on being a silent investor only, or if he had also planned on becoming one of the Green Goat's active partners, but Nelson didn't pause long enough.

'I probably haven't told you anything new. You were probably already aware of Collin's purpose in coming to Asheville, considering that you generously allowed him and his travel companions to camp outside your home.' He gestured in the direction of the van and the Airstream.

Up to that point, Dylan had been listening intently without comment, but at the reference to the camping and Collin's travel companions, he expressed his feelings toward both subjects with a derisive snort. Although too quiet to reach Nelson, Hope had no difficulty hearing – or understanding – it.

'You were also generous to your friend Megan,' Nelson continued. 'Or, more accurately, generous to Daniel and me when you agreed to combine your Halloween party with our Halloween party. We greatly appreciated it. Thank you.'

Hope looked at him in surprise. She hadn't expected him to express such gratitude.

'Even the most successful party wouldn't have solved all of our problems,' he told her, 'but it certainly would have helped, especially when combined with a new investor. But finding someone to invest a substantial sum in a relatively unproven business with a limited track record – particularly a restaurant – is far from easy. We've had a number of interested persons, but one after another, they've all fallen by the wayside for a variety of reasons. Finally Collin came along, and it looked as though we might get a lifeline at last. But then yesterday evening happened, and now it's too late.'

Nelson's manner was so sincere and his tone so heartfelt that Hope had considerable sympathy for his struggles, especially since she was a small business owner herself and understood the numerous difficulties that it entailed. Megan had told her how hard Daniel had been working to keep the Green Goat afloat. Clearly Nelson had been working hard, too. Unless Hope was seriously mistaken, it didn't sound to her as though Nelson had been planning on replacing Daniel as a business partner. On the contrary, it sounded as though Daniel had been fully involved in the search for a new investor.

But if Daniel had known about the new investor, why hadn't he told Megan? And more importantly, why hadn't Daniel told them in the wine cellar that he knew Collin? Hope remembered seeing what had appeared to be a flicker of recognition when Daniel had looked at Collin lying on the cellar floor. Could she have misread his reaction? Was it possible that Daniel didn't actually know who Collin was? Nelson's contact with Collin had been predominantly electronic, so perhaps Daniel hadn't previously seen Collin.

'And now it's too late,' Nelson repeated with a sigh. 'The ship has sailed from both ports, so to speak. Any other investor will be too late. And obviously tomorrow will no longer be Halloween, so any other party will be too late, as well.' He took a step toward Hope, as though to emphasize his next point. 'I'm truly sorry about the party. I'm sure that your shop relies at least to some degree on your party each year also, and you'll be forced to suffer the consequences when there is no party tonight.'

'No party tonight!' Rosemarie exclaimed. She may not have comprehended any of the sentences that had preceded them, but she had no difficulty understanding Nelson's all-important last three words. 'How can there not be a party tonight?'

Hope felt somewhat relieved. At least she hadn't been the one to deliver the unhappy news to Rosemarie. And it turned out that she didn't have to give any further explanation to her, either. Nelson voluntarily took the burden on himself.

'There can't be a party tonight due to events beyond our

control,' he told Rosemarie. 'I know that it's dreadfully sad and disappointing, but sometimes bad things happen to good people, and in those difficult moments, you need to find a way to turn the lemons into lemonade . . .'

Hope smiled to herself. It was exactly the sort of clichéd yet optimistic speech that would appeal to Rosemarie. Maybe Rosemarie's instinct upon meeting Nelson Hatch had been correct: she and Nelson were soulmates.

The sanguine speech continued, with Rosemarie listening raptly. Hope was debating whether she could somehow manage to quietly slip away to the brownstone for a much-needed cup of coffee when she caught a small movement by her feet. She looked down and found Summer looking up at her. Although she was still lying stationary on the rug, both of her sister's eyes were open and alert. The effects of the party punch had evidently worn off. Hope was about to ask her how long she had been awake and why she wasn't getting up when Summer shook her head slightly. Hope responded with a questioning frown.

Dylan leaned toward Hope. 'Don't,' he said in a low tone.

She turned her frown to him.

'He hasn't noticed that she's awake. Leave it that way.'

Considering that there was only one man present aside from himself, Dylan was apparently referring to Nelson. But why would Summer – and, for that matter, Dylan – care whether Nelson realized that she was no longer sleeping? Hope remembered that when she had confirmed their names to Nelson, he had looked at Summer quizzically on the rug. At the time, Hope had assumed that it was because he had found it odd for her to be sound asleep while surrounded by bright sunlight and chattering people. But maybe there had been a different reason for his quizzical look. It had almost seemed as though Nelson had recognized Summer in some way.

There was another small movement by her feet. Hope looked down at her sister once more. Summer repeated the slight shake of her head, and then she silently mouthed several words. Hope didn't understand them. Summer tried again.

Nelson is the murderer.

SIXTEEN

Nelson is the murderer? Hope was perplexed. Why would Summer think that? Dylan apparently thought it also – or at least, he thought that Summer had good reason for her belief. But it wasn't logical. Nelson had no motive for killing Collin. On the contrary, Nelson needed Collin alive and in fine fettle so that Collin could invest in the Green Goat. It was the same for Daniel. Collin's death was the last thing that either of them would have wanted if they had any hope of saving their business. And that was especially true as to the location of the death. Collin's murder on the Green Goat's premises was the worst thing that could have happened from a financial standpoint. It forced the cancellation of the Halloween party, closed the place for the indefinite duration of the investigation, and was horrible publicity. It made absolutely no sense for Nelson – or Daniel – to have been the murderer.

Hope studied Nelson. Although she freely admitted that appearance was often unreliable and illusory, Nelson didn't look like a deceitful and dangerous stranger who had attacked Collin with a box cutter in the wine cellar. In fact, he looked the exact opposite. With his earnest demeanor and upbeat oration, he had succeeded in accomplishing a nearly impossible task: comforting Rosemarie as to the loss of the Halloween party. Ordinarily Rosemarie would have been in the depths of despair as to the party's cancellation, but after only a few short minutes under Nelson's benign influence, she seemed tolerably resigned to the disappointing turn of events. She stood close by Nelson's side, her gilded butterfly antennae bobbing in agreement with everything that he said. Nelson had even managed to win over Percy, who had chosen the man's pleasurable pats and scratching under his chin around the edge of the bumblebee suit over a continued nap on the rug. Perhaps Percy had sensed Summer's tension and realized that no treats were in the offing, so he would try his luck elsewhere. The pug's continual quest for treats gave Hope an idea.

'Why don't we all go into the boutique?' she suggested.

Everyone – sans Summer – turned to her.

'Percy has been patiently waiting for one of his cookies, and the rest of us can sit down on a comfortable chair,' Hope said.

She had no doubt that Rosemarie would be in favor of the plan. Rosemarie was perpetually concerned that dear Percy might be hungry or thirsty, and she typically preferred sitting to standing, even when she was clad in less decorative and more pragmatic footwear. Today she had on strappy gold high heels that were a marvelous match for her costume but didn't do well in the soft grass on the side lawn, particularly over a prolonged period.

As predicted, Rosemarie wasted no time in voicing her approval for their change in location. She was apparently unwilling to take the chance that Nelson might have a different opinion on the subject and use it as an excuse to depart, because she scooped up the magician costume that he had deposited on the ground next to the shrubbery and immediately began herding Nelson and Percy in the direction of the brownstone.

'Have you been in the sisters' boutique before?' she chattered to Nelson. 'No? Oh, you'll love it! You should let Hope take a look at your palm. Yes, she does palm readings. Didn't you know? And she reads the Tarot, too. Yes, Tarot cards. It's quite exciting. You'll be amazed at what she can see. You can ask her any question, and she'll . . .'

Watching the pair, Hope smiled to herself. Rosemarie was carrying on the conversation with sufficient gusto for both of them. When given the opportunity, Nelson would respond with a word or two, but his contribution mostly consisted of keeping a sturdy hand under Rosemarie's elbow so that each time she wobbled and one of her heels sank precariously into the loose soil, he could steady her.

'I fear that you've made a grievous mistake,' Dylan said.

Hope looked at him.

He chuckled. 'Now you won't be able to get Rosemarie out of your shop for the remainder of the day. The butterfly, bumblebee, and magician will stay put until the bell tolls midnight and All Hallows' Eve comes to a close.'

'You're probably right,' Hope agreed, chuckling also. 'But I didn't have many options. If Summer didn't want to move from the rug while Nelson was out here, then the only option was to move Nelson elsewhere. And it was pretty clear that the best way to move Nelson was to move Rosemarie.'

Dylan chuckled some more. 'Maybe in addition to the boutique's other services, you should put *matchmaker* on the list of offerings. You seem to have sparked a budding romance between those two.'

'I hope you aren't too disappointed about that. If Rosemarie is infatuated with Nelson, then she won't be nearly as infatuated with you. Won't you miss the way that she giggles and blushes at you?'

'Not if I can get you to giggle and blush at me instead.'

Hope rolled her eyes. 'You are incorrigible.'

'I've never denied it. And while we're on the subject, with no party tonight, you can spend the evening alone with me instead. I'll protect you from the Halloween ghosts and goblins. A costume is optional.'

She rolled her eyes again. 'And with that you no doubt mean that all clothing is optional?'

Dylan grinned shamelessly. 'If that's what you'd like. I certainly have no objection to us passing the time together naked. I can think of plenty of things that we could do to entertain and occupy ourselves—'

He was interrupted by Summer, who had finally decided to quit playing a somnolent version of possum.

'Is Nelson gone?' Summer whispered. She had lifted her head a few inches above the rug, and her eyes darted about furtively. 'Is he far enough away that he can't see me?'

Hope looked toward the brownstone. Nelson, Rosemarie, and Percy were just turning the corner out of sight. 'You're safe. They're headed to the boutique.'

With a sigh of relief, Summer sat up and stretched her shoulders and back. 'My muscles are so stiff that they actually hurt. You can't imagine how hard it is to remain motionless for that long.'

'But why on earth did you want to remain motionless?' Hope said.

Summer frowned at her as though it was an inane question. 'Didn't you understand me before? Nelson is the murderer!'

'Even assuming that's the case, why would you—'

'Because he knows that I know that he's the murderer!'

It took Hope a moment to process her sister's words. 'You were pretending to be asleep because you didn't want a confrontation with Nelson?'

'Precisely!'

Now Hope frowned. Nelson hadn't seemed the least bit menacing to her. He had arrived on the side lawn wearing a shiny silver hat and cape with stars pasted on them and had talked about sharing a Halloween breakfast with his young son, all of which were far from ominous. But Summer was rarely intimidated by anyone, so if she was worried about a confrontation with Nelson, then Hope knew that there must be a good reason for it.

'Why do you think that Nelson is the murderer?' she asked her.

'Because I saw him.'

'You saw Nelson kill Collin?' Hope exclaimed, startled.

Summer hurriedly shushed her. 'Not so loud. Nelson will hear you.'

She glanced at the brownstone once more. No one was visible. 'They're gone, but they won't be gone for long if I don't open the boutique for them.'

'Dylan will have to go with you,' Summer said.

Hope cast her an irritated look. 'I don't require Dylan's assistance to unlock a door that I've unlocked ten thousand times before.'

Summer turned to Dylan. 'You need to go with Hope to the boutique. We don't want her to be alone with Nelson. He may have figured out that she talked to me.'

'Hmm?' Dylan murmured, his thoughts evidently elsewhere.

Laughing, Summer turned back to her sister. 'I don't suppose that we can expect too much of a response from him while he's still dreaming about spending the evening with you naked.'

Hope's irritated look repeated itself. 'Setting Percy aside, Rosemarie is currently alone with Nelson, so this is not the time for jokes if she's in any sort of danger and needs our help. How could you have seen Nelson kill Collin? You didn't know that Collin was dead until I told you and Lucas about what had happened.'

Dylan must have been at least partially listening to their conversation, because at her mention of Lucas, he visibly stiffened. Hope, however, was far more concerned about Rosemarie's safety at the moment than Dylan's possible annoyance, and she kept her focus on Summer.

'I didn't actually see Nelson kill Collin,' Summer told her.

'What did you see?'

'I was in the alley behind the Green Goat, trying to get an update from Gram and Morris about their trip.'

'And?' Hope pursued impatiently, already knowing that portion of the story.

'And I was walking back and forth, searching for a better signal on my phone, when all of a sudden, this man slammed straight into me from behind. It was clear that he had come from the Green Goat, because when I turned around to look at him, I saw that the back door of the place was standing wide open. The man seemed just as surprised to have crashed into me as I was, because he stared at me for a moment. Then he dashed down the alley and disappeared from view.'

'Did he speak to you?'

'No, aside from a sort of gurgling noise. As I said, he was too surprised, and he was breathing too heavily from running.'

'This man was Nelson?' Hope asked her.

'Yes.'

'You're positive? Because I was in the alley behind the Green Goat myself last night, and there was only one orange security light. The visibility wasn't great.'

'I know who I saw,' Summer responded, a touch indignantly. 'If the man standing at the edge of the gazebo this morning was Nelson, then the man who collided with me in the alley yesterday evening was Nelson.'

Hope considered for a moment. That explained why Nelson had looked at Summer quizzically on the rug. He had recognized her from the night before. But Nelson recognizing Summer and him being in the alley didn't mean that he was a murderer.

'So why do you believe that Nelson killed Collin?' Hope said.

'Because he had blood on him!' Summer replied.

'Blood?'

'*Blood*,' she repeated with emphasis. 'Obviously I couldn't collect a sample from him and take it to a lab for an analysis comparing it with Collin's blood, but why would Nelson have blood on him if he wasn't the one who had killed Collin? Why would he come charging out of the back door of the Green Goat if he wasn't guilty and racing away from the scene of the crime?'

'Maybe he stumbled across Collin's body and was so horrified by the discovery that he panicked and fled,' Hope suggested.

Summer sucked on her teeth doubtfully. 'Innocent people don't panic and flee. They stay put and call the police.'

'Not everyone reacts the same way. Take Rosemarie, for example. If she had found Collin lying on the floor of the wine cellar, she wouldn't have paused to check his vital signs and contact emergency services. She would have screamed her head off and galloped for the nearest exit in an absolute terror. And Rosemarie is about the last person in the world who would ever kill anybody.'

'Unless they threatened her beloved Percy,' Summer said.

'Unless they threatened her beloved Percy,' Hope agreed. 'But seriously, I don't think that we can put too much weight on Nelson sprinting from the scene, at least not all by itself. We need something more than that pointing to his guilt.'

'What about the blood?' Summer argued.

'How much blood are we talking about? Where exactly was it on Nelson? And are you sure that it actually was blood, because as we already discussed, there wasn't much light in the alley.'

Summer sucked on her teeth again. 'Why are you so determined to defend Nelson? Just because Rosemarie is suddenly enthralled with the man doesn't mean that he's overflowing with goodness and light. As we've seen on more than one occasion in the past, Rosemarie doesn't always show the most prudent taste regarding her romantic attachments. Plus, Nelson came here dressed as a magician. We don't like or trust magicians this weekend, remember?'

'Why don't you like or trust magicians?' Dylan asked them. 'You mentioned something about that yesterday, too. No magician costumes for the party. Why not?'

Disregarding Dylan, Hope said to her sister, 'I'm not defending Nelson. On the contrary, I have quite a few unanswered questions about him. I don't know when he and Collin separated yesterday in the Green Goat, where Nelson went afterward, and what or who he might have seen or heard during that time. But even with all of that, I'm hesitant to accuse Nelson of attacking Collin when he – and Daniel – have the weakest motive out of everyone involved in the matter. For the survival of their business, they needed Collin to invest, not die.'

'The motive is weak,' Dylan concurred, not belaboring the subject of magicians. 'But the issue of the blood needs to be addressed.'

Summer nodded vigorously.

Hope looked at Dylan in surprise. 'Did you see blood on Nelson last night, too?'

'No, but I saw his shoes today.'

Her surprise grew. 'Nelson has blood on his shoes today? Right now, you mean? I can't claim to have studied his clothing in great detail, but I thought that he was wearing reasonably new and clean athletic shoes. I noticed them when he was helping to steady Rosemarie on the grass in her strappy high heels.'

Summer nodded again, with slightly less vigor. 'You're right. Even from a distance and with my eyes closed a majority of the time, I got a pretty good view from the rug of everybody's feet on the lawn. There was no visible blood on Nelson's shoes.'

Hope shook her head in confusion. 'So what blood did you see yesterday?' She turned to Dylan. 'And what did you see today?'

'I saw blood on Nelson's shoes last night,' Summer told her. 'As he ran away from the Green Goat, he left marks behind in the alley. Granted, they weren't perfect footprints. They were just wavy smears. I wasn't sure that it was blood then, but after seeing Nelson today, I'm now convinced.'

'That matches what I saw last night,' Dylan said. He looked at Hope. 'Do you remember the pool of blood in the wine cellar?'

'Yes, of course. It isn't something that I'll ever forget—' She broke off, her eyes widening with a sudden realization. 'Just before I left the cellar, I had the impression that you had spotted something important. You kept examining the floor, and you seemed to be more focused on the blood than Collin himself.'

It was Dylan's turn to nod. 'Although it was only along one edge, the pool of blood appeared to me to have been disturbed.

When Nate and his colleagues arrived, and we finally got some good light in the place, it was clear that somebody had indeed come into contact with the blood. They didn't step into the middle of the pool, so their shoes wouldn't have been saturated. As I said, it was only along one edge, but as the person moved away afterward, they left behind shoeprints. The prints weren't well defined. They were wavy smears.'

'Wavy smears!' Summer exclaimed. 'That's exactly what I saw in the alley.'

'If you take a look at Nelson's feet when you unlock the door of the boutique for him and Rosemarie,' Dylan continued to Hope, 'you'll see that his athletic shoes are the type with a wavy sole that would create a wavy smear.'

'I told you,' Summer declared triumphantly. 'Nelson is the murderer!'

'Not necessarily,' Dylan countered.

Summer frowned at him. 'But you just said—'

He didn't let her finish. 'I said that the shoes Nelson is wearing today may match the prints left in the wine cellar and the alley last night. But there are a lot of athletic shoes in this country with wavy soles. Even if we tested Nelson's shoes now, and there was enough residue on the soles to match Collin's blood, it only proves that Nelson was in the wine cellar. We already know that he was in the Green Goat generally. You saw him in the alley, and Hope and Megan saw him in the bar talking to Collin. It doesn't prove that he killed Collin.'

'There are too many coincidences,' Summer contended stubbornly. 'And I don't believe in coincidences.'

'If Nate were here,' Dylan replied, 'he would tell you that coincidences are helpful but don't hold up in a court of law. And that's especially true in this case, considering that there were a second set of shoeprints in the wine cellar.'

Summer was momentarily rendered speechless.

'A second set?' Hope asked Dylan.

'A second set,' he confirmed. 'Similar to Nelson's – assuming that the first set indeed belongs to Nelson – they're poorly defined and more smears than actual prints. But there is no doubt that a second person came into contact with the pool of blood. The problem with the second set of prints, however, is that they only travel a short distance. Unlike Nelson's, which can be followed up the back stairs and into the alley before they disappear, the second set makes it no further than the edge of the wine cellar. There is no trace of them in the corridor or beyond, so the person who created them could have gone in any direction, and there wouldn't have been enough blood remaining on their shoes for anyone – including us – to have noticed it.'

There was a pause as they all considered who the second set of shoeprints might belong to.

Finally, Hope headed toward the shop. 'I'd better open the door for Rosemarie.'

'Dylan,' Summer began, 'I still think that you should go with Hope. I know that you're not convinced about Nelson's guilt, but I'm sure that we can all agree it's better to be safe than sorry when a possible murderer is—'

She was interrupted by a piercing scream.

SEVENTEEN

At the scream, Hope froze mid-step on the grass. For a brief moment, she wondered if her ears might have been playing a trick on her. Then came a second scream, even shriller than the first. She had no doubt who both of the screams belonged to: Rosemarie.

'I told you that Nelson is dangerous,' Summer cried. 'But you didn't want to believe me! I warned you that he—'

The remainder of her sister's reprimand was lost to Hope as she began to race across the side lawn in the direction of the boutique. Why would Nelson attack Rosemarie? Rosemarie hadn't seen or heard anything that could incriminate him – or, for that matter, anyone else. She had never even met Collin. She didn't know whether Collin was a conspiracy theorist, or about his travels in the camper van with Amber and Erik, or that he had planned on investing in the Green Goat. Thank heaven Dylan was at hand. With his medical training, he could help Rosemarie if she was injured. Surely nothing too grievous could happen to her before Nelson could be stopped.

At top speed, Hope rounded the corner of the brownstone. She looked past the shrubbery and down the front walk. There were people standing at the door of the boutique. Rosemarie was among them. When she let out a third scream, Hope promptly slowed to a walk. They weren't screams of fear or pain. Rosemarie wasn't in the process of being stabbed or strangled. On the contrary, with the way that her arms were wrapped around Nelson, there seemed to be a good chance that she might injure him instead. Rosemarie was hugging Nelson with such unbridled enthusiasm that a cracked rib and punctured lung didn't appear at all unlikely.

Dylan – who had also started to sprint across the lawn at the first indication of distress – similarly slackened his pace when he reached Hope. His interpretation of the situation was evidently the same as hers, because he remarked dryly, 'If Rosemarie squeezes the man any harder, we're going to have another dead body on our hands, albeit this one slightly more accidental.'

From the distance that separated them and the noise that she was making, it was improbable that Rosemarie heard Dylan's words, but she noticed his and Hope's arrival. 'Oh Hope!' she exclaimed. 'And Dylan! Just wait until you hear! It's wonderful! It's the most wonderful news!'

The only wonderful news that Hope could imagine at that moment would be if it turned out that they had all made a terrible mistake the night before, and Collin wasn't really dead. Sadly, she knew that wasn't possible.

Rosemarie turned to Nelson for confirmation. 'Isn't it wonderful news?'

Although Nelson tried to speak, he managed no more than an affirmative squeak while trapped in Rosemarie's bear hug.

Perhaps Percy had developed his own soft spot for Nelson and observed that the man's face was growing increasingly purple, because he raised his head toward Rosemarie and give a little yip.

'What is it, Percy?' Rosemarie asked, immediately focusing her attention on the pug. 'What's bothering you?'

Percy couldn't give a direct answer, of course, but if his aim had been to help Nelson, he succeeded nonetheless. As Rosemarie leaned down to check that Percy's collar wasn't choking him and his costume wasn't cutting off the circulation to any of his appendages, she simultaneously released her hold on Nelson.

Nelson took a couple of deep breaths – and a cautionary step backward in the event that Rosemarie suddenly decided to start squeezing him again – but he didn't appear to be in need of emergency medical assistance.

'Percy is thrilled,' Rosemarie announced as she straightened back up, fully satisfied as to the pug's well-being. 'You can see it in his expression. It's sheer joy.'

Percy yawned.

'We're all in a state of sheer joy,' Rosemarie maintained. As she looked between Hope and Dylan, her expression dimmed slightly. 'Where is Summer? Is she still sleeping? Maybe we should wake her. I'm sure that she'll want to hear this as soon as—'

'I'm here,' Summer interjected.

Everyone turned toward her in surprise. Summer had likewise come running from the gazebo at the sound of Rosemarie's screeches, but in contrast to Hope and Dylan – who had reached the front walk – she had halted close to the corner of the brownstone, as though to maintain a safe distance from the group. Hope noted that her sister studiously avoided any eye contact with Nelson.

'I'm here,' Summer repeated flatly. 'So go ahead and tell us your supposedly wonderful news, Rosemarie.'

'Well, it isn't really *my* news,' she clarified. 'It's *his* news.'

The kerfuffle with Rosemarie and Nelson had taken so much of Hope's attention that she had failed to notice there was a person standing to the far side of the pair, partially obscured by them and the recessed entrance to the boutique. As Rosemarie gestured toward the person, he stepped forward into full view. It was Lucas.

'Kiss me,' he said, looking at Hope. 'I've saved Halloween.'

'You've saved Halloween!' Rosemarie cried – and promptly rewarded Lucas with a large smacking kiss on his lips.

Lucas responded with his crooked smile. 'Actually, I was speaking to Hope, but I always appreciate receiving a warm kiss from a beautiful woman.'

'Oh, well, I . . .' Rosemarie giggled and blushed.

Hope couldn't help smiling also. It wasn't because Lucas had wanted her to kiss him. It was because Gram had been correct yesterday about Lucas being a smooth talker. He had managed to flatter both her and Rosemarie in the same sentence.

Dylan muttered something under his breath. Hope couldn't make out the words, but she had no doubt that they weren't flattering toward Lucas.

While continuing to giggle and blush, Rosemarie proclaimed, 'It's true! He's saved Halloween! There's going to be a party tonight, after all.'

Hope's smile faded. 'No, Rosemarie, there isn't going to be a party tonight.'

'Yes, yes, there will be,' she insisted. 'Lucas has arranged it. He's organized everything. It's all fixed.'

'It can't be fixed,' Hope told her.

'Yes, yes, it can—' Rosemarie began again before being interrupted by Lucas.

'You're right, Hope,' he said. 'It can't be fixed. The events of last night can't be undone. If they could be, we would all return to yesterday evening and alter the heinous outcome. But regrettably, none of us has that ability – not even Erik, no matter how close he might be to achieving a breakthrough in interdimensional time travel.'

There was more muttering from Dylan.

Lucas went on, 'We certainly don't mean to belittle a death by discussing festivities and business affairs. But the wheel of life continues to turn. Collin would recognize that. He would want us to march forward with happiness, not stagger backward in sorrow.'

Both Rosemarie and Nelson appeared to be engrossed by the speech. Summer, on the other hand, raised an eyebrow at it.

'So after we've paid our homage and the moment of grief has passed,' Lucas concluded, 'we must look to the future and take a step toward tomorrow.'

Now Hope also raised an eyebrow. The smooth-talking was perhaps a bit too smooth and glib under the circumstances.

'Those were my thoughts exactly, only you've expressed them much better than I ever could have,' Nelson said earnestly to Lucas. 'I came here to offer my condolences, and then I began talking about Collin investing in the Green Goat and how without him and without the party, our business would suffer. It must have sounded callous, terribly callous.'

'Not in the least!' Rosemarie protested. 'I thought that your words about finding a way to turn lemons into lemonade were lovely. And there's no shame in wanting your business to not only survive but also to thrive. It's completely natural.'

'Completely natural,' Lucas agreed. 'That was my intention as well. I want Hope and Summer's business to thrive, which is why I've arranged and organized everything. The party for tonight is no longer canceled!'

There was a pause.

Lucas's crooked smile reappeared. 'You can kiss me now, Hope, because I have in fact saved Halloween.'

Hope didn't kiss him. She wasn't sure how to respond, because she wasn't sure what he meant. How could the party no longer be canceled?

Dylan's reply was terse. 'You can't reinstate the party.'

'That just shows how little you know,' Lucas rejoined.

Summer frowned at Lucas. 'I haven't spoken to Nate about it, but I'm quite certain that he and his colleagues wouldn't allow any party to take place at the Green Goat while the investigation into Collin's death was ongoing. It wouldn't matter how desperately someone pleaded with them, or how much Nate wanted to help the boutique, or how securely the lower level of the Green Goat could be separated from the upper level—'

'I never said that the party was going to take place at the Green Goat,' Lucas interrupted her.

Hope sighed, frustrated. 'We already discussed this earlier. The party can't be moved back to the boutique on such short notice.'

'I didn't say that the party was going to be at the boutique, either,' he replied.

Now both Hope and Summer frowned at him. Lucas's crooked smile broadened as though he was in possession of a great secret, but before he could divulge it to them, Rosemarie jumped in, having apparently exhausted her patience and too giddy about the news to delay sharing it any longer.

'Lucas told Nelson and me all about it while we were waiting for Hope to unlock the door,' she explained. 'The party is going to be in an entirely new location. It's going to be outside!'

'Outside?' Summer echoed with surprise.

Hope turned to Lucas questioningly.

He inclined his head in confirmation. 'It's also as we discussed earlier. We agreed that a party could be pulled together for this evening if the entire event would take place outside. And that's where your party will be: outside.'

'But—'

Lucas preempted her misgiving. 'Before you protest that there isn't enough room on the side lawn and in the back garden and alley for everyone, let me add that it's not outside here. It's outside elsewhere—'

Rosemarie jumped in a second time, clapping her hands excitedly. 'The party is going to be at the pumpkin patch!'

'The pumpkin patch?' Summer echoed with even greater surprise than before.

'Isn't that absolutely perfect for Halloween?' Rosemarie exclaimed. She went on clapping her hands and looked so elated at the prospect that she moved toward Nelson as though she was about to clasp him in another suffocating bear hug. Thankfully for him, he was a step too far away to be easily embraced.

Hope knew of only one pumpkin patch in the area. 'The Lambert pumpkin patch?' she asked Lucas.

Again, he inclined his head in confirmation.

'And Richard Lambert agreed to this?'

'He did.'

Hope and Summer exchanged a glance.

'Are you sure?' Summer said to Lucas doubtfully. 'Because Richard Lambert doesn't usually allow people on his property. The pumpkins are just left to rot in the patch every autumn. It's always been a mystery why he plants them but doesn't harvest them or let anyone else harvest them. And it's been going on that way for years. When his uncle used to own the place, he would run trespassers – including Hope and me and other curious kids – off his land with a shotgun.'

Dylan gave a derisive snort in Lucas's direction. 'Your idea of saving Halloween is to get everybody either shot at or arrested for trespassing? You are aware that Summer's boyfriend is a police detective?'

'I'm aware of that,' Lucas snapped. 'And nobody is going to get shot at or arrested for trespassing. I talked to Richard about the party at length this morning, and he's happy for the pumpkin patch to be of use.'

Hope and Summer exchanged another glance.

'Are you sure?' Summer said again, no less doubtful than the first time.

'Of course I'm sure.' Although he didn't snap at Summer to the same degree that he had at Dylan, Lucas was clearly growing exasperated by their continued skepticism. He turned to Hope. 'Do you remember yesterday in the Green Goat when I recognized someone and went to talk to them?'

'Yes.'

'That person was Richard. My father and his uncle knew each

other many years ago, and Richard and I have subsequently run into each other at various events in various locales.'

The derisive snort from Dylan repeated itself. 'So what type of conspiracy theorist is Richard?'

Although Hope winced slightly at the question, she was interested in hearing the answer.

'I misspoke,' Dylan corrected himself. 'What type of *truth* is Richard *seeking*?'

His tone was unabashedly mocking, but Lucas wasn't intimidated.

'Richard is an alien contactee,' he told them.

The horn from a delivery truck sounded down the street and the siren from a fire engine wailed in the distance, but among the group outside the brownstone and boutique, there was a deafening silence. Both Hope and Summer shifted uncomfortably. Nelson appeared puzzled at the direction of the conversation. Dylan squinted at Lucas as though he was beginning to think that there might be something medically wrong with him. Rosemarie was the only one who seemed to find the mention of aliens wholly uncontroversial.

'My cousin Anastasia—' Interrupting herself, Rosemarie explained to Hope and Summer, 'She's the one with the wire-haired dachshund, Bella.'

The sisters nodded, having heard of Rosemarie's cousin and her wire-haired dachshund on more than one occasion previously.

'Anastasia,' Rosemarie continued, 'has seen numerous spacecraft hovering over a hill behind her home. One of her neighbors told her that they were weather balloons from the local university, but Anastasia doesn't believe it.'

'Did she document her experience?' Lucas asked her.

'Oh, yes! She wrote all about it in her journal.'

'I'd like to read that, if she'll let me. And I know that Richard would be extremely interested also. Perhaps she could bring the journal to the party tonight?'

'Oh, no. Anastasia and Bella live in West Virginia. They're too far away to come to the party. I did invite them, of course, but Bella doesn't do well on long car rides. She much prefers the train – as does Percy – except there isn't a good train connection between their home and ours . . .'

As Rosemarie mapped out the logistical difficulties of train travel between West Virginia and North Carolina, Dylan turned to Hope.

'I need to talk to Nate,' he said quietly. 'Will you and Summer be all right alone here for a while?'

'We'll be fine,' Hope assured him.

Dylan cast a wary eye first toward Lucas, and then at Nelson. 'I don't trust either of them.'

'You don't have to trust them. It's the middle of the day, and we'll be in the boutique. What could happen?'

'Collin probably believed the same thing in the wine cellar yesterday evening.'

Hope had no response for that. It certainly wasn't a comforting thought.

'I won't be gone long.' Dylan took a step in the direction of the street and his car. 'You can tell Summer that Nate is—'

Rosemarie must have noticed Dylan's movement and correctly interpreted it as a signal that he was on the cusp of departing, because she cut both herself and him off simultaneously. 'Here I am prattling on about train schedules when there is important work to be done! Dylan, I can see that you're diving straight in, and we must follow your spirited lead. We have to start contacting people and inform them about the party's new location. And we need to make signs to indicate the change. Lots and lots of signs! We'll put one or two up here. I don't think that more are necessary, because most people were already aware that the party had been moved from the boutique to the Green Goat. Wouldn't you agree, Hope?'

Hope didn't have a chance to agree or disagree, because Rosemarie went on without pausing.

'But we'll have to plaster the Green Goat's windows and doors with signs giving directions.'

Nelson began to volunteer his assistance with the Green Goat's signs, but Rosemarie shook her head.

'No, no, you're needed for other things. The food and drink can't be forgotten. What did the Green Goat have planned in that regard?' She didn't wait for Nelson's reply any more than she had Hope's a moment earlier and promptly turned to Lucas. 'What did you have in mind for the food and drink at the pumpkin patch?'

'A barbecue,' Lucas answered as Rosemarie took a breath. 'Hope and I discussed it last night, and I discussed it with Richard this morning. He's on board with the idea, and he's hosted groups before—'

'Probably groups of aliens who were making pumpkin patch crop circles,' Dylan said.

Thankfully, his tone was low enough that only Hope heard the remark.

'—So the grills and fuel are taken care of,' Lucas continued. 'And there are stacks of foldable chairs and tables in one of the sheds on the property. I took a look at them. They're not fancy, but they're fully functional and will serve the intended purpose.'

'The Green Goat is stocked with meat and buns,' Nelson told them. 'Condiments and paper products, too. They're all easy to move.'

'Excellent. That's excellent,' Rosemarie commended him.

Nelson looked quite pleased at her praise. 'I'll have to check on how we can transport the beverages.'

'Having personally sampled it, I can confirm that Hope has a first-class supply of party punch ready and waiting,' Lucas said.

'Which leaves us with lighting and decorations. I know plenty of ladies who can bring a string or two of twinkle lights on short notice. Is electricity available at the patch?' Rosemarie asked Lucas.

'I'll talk to Richard about how it's set up.'

'As for decorations, I'm sure that most of the ladies can also bring some extras from their homes.' Rosemarie turned to Nelson. 'Does the Green Goat have anything appropriate for outdoor use?'

'Daniel was working on the decorations previously, so I'll check with him when I check on the beverages.'

'Excellent. That's excellent,' Rosemarie said again.

Hope was impressed. Usually Rosemarie tended toward the jumbled and mildly chaotic. But something about the Halloween party had brought out her hidden organizational talents. Maybe it was because she was determined to show off her and Percy's costumes to a large audience.

Rosemarie looked up at the cloudless sky. 'At least the weather today is good, and there isn't any chance of rain later. That's the one thing we have no control over. As I said to Hope earlier, it would be such a hassle to need raincoats and umbrellas this evening – and that was before I knew we would be outside!'

Nelson and Lucas nodded in agreement.

For no explicable reason, Hope suddenly found herself wishing that a freak thunderstorm would wash out All Hallows' Eve and the party.

EIGHTEEN

'I don't have a good feeling about tonight,' Hope said.

Summer trumped her. 'I haven't had a good feeling about it since yesterday when we were carrying Gram's luggage down the hall stairs.'

'We should have gone to Charleston with her and Morris.'

'We never should have agreed to participate in any Halloween party that wasn't at the boutique.'

'It isn't really our party anymore.'

'No, now it's Lucas's party with Richard's pumpkin patch, Nelson's food, Daniel's decorations, Rosemarie's signs, and assorted ladies' twinkle lights. Our sole contribution is the party punch.'

'On the upside, we have a lot less work than if we were still the hosts. And we have pie,' Hope added, digging her fork into the contents of the aluminum pie tin that was sitting in front of her on the brownstone's kitchen island.

'And we have pie,' Summer echoed, pulling her stool closer to the island and likewise digging her fork into the tin.

'I suppose that we should have cut it into polite pieces and put them on plates,' Hope said.

'Any other day, yes. But not today. Consider it our Halloween treat.'

'This pie is really good, so if it's our treat, then we should be expecting a correspondingly bad trick.'

Summer gave a little shrug and took another forkful of pie. 'There's already been one murder. How much worse of a trick can there be? A second murder?'

'Don't joke about that.'

'I certainly won't joke about Gwen Podolski – or her niece – ever again. Gwen makes an absolutely fantastic pie. I know that apple is more traditional at this time of year, but I've never had an apple pie that's even half as good as this peach one. Gwen must have been exceedingly pleased with the Tarot reading yesterday to bring us a freshly baked pie today. You apparently succeeded in making the Seven of Swords sound highly auspicious for her.'

'At least there's one person who's happy with the Tarot cards this weekend,' Hope remarked.

'I saw on the appointment calendar that Gwen is scheduled for another reading next week. If you make it a happy reading again, maybe we'll get a second pie. Do you think that Gwen can do a raspberry one? I love raspberries.'

Hope responded by eating some more peach pie.

After breaking off a large piece of buttery crust, Summer said, 'What's going on with Lucas?'

'I assume that he's at the pumpkin patch directing the arrangement of the grills or chairs or twinkle lights. When I asked him if we could lend a hand, he told me that between Richard's friends and the Green Goat's staff and Rosemarie's battalion of helpful ladies, there were more than enough people for every task.'

'I wasn't referring to Lucas's present location and activity,' Summer replied. 'I was referring to you and Lucas.'

'Me and Lucas?'

Summer gave her sister a meaningful look. 'The two of you seemed pretty cozy under the gazebo last night.'

Hope frowned. 'I had a chill, and Lucas spread a blanket over my legs. It wasn't a big deal.'

'Did you also have a chill when he wrapped his arm around your shoulders and you curled up with him on the cushions?'

The frown deepened.

'Don't be angry with me,' Summer said. 'I'm not chastising you for a bit of snuggling on a comfy rug. I just want you to be careful. Talking about the Tarot reminded me of the warning we had from the Magician. We can argue about whether Lucas is considered a stranger, but stranger or not, there isn't much doubt that he won't be available for many more cozy nights under the gazebo.'

The remark surprised Hope. 'Do you think that Lucas might be arrested? You can't seriously believe that he killed Collin?'

Summer spread her hand ruefully. 'At this point, I don't know what to believe. Between Amber's jealous streak and her threats, the blood on Nelson's shoes and in the alley, and the unidentified second set of shoeprints in the wine cellar, I honestly have no clue who to trust and who to be wary of. There are so many questions without answers right now. For instance, where are Amber and Erik? Neither one of them has been seen or heard from since last night in the bar. Are they even aware that Collin is dead? And then there's Richard Lambert. He never lets anyone near that pumpkin patch of his, and now all of a sudden at Lucas's request, he's agreed to allow a Halloween party there?'

'Maybe Richard was amenable because Lucas is a fellow conspiracy theorist,' Hope suggested.

'Even assuming that you're right,' Summer replied, 'and there's nothing fishy about his connection to Richard, Lucas still won't be available for many more cozy nights with you under the gazebo. I didn't mean before that I thought he would be arrested for killing Collin. I meant that Lucas wasn't going to remain in Asheville for much longer. As soon as the police allow him to leave the city, Lucas will pack the gazebo back into the Airstream and drive off to continue his search for the chupacabra or whatever other cryptid he's decided to study next.'

Hope was silent.

'You're not too upset about that, are you?' Summer asked her, with visible concern. 'I know that Lucas has said some nice things about Asheville, and he indicated yesterday that he was going to schedule a viewing of the Larsons' brownstone and possibly put in an offer on the place, but I'm not sure how seriously we should take any of that from him. His dad spent decades on the road before finally settling down in Maine. Lucas doesn't seem to me to be quite at that stage yet.'

'I agree. I don't think that he's ready to grow roots or tomatoes next door.' When her sister breathed an audible sigh of relief, Hope smiled. 'There isn't any need to worry. I haven't fallen desperately in love with Lucas only to have my heart crushed when he abruptly departs. There was just something warm and steadying about him last night. And there might be something warm and steadying about him again before he leaves. But I have no illusions that he's going to unhitch his Airstream here permanently—'

'You may not have fallen desperately in love with Lucas, but he's going to fall desperately in love with you when he sees you in that costume,' Megan interjected drolly.

Startled, Hope and Summer spun on their stools toward the open doorway that led from the kitchen into the main hall.

'He'll face some stiff competition from Dylan, of course,' Megan continued. 'And Nate will forget all about his investigation, because he'll be too busy drooling over Summer in her costume to think of anything else.'

The sisters laughed.

'There was no one in the boutique, so I came through the brownstone when I heard your voices—' Megan broke off in the middle of her explanation. 'Good golly, it smells heavenly in here. Is that fresh pie?'

'Grab a fork and a stool,' Hope answered.

Megan wasted no time in taking one of the empty seats at the island and digging into the pie.

'While we're on the subject of drooling,' Hope said, 'Daniel won't be fretting about party decorations or the state of the Green Goat's finances when he sees your costume, Megan. That walnut-brown jumpsuit is sexy.'

Summer nodded in agreement. 'I have to admit that I was doubtful of your idea at the outset, but I was wrong. You make an outstanding broom. You got those bristles to match your hair exactly. It's really quite gorgeous.'

'Thank you. I had a little trouble with the—'

'So you're a broom?' Dylan said.

No less startled than when Megan had appeared a minute earlier, Hope and Summer once again spun on their stools toward the open doorway. Megan glanced over at Dylan but kept on eating.

'You were entering the boutique as I was pulling up to the curb,' he told Megan, 'and from a distance, I wasn't sure about your costume. But Hope is right. Daniel will definitely be drooling when he sees you.'

'Then I chose correctly,' Megan replied, in between bites of pie. 'I was originally debating between a broom and a cauldron, but truth be told, vanity made the decision for me. I figured that I could be tall and slender as a broom. As a cauldron, I would end up short and portly.'

They all laughed.

'Out of curiosity, why a broom or a cauldron?' Dylan asked.

Megan smiled. 'Do you not see the theme? What are the three quintessential possessions of a witch? A cauldron, a broomstick, and' – she motioned toward Hope and Summer – 'feline companions.'

Dylan turned to the sisters. They were dressed as cats in form-fitting black, with a curling tail, whiskers, and ears. Hope couldn't help feeling somewhat pleased, because there was no mistaking the way that Dylan was looking at her. He may not have actually been drooling, but he certainly liked what he saw.

'I stand corrected from yesterday,' he said. 'With your emerald eyes and that costume, Hope, you can bring any man to his knees.'

Her cheeks began to flush, and in an effort to divert attention from it, she responded, 'Speaking of costumes, where is yours?'

'Nate has it. He has both of ours. The desk sergeant at his station knows the owner of a costume shop, and he arranged the costumes for us. Nate is running late because of the investigation, so he told me that he'd bring the costumes to the party and meet us there.' Dylan turned to Summer. 'I assume Nate told you that also?'

'He did,' she confirmed. 'But he didn't tell me what the costumes were.'

The sisters exchanged an apprehensive glance.

Dylan chuckled. 'Don't bristle your kitten fur. Nate and I aren't going to be dressed as aliens. We won't grossly offend Lucas and Richard and their ilk.'

'They'll probably be dressed as aliens themselves,' Megan remarked. 'As part of my duties at the hotel, I assisted in organizing a UFO convention there last year, and nearly all of the attendees wore some sort of an alien costume. Spacesuits covered in blinking lights, metallic robes and headdresses, green masks with giant reflective eyes. One interesting fact I learned during the convention, by the way, is that they don't call them UFOs anymore. Instead of unidentified flying objects, they're now UAPs.'

'UAPs?' Summer asked.

'Unidentified anomalous phenomena. Apparently it was unidentified *aerial* phenomena for a short while first before the government officially changed it to *anomalous* to include items in the sea and space, in addition to the air.'

'Huh?'

Megan shook her head. 'Don't ask me to explain the difference. I neither know nor care. When it comes to conventions, my job is to make sure the attendees have sufficient nametags and coffee mugs, and that they don't burn the hotel down with either a rave or a riot. Beyond that, I keep my nose out of it, regardless of whether they're visitors from another planet, orthodontists, or stamp collectors.'

'A wise move,' Dylan told her.

'Wise enough to remain gainfully employed,' Megan responded.

Summer turned to her sister. 'All things considered, maybe it's for the best that the party this evening no longer has much of a connection to the boutique. We have enough problems with skeptics of the spiritual world. We don't need to add problems with alien devotees versus alien debunkers.'

Hope nodded. 'Be grateful for small favors, I guess.'

Megan set down her fork and pushed her stool away from the kitchen island. 'I'm stuffed.'

'You should be,' Hope said with a laugh. 'You ate nearly half the pie.'

'I needed to,' Megan answered matter-of-factly. 'I can't drink the Halloween party punch on an empty stomach.'

Now Dylan laughed, too. 'You've got that right. I tasted the punch this morning. The stuff is practically lethal.'

'You've got that right,' Megan echoed him. 'It would make an excellent murder weapon!'

Dylan laughed harder.

'I know that you're trying to give me a stern look for being so flippant about murder under the circumstances,' Megan said to Hope, 'but it isn't working. Beneath the half-hearted attempt at a disapproving stare, I can see that you're laughing with us.'

'Maybe a little,' Hope admitted. 'In any case, the punch is gone.'

'What!' Megan exclaimed. 'It's gone already? How could you and Summer possibly have consumed it all? You wouldn't be sitting on that stool, talking coherently. You'd be lolling on the floor, singing showtunes.'

'I would say that *you've* had too much punch,' Hope responded dryly. 'Except I know that you haven't had any. Neither has Summer or I today. What I meant was that the punch is no longer at the brownstone. Nelson – and Rosemarie – picked it up a little while ago, adding it to the food and other beverages that they were transporting from the Green Goat to the pumpkin patch.'

At the mention of Rosemarie and Nelson, Megan's amusement faded. 'I was at the Green Goat earlier this afternoon with Daniel, and I saw Rosemarie there. She was hanging up signs in the windows and on the doors informing people about the new location for the party. She was also hanging on to Nelson a lot.'

Hope nodded. 'Even for the short time that they were here to collect the punch, she was quite clingy with him. I don't think that she let go of him once.'

'Not once,' Summer confirmed. 'I noticed that, too.'

'I'm worried about her,' Megan said. 'Rosemarie can be far too obtuse for her own good, especially when it comes to men. She automatically assumes that everyone is as kind-hearted and sweet-natured as she is, even though she knows nothing about the person.'

'She knows that she likes Nelson's Halloween costume,' Summer remarked wryly. 'She thought that he was *so fun and festive* as a magician.'

Megan rolled her eyes. 'That's exactly what I mean about her being obtuse. Rosemarie knows nothing of substance about Nelson. For that matter, what do any of us know about Nelson?'

'Daniel must know something about him,' Hope said. 'He and Nelson are business partners, after all.'

'Daniel won't talk about Nelson now. He told me that the police instructed him not to discuss the events from yesterday evening, and to him that includes all aspects of the Green Goat. But it's clear to me that Daniel is uncomfortable with Nelson. Whenever Nelson – together with Rosemarie – came within eyeshot or earshot this afternoon, Daniel deliberately turned away from them, studiously focusing his attention elsewhere.'

'How did Nelson react to Daniel?' Dylan asked her.

Megan considered for a moment. 'It's difficult for me to judge, because I haven't been with Nelson enough to be familiar with his mannerisms, but I had the impression that he was uncomfortable, too.'

'It might have been the place rather than the person,' Hope suggested. 'I would assume that most people are ill at ease spending extra time at the scene of a murder.'

'That's true,' Megan agreed. 'And I know that the murder has been preying on Daniel's mind, because he's been terribly worried about who I'm going to the party with. At first he insisted that he take me himself, but then he realized that he had to wait until everybody else had finished their work at the Green Goat so that he could make certain the place was locked and secured. I told him that I was going to the party with you and that I would meet him there, but that didn't seem to reassure him.'

Summer's brow furrowed. 'Why wouldn't that reassure him? Does he imagine that Hope and I had something to do with Collin's death?'

'Of course not. Daniel is just being protective.' Megan was thoughtful. 'Did you say a minute ago that Nelson's costume is a magician?'

'Yes,' Summer answered. 'Didn't you see it when he was at the Green Goat with Rosemarie?'

'No. Rosemarie was in her butterfly costume, but Nelson was wearing his regular clothes.' Again, Megan was thoughtful.

'What is it?' Hope asked her.

Now Megan's brow furrowed. 'It's an odd coincidence,' she said. 'Daniel's costume is also a magician.'

NINETEEN

Unlike Rosemarie's opinion of Nelson's Halloween costume, the drive to the party was not fun and festive. Since his car was already at the curb, Dylan volunteered to act as their chauffeur for the short journey from the boutique to the outskirts of the city and Richard Lambert's pumpkin patch. Hope sat beside Dylan in the front passenger seat, with Summer and Megan in the seats behind them. They were all quiet and subdued, each lost in their own thoughts.

'Remind me to thank Gram,' Summer said after a while.

Hope turned to her questioningly.

'I was annoyed when Gram insisted yesterday that Dylan go with us to the party, but she was right: a large group of friends is comforting in case there's a problem.'

'There won't be a problem.' In an attempt to sound more confident than she felt, Hope forced a little laugh. 'At least we're officially invited this time, so Richard can't accuse us of trespassing on his land.'

'Did his uncle really run you and the other curious kids off his property with a shotgun?' Dylan asked her.

'Oh yes. He didn't fire the gun – at least not when Summer and I were there. I don't know whether it was actually loaded. But he waved it around while cursing up a storm, and to us and the rest of the kids that made quite an impression.'

'He frightened the stuffing out of me,' Summer admitted frankly. 'It gave me nightmares for a week. I never went back to the place. Hope was braver than I was.'

Dylan looked at Hope in surprise. 'You went back?'

'Once,' she told him.

'And did the uncle run you off again?'

'No' – she forced another little laugh – 'the pumpkins and rats did.'

'What does that mean?'

'Summer wasn't exaggerating when she said earlier that

Richard – the same as his uncle did before him – leaves the entire crop of pumpkins to rot in the patch every autumn. The night that I was there, the pumpkins were stinking to high heaven. But the smell didn't deter any of the critters from eating them. I have no trouble with raccoons and opossums; Summer and I frequently see them roaming through our back garden after dark. However, the rats in the pumpkin patch were scary. They weren't cute little field mice. They were big, ugly sewer rats.'

Dylan grimaced. 'Those sorts of rats are notorious transmitters of disease. You're lucky that you weren't bitten.'

Hope nodded. 'At the time, I didn't fully understand how dangerous they can be. But I knew that I wanted to get away from the stench of the pumpkins and the scurrying beasts, so I scurried away myself and haven't returned.'

'Has anybody ever complained to the authorities?'

'I don't think so, and even if they did, I'm not sure what the authorities could do. As you'll see, it's a large piece of hilly farmland. As far as I'm aware, there's no law against planting crops and then not harvesting them.'

'But it's weird,' Summer said. 'Really weird. And it costs a considerable amount of money. Richard has to plow the field and buy the seed annually. Why would he do that year after year for no purpose?'

'Maybe his purpose is to terrify the children of Asheville, encourage the rats, and thereby keep everyone away from his land,' Megan suggested.

'If that's the case, then he's succeeded,' Summer replied, 'because Hope and I have heard from more than a few of our clients at the boutique that they and their families and friends deliberately give the property a wide berth.'

'Which makes me wonder whether any of our customers – or the Green Goat's customers – will voluntarily go to the pumpkin patch tonight for the party,' Hope said. 'There could end up being only the four of us in this car, plus Nate and Daniel, Rosemarie and Nelson, and Lucas and Richard.'

'Don't forget about the sewer rats,' Summer reminded her.

'The first sewer rat that I see,' Dylan informed them brusquely, 'we are turning around, getting right back in the car, and driving the hell away from there. And I don't want to hear a word of argument about it. I've witnessed infected rat bites at the hospital, and let me tell you that they aren't pretty. I promised your grandmother that I would accompany you to the party, and I have no intention of incurring Olivia's wrath by leaving any of you behind in a field of rotting pumpkins and hungry rats.'

He received no argument. On the contrary, the mood in the car lightened considerably, because they all felt better knowing that there was an exit plan in place if necessary.

'On the bright side,' Megan remarked after a minute, 'if it's only a small group of us, then there will be enough party punch for everyone.'

Summer grinned. 'Maybe we could use the punch to disorientate the rats and send them scampering – or wobbling – from the field back to the storm sewer.'

'While we're on the subject of the field,' Megan said, 'I know that there was some mention of tables and chairs being available, but are they going to be directly in the middle of the pumpkins?'

'I'm not sure. According to Lucas, Richard has hosted groups before – hence the stock of tables and chairs – but he didn't give any further details. I can't imagine that many groups would be willing to sit for an extended stretch in the pumpkin patch, regardless of the season, which means that some other area must also be usable. I haven't been to the property for so long that I don't know how it's been developed. When you last spoke to Daniel this afternoon, had he been there yet?'

'No. Some of the Green Goat's staff went to the place to help set up, but they hadn't come back by the time that I left, so there weren't any current reports on its condition or facilities . . .'

Hope didn't hear the remainder of their conversation. Her attention shifted as Dylan steered the car through a sharp bend in the road. The bottom rim of the sun was just beginning to dip below the edge of the horizon, illuminating the yellow-leafed sugar maples that dotted the landscape in an ethereal golden glow. The sunlight also glinted off the windshields and metallic trim of the long line of parked vehicles that appeared unexpectedly on both sides of the road ahead of them.

'What are they all doing here?' Hope said in surprise.

'Probably the same thing we are,' Dylan told her. 'I doubt that there's another large event this close by.'

'But how could word of the new location have spread so quickly? Rosemarie's signs were hung up at the Green Goat and the shop just a few hours ago. In the past, the turnout for the party at the boutique has been robust, but this is extreme.'

Megan stared out the window as they drove along the two continuous rows of vehicles. 'Forget my comment about it being only a small group of us. This crowd is going to be worse than at the Green Goat last night.'

Summer groaned.

Knowing how much her sister disliked crowds, especially for any prolonged period, Hope tried to put a positive spin on it. 'We'll be outside, Summer, so the noise won't be overwhelming. Plus, there will be plenty of air and elbow room.'

'Air but not necessarily fresh air,' Megan responded drolly. 'The only uncongested area could be a corner of rotting pumpkins. But at least it will be a quiet corner, because the rats can't talk, just nibble. And if there aren't any chairs remaining, we can always pull out the floor mats from Dylan's car and sit on those.'

Dylan laughed. 'That's an excellent idea.'

Although Summer tried to laugh, too, it came out weak and shaky. 'I wonder if Nate is here.'

'Didn't he tell you and Dylan that he was going to be late?' Hope said.

'He did, but I'm not certain what that means anymore. Doesn't it seem as though *we* are the ones who are late?'

Megan nodded. 'It's not even dusk yet, and apparently everybody has already arrived. Since when does a Halloween party for people over the age of ten get into full swing before the sun has set? After all, half the fun of a good Halloween party is spooky lighting and shadowy nooks where you can—' She broke off abruptly. 'There's an open spot, Dylan! Up ahead on the left in front of that old paneled station wagon. Do you see it? Is it big enough for us to squeeze into?'

'Yes, I see it. It's big enough.'

Dylan skillfully maneuvered the car into the narrow space on the side of the road and turned off the engine. They all remained seated with the doors closed. Although none of them acknowledged it out loud, there was a palpable sense of foreboding among the occupants of the vehicle.

Finally – albeit reluctantly – Hope opened her door and began to climb out. 'The boutique is still to some degree associated with the party, Summer, so we have to make a public appearance, even if it's only a brief one.'

Summer agreed with a sigh.

'The party is important for Daniel's business, too,' Megan reminded them, likewise opening her door and climbing out.

Standing on the thin strip of gravel that bordered the road, Hope looked around and saw a woman exiting a hatchback across from them. One knee-high white boot appeared, followed by a second knee-high white boot. Then came a pair of mint-green tights, which were topped by a matching mint-green bodysuit with long sleeves. The woman's brown hair was gathered together in a tight bun. Stuck into the crown of the bun were two bobbling white antennae constructed of wire pipe cleaners and plastic table tennis balls.

Dylan chortled. 'You were right with what you said before, Megan: they're dressed as aliens.'

Megan chortled with him. 'We'll certainly be able to distinguish the boutique's guests and the Green Goat's guests from Richard's guests.'

Although the woman was too far away to hear their muffled words, she must have caught their laughter, because she looked over at the group. She studied their costumes for a moment and seemed to debate with herself whether to comment on them, but then she apparently decided against it.

'I'm glad that I'm not the only one who's running a bit late,' she said sociably. 'At least we managed to find a pair of parking spaces close by. Last time I was stuck all the way at the end of a row.'

'Last time?' Megan asked her, adopting a similar friendly, chatty manner.

'Last week,' the woman answered. 'Were you here for that one?'

Hope and Summer exchanged a glance. Did she mean another party? It obviously couldn't have been a Halloween party.

'No, unfortunately I missed it,' Megan told the woman.

'Oh, what rotten luck!' she exclaimed. 'I don't want to sound as though I'm gloating, but it was a wonderful experience. It was one of the best this month, possibly even for the last couple of months.'

Hope and Summer exchanged another glance. *One of the best this month?* How many parties was Richard hosting in the pumpkin patch?

'The lights were outstanding,' the woman went on. 'And it wasn't just a few flashes. They appeared intermittently for at least an hour. It made the long walk from the car and up the hill well worthwhile.'

'Up the hill?' Megan said. 'So you weren't in the pumpkin patch?'

The question seemed to confuse the woman, and she frowned. 'Of course not. Why would I be in the patch? No one is ever in the patch.'

Megan hesitated briefly, then with a wink at Hope, she replied, 'When one of my friends was last here, she was pretty sure that someone was in the patch.'

'That isn't good.' The woman's frown deepened. 'Richard won't be happy about it. Over the years, he and his uncle have been forced to deal with so many troublesome children and snooping adults . . .'

Dylan leaned toward Hope. 'Did you hear that? You and Summer were troublesome children.'

She smiled. 'Some people still consider us to be troublesome.'

'Richard does everything he can to keep their prying eyes away from the patch,' the woman continued. 'Has your friend told him about what she saw?'

'I believe that he's aware of it,' Megan responded somewhat vaguely.

'It's important for him to know. Very important. The patch can't be disturbed. It must be protected at all costs.'

'At all costs,' Megan echoed, nodding with feigned gravitas.

The woman nodded back at her, the white antennae in her bun bobbling wildly. 'Without the patch, we wouldn't see any lights.'

'No lights?' Summer said, jumping into the conversation. 'But why not?'

The woman turned to her with a startled expression as though the answer should have been obvious. 'How would we see the visitors' lights if their spacecraft couldn't land in the pumpkin patch?'

TWENTY

There was a pause. Dylan cleared his throat. Megan gave a little cough. And Hope and Summer looked at each other. They no longer had to wonder why Richard Lambert had agreed to Lucas's request regarding the party. Richard was already hosting aliens and alien contactees, so he could easily add a few Halloween revelers to the list, as long as they stayed out of his treasured pumpkin patch. It also explained the large number of vehicles that were parked alongside the road. They weren't there because they had seen Rosemarie's signs and learned about the new location for the boutique and Green Goat's festivities. They were there to watch for the landing lights of the visitors' spacecraft.

About a third of the sun had now disappeared below the horizon, and its rays ceased to glint with the same intensity off the row of windshields and metallic trim. The woman must have noticed the change, because she cried out in alarm.

'It's getting late!' she exclaimed. 'The lights often begin to appear at dusk, and we still need to get up the hill. We must hurry!'

She grabbed a pair of fleece blankets from her car, slung a little rucksack over one shoulder, and hastened across the road toward their side.

'Don't forget your sweaters and jackets,' she reminded them as she rushed by. 'It can get breezy after dark.'

Just as she was about to descend into the gully, the woman stopped and turned back toward the group. As she had before, she studied their costumes for a moment and appeared to debate with herself whether to comment on them. This time she spoke her mind.

'If you're dressed as a twig or a branch from a tree,' she said to Megan, 'then I don't think there will be a problem, because the visitors like nature.' Her gaze moved critically to Hope and Summer. 'But those cat outfits are a poor choice. Very poor.' She clucked her tongue in disapproval. 'The visitors hate cats. If they don't show up tonight, you two could be to blame for it.'

Not waiting for their response, the woman clucked her tongue again and set off into the gully. Hope saw that one of the table tennis balls from her antennae had fallen off its pipe cleaner and was lying on the gravel. Under other circumstances she would have retrieved the ball for her, but being a hated cat, she decided against it.

'A twig or a branch,' Megan muttered, glaring after the woman.

'If you'd been dressed as a cauldron instead of a broom,' Summer remarked jovially, 'she might have called you a soup pot or a tea kettle.'

Megan was not amused and muttered some more.

'You should consider yourself lucky,' Hope told her. 'At least the aliens like you. You aren't an arch-enemy feline.'

Dylan laughed. 'Which must prove that I'm not an alien, because I'm a great fan of felines.' He added in a low tone toward Hope, 'One feline in particular.'

She smiled at him warmly.

'It turns out that you – and Nate – are the smart ones,' Summer said to Dylan. 'Since you aren't wearing a costume, nobody knows whether you're here for the boutique, the Green Goat, or the visitors.'

He laughed again. 'Maybe I'm secretly a daredevil, and I'm here to steal a prized pumpkin from the patch.'

That made them all laugh, even Megan.

The sun sank a little further, and long shadows began to creep across the road.

'So into the gully and up the hill while it's still light enough for us to see where we're going?' Megan asked.

Hope shook her head. 'That might be the best route for those on the hunt for spacecraft, but I'm on the hunt for the boutique's clients, so I vote for a path with less climbing and no stumbling over uneven ground. Let's walk on Richard's driveway. It's just a short distance ahead of us.'

'That's my vote, too,' Summer said. 'I'm sure Nate will be that way, as will Daniel and anyone else that we know. They won't go rambling over hills, staring into the pumpkin patch for the arrival of intergalactic lights. They'll stay close to the—' She interrupted herself with a demonstrative sniff. 'I smell barbecue!'

Without further discussion, the group set off at a quick pace toward Richard's driveway. It wasn't because they were ravenously hungry. It was because the barbecue was a heartening sign that at least some portion of the party was proceeding as anticipated. The driveway was wide and unpaved, but its dirt was so solidly packed and well maintained that it was almost as smooth as asphalt. Although it also headed up the hill, it had a much gentler slope. Similar to the road, both sides of the driveway were lined with parked vehicles. To the group's collective disappointment, they didn't see any familiar cars or trucks. Plenty of other people were walking on the driveway – both to and from the hill – but none wore traditional Halloween costumes. There were no comic book heroes, princesses, or ghosts. They were dressed either in regular clothes like Dylan, or in alien garb similar to the woman from the hatchback, especially with regard to color. In addition to a large number of mint-green tights and bodysuits, there were mint-green masks, mint-green headdresses, mint-green robes, and mint-green spacesuits. There were even a handful of bold souls who had dyed their hair mint green.

'Does anybody else feel as though we've stepped into a really bizarre dream?' Summer said.

Hope nodded. 'The woman told us that the visitors like nature, so I guess that makes green the hue du jour.'

'But *mint* green?'

Megan smiled wryly. 'We should be serving mint-chocolate-chip ice cream with the barbecue.'

'I'm curious about the aluminum foil,' Dylan said. 'A lot of them have foil wrapped around their waists as a sort of a belt, and also crinkled around their ankles and wrists. They can't honestly believe that it serves any scientific purpose. It must be decorative or a spoof, right?'

'If it's not decorative or a spoof,' Hope replied, 'then Summer and I might be in trouble, because some of them aren't looking at us in a very friendly manner. If they take aluminum foil that seriously, then they could take our cat costumes seriously, too – in a bad way.'

'My thoughts exactly,' Summer agreed. 'They have that pitch-forks-and-blazing-torches expression. Instead of burning us at the stake as witches, they'll drown us in the nearest well as cats.'

Dylan raised an eyebrow at her.

'You may not understand our concern,' Summer responded

tetchily, 'but that doesn't make it any less valid. As physicians, you and your father worry about aggrieved patients suing you for medical malpractice. As Baileys, Hope and I worry about angry villagers storming the boutique – or, in this case, angry alien contactees blaming us when the aliens don't show up as expected in the pumpkin patch.'

Dylan's eyebrow remained elevated.

'You're right that some of them aren't looking at us in a very friendly manner,' Megan said to the sisters, 'which is odd because it's the complete opposite of my experience at the hotel last year. I didn't meet a single UFO convention attendee who was surly or hostile. Unlike most of the regular hotel guests who tend to be spoiled and bratty, the convention attendees were all polite and down-to-earth and—'

'Speaking of down-to-earth,' Hope interjected, 'up ahead near the top of the driveway on the left, there's a man with shoulder-length hair and a sweatshirt who appears to be headed in our direction. Isn't that Erik?'

The group stopped walking and turned toward the person in question.

'That's Erik,' Megan confirmed. 'And if I'm not mistaken, that's the same sweatshirt – and cut-off jeans – he was wearing yesterday in the Green Goat.'

'They certainly look the same,' Hope agreed. 'So he hasn't changed his clothes since we left him at the table in the bar last night. That makes sense, considering he didn't return to the camper van today, at least as far as I'm aware.'

'I wonder how he knew to come here?' Megan mused.

'Lucas probably told him—' Hope began.

'It doesn't matter how Erik knew to come here,' Summer interrupted her sister in agitation. 'The far more important point is whether Amber has come here with him. Do you remember all of her accusations that I was stealing Collin from her? Her accusation now might be that I killed Collin!'

'It would be smart of her to try to push the blame on to you,' Megan said, 'if she herself killed Collin.'

Hope was doubtful. 'But would Amber have killed him? I'm inclined to think that she loved Collin too much for that, even with her wicked jealous streak.'

'Love causes people to do some very stupid things,' Megan replied. 'You and I both heard Amber threaten to kill Collin – and Summer. For all we know, Amber and Erik killed Collin together.'

Dylan shook his head. 'Erik didn't kill Collin.'

Megan frowned at him. 'How can you be sure of that?'

'Because you told me so a minute ago. You – and Hope – said that Erik is currently wearing the same sweatshirt and jeans that he had on last night. Whoever killed Collin surely got some of his blood on them. It may not have been a large quantity of blood, but regardless of the amount, no murderer would voluntarily remain in the same clothing for an entire day afterward. The chance of getting caught is simply too high. If Erik had killed Collin, that sweatshirt and those jeans would have been in a dumpster, a ditch, or a bonfire long ago. Between the Green Goat and this place, there are a hundred good disposal spots.'

'Would that apply to shoes, too?' Summer asked him. 'Because as we talked about this morning, I think Nelson is wearing the same athletic shoes with wavy soles today that he was wearing last night.'

'If I were a murderer,' Dylan answered her, 'I would get rid of my shoes with the rest of my clothing. But according to Nate, a lot of criminals destroy everything they're wearing *except* for their shoes. They falsely believe that they can adequately clean them to remove all evidence – which they can't, of course. But as we also talked about this morning, finding traces of Collin's blood on a pair of shoes only proves that the person was in the wine cellar. It doesn't prove that the person killed Collin.'

Summer turned to her sister. 'Do you remember what kind of shoes Erik was wearing last night? Were they athletic shoes with wavy soles?'

'No, he was wearing hiking boots.'

'He's still wearing hiking boots,' Megan said. 'Old, muddy, heavily used hiking boots. And in another second, he and his boots will be close enough to hear us.'

She had barely finished the sentence when Erik called out to them.

'Dude, I noticed you from the top of the driveway, and I thought to myself: *Dude, they sure look familiar.*'

Now that he was directly in front of them, Hope could see for certain that Erik was wearing the same sweatshirt, jeans, and hiking boots as the previous day. Both the sweatshirt and the jeans were wrinkled and baggy from having been lived in for so long, but they were clean. There was no visible blood on them. There also wasn't any indication that Erik had attempted to wash out a dirty spot or that he had been in an altercation in the clothes.

'I was lucky to notice you at all,' he went on. 'In another few minutes, it will be too dark to tell the difference between a shrub and a bear from a distance. Dude, Lucas will be happy. He asked me to keep an eye out for you.'

Erik looked at Hope as he spoke, giving the impression that Lucas had been referring to her specifically rather than the entire group. Dylan's gaze narrowed with annoyance.

For her part, Hope was interested in learning where Erik – and Amber – had been since the prior evening, and she used the mention of Lucas as an opening. 'So you came here with Lucas?'

'No, I came with Richard.'

'Richard?' she echoed in surprise. 'You know Richard Lambert?'

'Sure, dude. Richard and I have known each other for a long time. We travel to a lot of the same meetings and events. He's interested in interdimensional crossings, too.'

Dylan's gaze narrowed further.

'When we first arrived in Asheville,' Erik continued, 'I was thinking that I should get in touch with Richard, but then all of a sudden, there he was standing in front of us in the bar last night. You and she' – he nodded toward Megan – 'left the table, and a minute later, Richard appeared. What a coincidence!'

Now Summer's gaze narrowed. She was always suspicious of coincidences.

'Richard said that I should come over and see this place, so that's what I did. Which reminds me, dude' – Erik looked from one sister to the other – 'even though I didn't camp by you last night, I still appreciate you offering me a space to roll out my tarp and sleeping bag. Not everybody is that generous. Plenty of people would have sent me packing.'

'You're still welcome to the space whenever you want to use it,' Hope told him. She didn't mention that the space was currently occupied by Lucas's gazebo.

'Thanks, dude, but I'm all set. Richard invited me to stay here for the next couple of days. I like it; there's plenty of room to roam.'

Hope noted that he made no reference to the camper van, Collin, or Amber. Was it possible that Erik didn't know about what had happened to Collin? And where was Amber all this time?

Summer's thoughts must have been along the same line, because she cleverly said to Erik, 'Since you're staying here, if there's anything that you need Hope and me to do with regard to the camper van, just let us know. We're happy to help in any way.'

He shook his head. 'Again I appreciate the offer, dude, but there's nothing to be done. Collin didn't have many personal items in the van, so not much has to be packed up.'

That resolved one outstanding question: Erik knew that Collin was dead.

'It's not a problem if we keep the van parked on your street a little while longer, is it?' Erik asked them.

'It's not a problem at all,' Summer replied. 'There's no rush whatsoever to move it. We know that this is a difficult time. As I said before, if there's anything that Hope and I can do to help, either for you or for Amber . . .'

Hope was impressed at how smoothly her sister had slipped Amber's name into the conversation, as though it was an entirely natural and innocent inquiry into the woman's well-being.

Erik shook his head once more. 'There's nothing to be done,' he repeated.

Although they waited for him to continue – particularly as to Amber – he didn't. Was he deliberately not mentioning Amber, or was he simply being obtuse? Perhaps he didn't know where Amber was any more than they did. Hope looked at Erik closely, but his placid expression gave her no answers.

Summer made another attempt. 'Well, if you change your mind, and you or Amber want us to pick up a change of clothes or check on something in the van, don't hesitate to—'

'So this is where you disappeared to!' a voice cut her off. 'I've been searching for you *everywhere*. On the hill, by the grills, along the top of the driveway – and finally I find you down here!'

In unison, Hope and Summer winced. There was no mistaking the bellowing voice. It belonged to Amber.

TWENTY-ONE

If Hope and Summer were expecting a weeping and subdued woman as a result of Collin's death, they were in error. Even in the dwindling light, they could see as Amber drew near to them that her cheeks were not stained with tears, nor was she passive and despondent from grief. On the contrary, she was animated and voluble.

'Lucas was asking about you,' she said to Erik, 'and Richard was asking about you, but I couldn't tell them anything, because you seemed to have vanished from the face of the earth.' Amber gave a high-pitched laugh. 'There were rumblings among the crowd that the visitors had taken you aboard one of their spacecraft.'

Erik's response was earnest. 'No, I haven't traveled anywhere. I've been on the driveway the entire time.'

'Yes, I realize that now, darling.'

Darling? Hope and Summer exchanged a glance. Had Amber shifted her affections from Collin to Erik so swiftly?

'You noticed friends and went to greet them,' she continued. 'How nice.' The high-pitched laugh repeated itself.

Summer took a step backward. Hope followed suit. Although there wasn't anything imminently menacing about Amber, they certainly hadn't forgotten her threats from the previous day. It seemed wise to provide a thundering elephant – to use Lucas's description of her – with extra room in case it suddenly decided to charge.

Amber gave the sisters an appraising look. Summer took another cautionary step backward.

'I really like your costumes,' Amber said to them. 'I wish that I had my costume tonight. I have a fabulous Tinker Bell outfit with wings and matching ballet slippers. But it's in the van by you, and I haven't been there since yesterday.' She turned to Erik. 'I've always enjoyed Halloween. Next October, we have to come back to Asheville for the boutique's party. Promise me that we will, Erik. We need to put it on our schedule now so that we can be in this part of the country in autumn and the trip won't take us too far out of our way.'

Hope and Summer exchanged another glance. Apparently Amber and Erik planned on continuing to travel together in the camper van. Of even greater interest was Amber's announcement that she wanted to attend next year's Halloween party at the boutique. That seemed to be a pretty good indication that she was no longer intent on killing Summer for supposedly stealing Collin from her.

'We'll put it on our schedule,' Erik promised her. 'And we'll let Richard know so that we can park the van here. But I'll need a costume; I don't have one.'

'Oh, that's not a problem,' Amber told him. 'You can be a pirate or a cowboy. There are so many costumes to choose from.'

'But not a cat if you're expecting alien visitors,' Summer grumbled as two people dressed in mint-green spacesuits passed by the group and glowered at the sisters.

Although she had spoken in a low tone, Erik must have heard her, because he replied, 'Dude, they don't understand that you're wearing the costumes for the Halloween party. They think that you're wearing them to deliberately keep the visitors away, the same as the ancient Egyptians did.'

Summer squinted at him. 'Huh?'

'The reason the ancient Egyptians had such a great love of cats,' he explained, 'and decorated their tombs with cats, and created so much art containing cats was to dissuade the visitors from visiting them.'

'But I was under the impression that aliens built the pyramids,' Dylan said.

Erik didn't appear to notice the laughter in his voice. 'No, dude, that's only an old myth. The ancient Egyptians built the pyramids themselves – with ramps.'

'Well, it all seems pretty silly to me,' Amber remarked. 'How could a little statuette of a cat drive away a spacecraft? And with regard to this evening, how could the visitors distinguish cat costumes in the dark?' She shook her head at the sisters. 'Don't pay attention to anyone's sour looks. I still really like your costumes, and I'm sure that Lucas will like them, too.' She winked at Hope. 'Especially yours. Now let's go up the hill and see him.'

Amber slipped one of her arms through Hope's. Slipping her other arm through Summer's, she said to her, 'Your boyfriend is also on the hill.' And before either of the sisters could respond, she began to propel both of them up the driveway. She gave a quick glance back at Erik. 'Come along, darling.'

When Hope likewise took a quick glance back, she saw that Erik was following obediently, close behind them. Dylan and Megan were following, too, slightly further back. Megan was looking at everyone that they passed, no doubt in search of Daniel. Dylan wasn't looking at anybody, and his expression was more thoughtful than perturbed. Either he hadn't heard Amber's comments about Lucas, or he had more pressing issues on his mind.

There were several issues on Hope's mind, as well. For starters, what had brought about the radical transformation in Amber's behavior? Yesterday she had been roaring with rage and jealousy, hurling dishes in the camper van and threats in the bar, but today – albeit still a bellower – she was friendly and pleasant. Even more startling was Amber's treatment of Collin. There was no mention of him whatsoever. Amber's love for Collin had been intensely possessive, but it didn't appear to have been deep or long-lasting, because he had been rapidly and summarily replaced by Erik. Perhaps it was the only way that Amber could deal with Collin's death. If she didn't think about what had happened to him, then she could manage to carry on with daily life. Or perhaps it was an indication that she was the one who had killed Collin.

There was a bright flash of lights ahead of them.

Megan gave a little laugh. 'Was that the first spacecraft of the evening?'

Erik took the question seriously. 'No, dude, that wasn't a spacecraft. The spacecraft are only visible from the top of the hill, looking down the opposite side into the pumpkin patch. Those were twinkle lights that we just saw. Another string must have been hooked up by the grills.'

'Your friend Rosemarie brought enough twinkle lights to illuminate the entire property twice over,' Amber told the sisters. 'But some in the crowd were complaining that too many twinkle lights would hinder their view of the landing lights, so in the end, only a few strings have been used. Your boyfriend' – she tugged on Summer's arm – 'helped to hook them up. He's very handy. It's nice to have a handy boyfriend. Erik can fix almost anything in the camper van. And do you know' – this time she tugged on Hope's arm – 'that Lucas does all the maintenance on the Airstream himself?'

Hope didn't respond. She was beginning to feel rather uncomfortable. It had nothing to do with Lucas and his ostensible handiness with his Airstream. It was Amber's artificial, sing-song manner.

'Rosemarie's butterfly costume is fantastic,' she continued chirpily. 'And that pug of hers is absolutely adorable in his bumblebee suit! Is it true that she made both of their costumes by hand?' Not pausing for an answer, Amber heaved a loud, wistful sigh. 'I wish that I could sew properly. And I wish that I could have worn my Tinker Bell costume. I could have compared my wings with Rosemarie's, and she could have shown me how to improve them to be as nice as hers. Such a shame!'

Amber concluded the speech with another wistful sigh, which was as exaggerated as the first. The more time that Hope spent with her, the more she realized how accurate Erik's description of her on their initial meeting had been: Amber loved drama. It was almost as though she was bored without drama. Big tempestuous drama and little bubbly drama. The question was whether Amber's dramatics went so far as to include the use of a box cutter in the Green Goat's wine cellar.

Megan quickened her pace until she was alongside Hope, who used it as an excuse to detangle her arm from Amber's.

'I think I see Daniel up ahead,' Megan said to her. 'Isn't that him?'

They had almost reached the top of the driveway, and with it, the top of the hill. The barbecue had been set up at the end of the packed dirt. A trio of large charcoal grills stood in a row with smoke rising from them. The alien contactees may not have been fond of cats, but they were clearly not averse to bratwursts, because there was a long line of mint green in front of the grills, waiting with a plate and a bun for a sausage.

As Amber had indicated, the twinkle lights were sparse. The

majority had been strategically placed around a pair of long tables that were situated to the right of the grills. One table held condiments and an assortment of snacks. The second table held bottles of soda and beer. There was no sign of the party punch. In the other direction, to the left of the grills, several dozen plastic folding chairs had been arranged to face away from the road and the driveway, looking down the opposite side of the hill into the pumpkin patch. Beyond the chairs, countless blankets had been spread on the crest of the hill, also looking down into the patch. The chairs and the blankets were occupied by those in mint green. The visitors' landing lights had yet to be spotted evidently, because everyone was eating and drinking and chatting together merrily. No one was gazing toward the patch.

'I've lost him,' Megan said in disappointment. 'I thought Daniel was standing near the grills, but then he disappeared.'

'I didn't see him at all,' Hope told her. 'There are too many people moving around in too little light. It's difficult to discern anyone unless—'

She was interrupted by the distinctive yips of a dog.

Megan chuckled. 'Unless you've got a pug's sense of smell and are on the hunt for your favorite treats.'

An instant later, Percy in his fuzzy bumblebee suit burst out of the shadows, racing toward them.

'Rosemarie won't be far behind.' Megan dropped her voice so that only Hope could hear her. 'And Nelson, too, in all likelihood. I'm still not sure what I think of him or his shoes, regardless of what Dylan says about the shoes not proving anything. While I have the opportunity, I'm going to sneak away and look for Daniel.'

Hope reached out and squeezed her hand. 'Good luck.'

Megan squeezed her hand in return, and then as swiftly as Percy had appeared out of the shadows, she vanished into them.

Her departure wasn't a minute too soon. As expected, Rosemarie followed after the pug, jogging awkwardly on the same strappy gold high heels that she had been wearing earlier that day to match her costume. The shoes didn't perform any better on the packed dirt of Richard's driveway than they had on the soft grass of the brownstone's side lawn. They were now dirty and scuffed, but the remainder of the butterfly costume was

The Magician's Deception 179

still in good condition even after climbing in and out of vehicles at numerous locations and organizing twinkle lights.

'I knew that you were here!' Rosemarie exclaimed sunnily to the sisters. 'Percy was snoozing in Nelson's lap while we were relaxing on our blanket, and all of a sudden, his little head popped up, his nose twitched, and a second later, he set off at a sprint. I told Nelson that it was a sure sign the two of you had arrived. Percy wouldn't interrupt his nap for anybody else. Didn't I tell you that, Nelson?'

'You told me that,' Nelson confirmed.

Having walked rather than jogged, Nelson was a few paces behind Rosemarie. Hope didn't know whether it was primarily his decision or at the insistence of Rosemarie, but he was once again wearing his Halloween costume with its shiny silver cape and coordinating hat covered in shiny silver stars. The long white fake beard was absent.

'Oh, my wings keep flapping from when I was running after Percy.' Rosemarie tried to reach around to her back, without success. 'Make them stop, won't you, Nelson?'

Nelson put a steadying hand on the fluttering gilded wings. When the wings had quieted, the hand slid down to Rosemarie's waist and remained there.

Hope smiled to herself. Clearly the budding romance between the pair was growing, not wilting. Her smile faded a moment later. What if Megan's suspicions about Nelson proved to be correct and he turned out to be a murderer? Rosemarie would be devastated.

Percy pressed his nose against Hope's leg.

She looked down at him apologetically. 'I'm sorry, sweetheart, but all of your treats are at the boutique.'

The pug responded with a cantankerous snort.

'Don't be so grumpy,' Rosemarie chided him. 'You should be grateful that Hope didn't bring any of your cookies with her, otherwise your belly would start hurting from too much food.'

'Has he already had a bratwurst?' Summer asked with a laugh.

'I had a difficult time stopping him at one!' Rosemarie replied.

Summer laughed some more. She was apparently just as uncomfortable as Hope had been standing so near to Amber, because she moved toward her sister and leaned down to pat Percy.

Watching Summer scratch under the pug's chin around the edge of the bumblebee suit, Rosemarie's tone turned melancholy. 'I haven't received a single compliment on Percy's costume.'

'None?' Summer said in surprise.

'*None*,' Rosemarie repeated with emphasis. 'Nor has anybody commented on my costume, even though I put so much time and effort into making it. And I would guess that nobody has commented on your costumes, either, even though you both look divine. Don't Hope and Summer look divine, Nelson?'

To his credit, Nelson didn't use the question as an excuse to ogle them. 'Their costumes are nice,' he answered politely.

'Aside from our little group,' Rosemarie continued to the sisters, 'there are almost no costumes at all. In my opinion, most of these strange alien outfits don't count. And if my cousin Anastasia – who, as you may remember, believes in aliens – were here right now with Bella, I have no doubt that they would agree with me.'

Hope was inclined to think that Bella the wire-haired dachshund would be in Percy's camp and show a greater concern for bratwursts than costumes, but she didn't dispute the point. Instead she said, 'This crowd doesn't seem to be very interested in celebrating Halloween, I'm afraid.'

'They certainly aren't interested in any of my Halloween decorations,' Rosemarie responded with more sadness than indignation. 'They objected to absolutely everything that I wanted to put up, including the twinkle lights. At least we eventually got a few strings of those placed around the tables by the grills. Without them, it would be pitch black on this hill, and we wouldn't be able to see our fingers in front of our faces. Speaking of which, I thought that I caught a glimpse of Megan a moment ago. Where did she go? I wanted so much to take a look at her costume.'

'She went to find Daniel,' Hope told her.

At the mention of his business partner, Nelson's brow furrowed.

Hope was about to ask him if he knew of Daniel's whereabouts, but Rosemarie spoke before she could.

'I also thought that I caught a glimpse of Dylan, but he's gone, too.'

'He's gone?' Hope spun around in surprise and discovered that Rosemarie was right. Dylan was no longer behind them. Similar to Megan, he had apparently used the arrival of Percy as an opportunity to slink away on his own business, except Hope didn't know what that business was.

'I wonder if Dylan has managed to locate Nate,' Summer said under her breath to her sister. 'I haven't been able to spot him anywhere.'

Either Amber heard Summer, or she guessed the direction of her thoughts, because she laughingly remarked, 'Are you looking for your boyfriend? Maybe Lucas can pull him out of his hat for you.'

Hope and Summer frowned, not understanding. Then Lucas stepped in front of them, dressed as a magician.

TWENTY-TWO

Aside from the fact that they both possessed a hat, Lucas's costume bore little resemblance to Nelson's. The latter was a storybook wizard, while the former was a stage magician. Lucas wore a dinner tuxedo with black tails, a starched white shirt and vest, and a crimson silk bow tie with a matching crimson silk handkerchief tucked into his left breast pocket. In contrast to Nelson's pointy silver hat decorated with shiny silver stars, an old-fashioned black felt stovepipe top hat was perched on Lucas's head.

'Dude,' Erik said, 'that's a really tall hat.'

Amber responded with one of her high-pitched laughs. It was so loud that some of the nearby mint-green crowd looked over at her. To Hope, the laugh had a screeching quality reminiscent of long fingernails being scraped down a chalkboard.

'Every woman knows,' Amber cackled, 'it's not the size of the hat that counts, but the skill of the magician.'

Lucas's mouth curled with his crooked smile. The sisters rolled their eyes. Nelson shifted uncomfortably. And Erik and Rosemarie looked perplexed.

Rosemarie started to inquire what Amber meant, but to Hope and Summer's relief, Erik preempted her.

'Dude, can you do any magic tricks?' he asked Lucas.

'Indubitably.'

Lucas drew a short black wand from his pocket, tapped it three times against his palm, and then – voila! – the wand transformed into a plastic red rose.

Amber and Rosemarie clapped their hands. Erik and Nelson nodded approvingly. And the sisters once again rolled their eyes.

'A beautiful flower for a beautiful flower who is presently in the form of a very sexy cat,' Lucas said, presenting the rose to Hope.

She laughed and accepted the gift.

His crooked smile grew. 'You can thank me with a purring kiss.'

Hope laughed some more, but she didn't kiss him. She was exceedingly grateful that Dylan had decided to disappear a few minutes earlier.

'I'm not discouraged,' Lucas told her. 'You can kiss me later, in private. I have all the time and the patience in the world.'

He sounded more earnest than he typically did, which confused Hope. It was difficult to know when he was being serious and when he was engaged in his usual smooth talk. Then she became earnest with him, although not on the subject of kissing.

'Thank you for all of your efforts with the Halloween party this evening, Lucas. Summer and I greatly appreciate it.'

'I'd rather have the kiss,' he replied, 'but I'll take a kind word, too.'

Hope smiled at him. 'You'll get plenty of kind words from us. You did a wonderful job setting up the barbecue.'

Summer nodded. 'Even though there aren't many customers from the boutique or the Green Goat here to enjoy it, we realize how much work it was for you to organize everything on such short notice.'

'Unfortunately you're correct about the boutique and the Green Goat's customers,' Lucas said, 'but there are a lot of other people here tonight. Some of them could turn into new customers for you.'

Hope was doubtful on that score. Although a few in the crowd might go to the Green Goat for an occasional lunch or dinner, they probably wouldn't go to the boutique for a palm or Tarot reading. There were, after all, no Tarot cards depicting aliens.

Lucas continued, 'Richard told me that he would spread the word about both places, so that should help.'

'That's awfully nice of him,' Rosemarie said. 'Nelson has explained the Green Goat's financial struggles to me, and under the circumstances, every bit of extra business makes a difference. Isn't that right, Nelson?'

'That's right,' Nelson agreed. 'And while we're on the subject, I have some good news to share—'

He was interrupted by Erik.

'Dude, I think I see Richard near the chairs.'

'Where?' Amber demanded. She looked in the direction Erik pointed. 'Oh, yes, there he is. Richard!' she bellowed. 'Richard!'

It was impossible for anyone on the hill to miss Amber's shouts, and a moment later, Richard Lambert appeared before them. He wore neither mint green nor a Halloween costume. But even without a costume, Richard could have been a cauldron to complement Megan's broom, because he was distinctively short and portly. He wasn't especially overweight; he was simply round. He had a round head, a round neck, and a round middle. Unlike the sisters' experience with his uncle, Richard didn't brandish a shotgun or curse up a storm. On the contrary, he seemed as jolly as he was round.

'Erik,' he chortled, 'you'll never have to be afraid of losing Amber in the wilderness. With those hearty lungs of hers, she'll be able to summon rescue parties and keep dangerous animals at bay at the same time.'

Erik chortled with him. 'So true, dude.'

Amber wasn't the least bit offended. 'I'm not one of those pathetic shrinking violets who doesn't know what they want or how to get it,' she declared.

As Richard and Erik – joined by Lucas – chortled some more, Rosemarie turned to Nelson.

'You started to say something about good news?' she asked him.

'Yes, in fact, it's very good news,' he told her. 'Do you remember when I mentioned this morning that a number of persons had expressed interest in investing in the Green Goat, but one after another, they all fell by the wayside for a variety of reasons?'

That caught Hope's attention, and she listened more closely.

'Certainly I remember,' Rosemarie replied. 'You and Daniel have had such bad luck.'

'Well, it seems that our luck has finally turned, because—'

Nelson was forced to stop by Amber, whose voice rose to dominate the group. Both Hope and Rosemarie looked at her with annoyance.

'I heard somebody talk about luck,' Amber remarked loudly. 'How has your luck gone this evening, Richard? Have there been any sightings?'

'No.' Richard shook his round head. 'No lights or other signs, and I don't expect any, either.'

'Why not, dude?' Erik asked.

'Because there are too many people,' he answered. 'Too much noise and commotion – and far too much mint green.'

Summer snickered.

Richard nodded at her. 'It's absurd, isn't it? You may have thought they were dressed that way for Halloween, but they're not. They wear those ludicrous costumes all the time, every damn weekend when they come up here.'

There was no more snickering from Summer. She frowned instead, as did Hope. It surprised them that Richard would disparage his fellow alien contactees.

'Thrill seekers and tag-alongs, eh?' Lucas said.

'Exactly.' Richard nodded again. 'There used to be only a small assembly of us who would watch from the hill and record our observations. We were serious and dedicated to our studies, the same as you are, Lucas.'

Lucas nodded back at him.

'We were determined that this location remain private and unknown,' Richard went on. 'We did everything in our power to discourage people from taking an interest in the property.'

Summer glanced at her sister. Hope knew what she was thinking, because she was thinking it, too: Richard's uncle and his shotgun had certainly discouraged them from taking an interest in the property.

'For a long time, we were successful in keeping our secret, and then a few months ago, it all changed.' Richard gave a weary sigh. 'Somebody in our assembly had loose lips and could no longer resist bragging about what we were witnessing. One mouth gossiped to the next, and in the blink of an eye, we were inundated with the masses that you see before you today. They all pretend to be greatly fascinated by the visitors, but they aren't really interested in learning anything about them. They just want to booze and yammer and get a photo or video to show off to their friends and followers. It's a carnival now.'

Lucas sucked on his teeth in disgust. 'And you probably haven't had a good sighting in ages.'

'Not a *genuine* sighting,' Richard told him. 'Every weekend there's always one person in the multitude who claims to see a light from the visitors, and in the next instant, everybody else claims to see that same light, followed by a dozen more lights. None of the lights actually exist, of course. In my opinion, it's a form of mass hysteria.'

'Mass delusion might be a better description for it,' Lucas replied.

Richard agreed with a small smile. 'Regardless of what it's called, the visitors haven't appeared since it began. I can't honestly blame them. Who would want to be a spectacle in this circus?'

Hope looked at the crowd on the crest of the hill. They were still eating and drinking and chatting together merrily the same as when she had first arrived. They also showed as little interest in the pumpkin patch as they had before. It turned out that the mint-green occupants of the chairs and the blankets weren't Richard's fellow alien contactees at all. They were only there for a picture and a story. Hope thought back to the woman from the hatchback with the bodysuit and the bobbling antennae. She had claimed that last week's lights were outstanding, the best of the month. Clearly the woman was just another thrill seeker and tag-along – and if Hope ever saw her again, she wouldn't hesitate to tell her exactly what she thought about her opinions on cats.

'Isn't there some way to get rid of all the people?' Erik asked Richard. 'I mean, dude, it's your hill, and you should be able to decide who gets to sit on it.'

Amber chimed in, 'Summer's boyfriend is a police detective. You should talk to him about it. He could help you to remove everybody and keep them from coming back.'

They turned to Summer for her thoughts on the subject. When she didn't immediately respond, Amber offered an alternative suggestion to Richard.

'Or do the opposite,' she said. 'Instead of removing them, remove yourself. Take a break from this place and come on the road with me and Erik and Lucas. We were planning on leaving tomorrow, but we could push it back a day or two if you need some extra time to put your affairs in order.'

The proposal surprised Richard enough to render him momentarily speechless. Hope was surprised, too. Lucas was leaving tomorrow?

Lucas shook his head at Amber. 'I can't leave tomorrow. I

have paperwork to sign that won't be completed until later in the week.'

Hope's surprise grew. Lucas had paperwork to sign? Did that mean he had put in a successful offer on the Larsons' brownstone next door? How would Dylan react when he found out about it?

'Ideally, it would be best to sign the paperwork in person,' Nelson said to Lucas, 'but if you really want – or need – to leave early, we could arrange to have it done electronically instead.'

Hope's surprise switched to confusion. How was Nelson involved in the sale of the neighboring brownstone?

Before Lucas could reply to Nelson, Megan rejoined the group.

'There you are!' she exclaimed to the sisters with an air of relief. 'It's awfully hard to find people in the dark, and it's so tricky to move safely around the obstacle course of blankets and chairs. We didn't realize it from the road or when we walked up the driveway, but the opposite side of the hill is seriously steep. As I was searching for Daniel and then for you, I almost fell down it – twice.'

Richard nodded at her. 'We've had a couple of accidents in the last month. Thankfully, they've been minor, only a twisted ankle and a few bumps and bruises. But if the crowds continue this way every weekend, I may have to put up some sort of a temporary guard rail, or at a minimum, post warning signs before anyone takes a really bad tumble—' He interrupted himself. 'You're supposed to be a broom, right? That is an absolutely brilliant Halloween costume.'

Megan beamed. 'Thank you! Aside from my friends, nobody here seems to understand the costume. Would you believe that one woman thought I was a twig from a tree?'

'Was she wearing mint green?' Richard replied. 'Because that would explain quite a lot . . .'

While Richard and Megan discussed the crowd's sartorial choices, Hope took a step toward the opposite side of the hill and peered down it. She didn't remember the slope being so sharp during her brief visit there many years earlier. Either her memory was faulty, or the hill had suffered significant erosion in the interim. In any case, Megan was correct, and the ground was seriously steep. It was covered in deep, unmown grass, and at the bottom lay the pumpkin patch. The pumpkins weren't visible.

'The only good thing about the large quantity of mint green,' Megan concluded, 'is that it allowed me to spot Daniel much more easily. Otherwise, I might have been walking back and forth along the hill for the next hour, and instead of almost falling down it twice, I would have almost fallen down it four or five times.'

'I still haven't spotted Nate,' Summer told her plaintively. 'Did you see him?'

Megan shook her head with regret. 'Did you see Nate, Daniel?'

Daniel – who had been in the shadows behind Megan – moved into view. 'No, I—' he began.

'You're not wearing your magician costume,' Rosemarie interrupted him.

He looked at her.

'I saw it in the office this afternoon. You should be wearing your costume,' she said. 'Half the purpose of this party is to support the Green Goat. Nelson is doing his part. Why aren't you doing your part?'

'Rosemarie—' Nelson objected.

It was Daniel's turn to interrupt. 'It's a fair point. To support the business, I should be wearing my costume. But it's been a long and difficult day, with far too much to do, and when I finally got here, I realized that I had left the costume in the office. Frankly, I was too tired to go back and get it.'

There was no irritation or anger in his voice. There was simply fatigue. Hope took a closer look at Daniel's face. His mouth sagged, his skin was sallow, and heavy circles ringed his eyes. He was exhausted and dispirited, and it was easy to understand why. His business was on the verge of failure, the prospective investor in that business had been murdered on the premises the night before, and the Halloween party that might have offered a brief respite was a dismal disappointment.

'It has indeed been a long and difficult day,' Nelson concurred, 'but there is also some good news.'

Everyone turned toward him.

'Finally we get to hear the good news!' Rosemarie exclaimed. 'I've been waiting and waiting.'

Nelson smiled at her, then he looked at the others. 'As I was saying to Rosemarie a few minutes ago, it seems that the Green Goat's luck has finally turned.'

Daniel's brow furrowed. 'What do you mean?'

Rather than respond directly to his business partner, Nelson spoke to the group collectively. 'Some of you may have already started to guess when we were discussing paperwork. It isn't official yet, because the paperwork hasn't been signed, but after all the worry and all the struggles, I believe that we have a lifeline at last.'

Lucas nodded in confirmation. 'I've agreed to be the new investor in the Green Goat.'

TWENTY-THREE

The reactions to Lucas's announcement were mixed. Rosemarie was the most outwardly enthusiastic of the group. She gave a great cry of delight and threw her arms around Nelson in excitement. Erik offered an easy-going, congratulatory: *That's cool, dude.* Amber's response was limited to an apathetic sniffle. She displayed no interest in the Green Goat's affairs, regardless that Collin had been killed there or that Lucas's business dealings might delay their departure from Asheville.

Lucas turned to Hope with his crooked smile, but when he saw her expression, the smile faded. 'You don't look as pleased as I thought you'd be.'

'I'm surprised,' she answered honestly. 'I distinctly remember you saying last night that you were glad you didn't invest in the Green Goat.'

'I remember that, too,' Summer corroborated.

'After some reflection and a more thorough reading of the financial documents that Collin had previously given me, I changed my mind,' Lucas told them. 'The Green Goat may be struggling now, but there's no question that its fundamentals are sound. In my opinion, it has the potential for significant growth and profits in the future. Not to mention' – his crooked smile resurfaced – 'an investment here gives me a good excuse to come back. You wouldn't mind if I visited more often, would you?'

Not providing Hope with an opportunity to reply, Lucas continued, 'Plus, I like your friends, and they all seem to have a connection to the Green Goat: Megan and Rosemarie and obviously Nelson—'

Summer interrupted him, keeping her voice low to avoid unwanted listeners. 'Nelson isn't really our friend. We barely know him.'

As she spoke, Summer's eyes went to Nelson's shoes. Hope knew that her sister was thinking again of the bloody footprints that had been left behind in the wine cellar and the alley. It made

Hope wonder about the second set of footprints in the cellar that Dylan had told them about.

'You barely know Nelson?' Lucas echoed in surprise. 'But I was under the impression that he and Rosemarie are in a relationship, and they . . .'

He didn't drop his voice the same way that Summer had, and Hope looked quickly at Rosemarie and Nelson. There wasn't any need for her to worry, however. Although Rosemarie was no longer hugging Nelson, she was chattering to him so effusively that neither one of the pair could have heard a word from Lucas.

Megan stood on the other side of Nelson. Similar to Rosemarie – albeit with slightly less volume and slightly more self-possession – Megan was telling Daniel how happy she was that the Green Goat had been saved by a new investor. Daniel didn't return her smiles or express any happiness himself. In fact, he showed no emotion at all. Either he was too astonished by Lucas's announcement, or he was too fatigued to fully comprehend its import. Perhaps it was some combination of both.

Hope was beginning to shift her attention back to Lucas – who was still talking to Summer – when she noticed a man moving in the shadows behind Megan. At first glance, she dismissed him as a random member of the crowd. But then the man moved closer, and she recognized him. It was Nate. He had found them at last. Summer would be thrilled! Hope was about to call out to him in greeting, but Nate met her gaze and shook his head. She squinted at him. He shook his head again, slowly and gravely. Nate didn't want her to point him out to Summer and the others? But why not?

There was more movement in the shadows. Looking carefully, Hope saw that Nate wasn't alone. A group of men were with him, including several uniformed police officers. Unless she was greatly mistaken, their uniforms were not costumes. Nate and the other men weren't wearing costumes, either. And that was when Hope realized they weren't there for the party. They were there on business. Had the police figured out who had killed Collin?

'Dylan,' Rosemarie cried, 'you just missed the wonderful news!'

Startled, Hope turned and found Dylan standing next to her.

'Lucas has come to the rescue of the Green Goat,' Rosemarie explained to him eagerly. 'He's their new investor. Isn't that marvelous?'

Under other circumstances, Hope would have dreaded Dylan's reaction to learning that Lucas was furthering his connection to Asheville, but her mind was still focused on Nate and his colleagues. Dylan had appeared in almost the same moment they had. That couldn't possibly be a coincidence.

'I plan to visit the city often to check on my investment,' Lucas told Dylan, 'so I'll be spending a lot of time at the boutique.'

Lucas was clearly implying that he intended on spending a lot of time with Hope, but Dylan paid no attention to him. Instead, he looked at Megan.

'Megan,' Dylan said, 'you should come over here by Hope and Summer and me.'

Megan frowned at him.

His tone grew sterner. 'Megan, come over here by Hope and Summer.'

Her frown deepened and became somewhat annoyed. It was obvious that she found Dylan's request odd. Hope found it odd, too, and she also frowned at him.

Dylan gave Hope a significant look and said to her under his breath, 'Megan needs to move.'

Why would Megan need to move? Then suddenly Hope understood. Dylan was working with Nate. The police were going to make an arrest, and Megan was blocking the angle from which they wanted to approach. She needed to move for her own safety.

Hope didn't hesitate. 'Megan, could you come here? I need to talk to you.'

Megan's frown turned toward her.

'Please, Megan. *Now.*'

Although the insistence in Hope's tone only seemed to add to Megan's confusion, it succeeded in convincing Summer that something serious was happening. She looked thoughtfully from her sister to Dylan and finally to Megan. It wasn't clear whether she noticed Nate and his colleagues in the shadows behind Megan, but she caught on to what Hope and Dylan were attempting to do.

'You're worried about where Megan is standing, aren't you?' she said to them. 'You're trying to get her away from Nelson.'

'What!' Megan and Rosemarie exclaimed in unison.

'Summer,' Dylan began, 'you should let the—'

He wanted her to let the police handle the matter. Hope wanted that, too. But either Summer hadn't seen the police, or she didn't have the patience to wait for them to intervene, because she cut Dylan off.

'I always suspected it was you,' she told Nelson. 'The others weren't convinced, but I knew you had done it.'

Both Megan and Rosemarie stared at Summer, but their subsequent actions went in opposite directions. Megan took a sizable step away from Nelson, further toward Daniel. Rosemarie, on the other hand, shifted nearer to Nelson, as if seeking reassurance by his proximity.

Although Rosemarie wasn't blocking the police's approach to the same extent as Megan had been, she was much too close to Nelson for Hope's comfort. This time Hope tried to get her to move, using Percy as an excuse.

'Rosemarie,' she said, 'it's awfully dark, and there are so many people wandering about the hill. Percy could get scared or even lost under foot. Why don't you scoop him up and come over here by me?'

Before Rosemarie could respond, Summer continued to Nelson, 'I saw you in the alley behind the Green Goat last night. I saw your bloody shoes and the bloody footprints you left there.'

Rosemarie's stare turned toward Nelson. 'What – what does she mean?'

There was a pause. Nelson pulled the pointy silver hat from his head and clasped it against his chest. To Hope's surprise, his face didn't cloud with anger nor did his muscles tense as though he was about to explode with rage and resentment at Summer's accusation. On the contrary, Nelson exhaled slowly, and with it, his body relaxed as though an enormous weight had been lifted from his shoulders.

'You're absolutely correct,' he answered Summer. 'I also saw someone in the alley last night, and this morning on the lawn under the gazebo, I realized that it had been you. I was ashamed then already, and I should have confessed everything immediately, but I didn't. So I'll do it now.'

Hope glanced at Dylan. Shouldn't he motion toward Nate and

his colleagues to come out of the shadows and listen to Nelson's confession? Maybe Dylan was concerned that if the police appeared, Nelson would be spooked into silence.

Exhaling again, Nelson said, 'Collin and I had a meeting yesterday evening in the Green Goat to finalize the details of his investment. We were downstairs in my office, and the phone rang. It was an important call from one of our suppliers that I had been waiting on for most of the afternoon and didn't want to put off until the following Monday. Collin said that he would take a look around the wine cellar while I spoke with the supplier. The call lasted a while, and when it was concluded, I went to the cellar. I didn't find Collin there, so I assumed that he must have gotten tired of waiting and gone back upstairs into the bar. Just as I was about to go upstairs, too, I noticed some liquid shimmering on the floor of the cellar. At first I thought that one of the kegs or the cases was leaking, but when I took a closer look, I saw that it was blood. And then I saw that the blood belonged to Collin.'

Rosemarie made a distressed little mewing noise.

Nelson nodded at her. 'It was horrible. Without question, it was the most horrible sight of my life. I'll never forget Collin lying on that floor – dead. And I'll never forget the shame that I feel at this moment confessing to you what I did at that moment. I didn't call an ambulance or stay with the poor man. I panicked, and I ran. I tucked my tail between my legs and fled from the cellar out into the alley. It wasn't until I got home that I noticed Collin's blood on my shoes. I must have gotten closer to him on the floor than I realized. And the whole time that I was cleaning the blood off, I was thinking to myself what a miserable coward I was. How would I ever explain to my son that instead of contacting the police as I always tell him that he should do in an emergency, I simply scampered away? I'm supposed to be his role model, but I ended up being nothing more than a frightened mouse.'

'You're not a mouse!' Rosemarie protested, grasping hold of Nelson's arm to offer him encouragement. 'A mouse would have stayed in his hole, cowering with his piece of cheese. You bravely stood up and told the truth in front of all of us. You can be tremendously proud of that, and I have every confidence that your son will be proud of it, too.'

Rosemarie believed Nelson without the slightest doubt. Summer must have believed him also – at least to a significant degree – because she didn't contradict or argue with him. Hope didn't argue, either. It certainly wasn't the story that she had expected to hear, but the story made sense and filled in many of the gaps in her knowledge. It explained the meeting between Nelson and Collin in the Green Goat, how Collin ended up in the wine cellar, why Nelson raced away in the alley with his bloody shoes and bloody footprints as witnessed by Summer. Hope had noticed the liquid shimmering on the floor of the cellar, initially thought that it was leakage from a keg or a case, and then discovered Collin's body in the same way that Nelson had. It all matched. Except it left a monstrous question. If Nelson wasn't the one who had killed Collin, then who was the murderer?

Nelson gave Rosemarie a grateful smile, then he turned to Lucas. 'I fully understand,' he said solemnly, 'that this might alter your decision to become our new investor. You may no longer wish to be involved in the Green Goat. Collin was your friend, after all.'

There was another distressed mewing noise, except it came from Amber rather than Rosemarie. Hope looked at Amber. Her face was pale, with a dark red spot on each cheek. It was the first time that she had shown any reaction to the mention of Collin since his death. Erik also looked at Amber, but the rest of the group didn't. Either they hadn't heard her, or they were too concentrated on how Lucas would respond to Nelson.

'Yes, Collin was my friend . . .' Lucas began in the same solemn tone as Nelson.

Amber's mewing grew louder, and the red spots on her cheeks became noticeably larger. Pausing his speech, Lucas stepped toward her and put a comforting hand on her shoulder. The mewing stopped.

Lucas turned back to Nelson. 'Collin was a friend to many of us. But he wasn't the type to hold grudges, and neither am I. My agreement to invest in the Green Goat stands. I have high hopes that—'

'No,' Daniel interrupted him.

Daniel hadn't spoken for such a long time that everyone looked at him in surprise. He looked back at them with an agitated expression.

'*No*,' he repeated to Lucas, 'you can't invest in the Green Goat.'

Lucas's brow furrowed, and he was momentarily silent.

Megan frowned. 'But, Daniel, without Lucas's investment, the business will almost surely fail.'

'Do you think I don't know that?' he retorted. 'Of course I know that.'

The sharpness of his tone visibly startled Megan, but unlike Lucas with Amber a minute earlier, Daniel did not reach out and put a comforting hand on Megan's shoulder.

'I also know,' he continued brusquely, 'that I'm tired. I'm damn tired of pretending to do everything for the supposed good of the business: updating menus, offering promotions, hosting useless events and asinine Halloween parties.'

Hope saw Dylan take a watchful glance at Megan and then make a small signaling motion toward Nate. A cold feeling spread through her as she realized what it meant. She and Summer had been wrong. Dylan hadn't been trying to move Megan away from Nelson. He had been trying to move her away from Daniel.

'You were pretending?' Megan said to Daniel, her voice almost inaudible.

'Obviously I was pretending!' he snapped. 'That was the entire reason I went to the restaurateur convention. It wasn't to learn how to save the business. It was to learn how to end the business. I *want* the business to fail and—'

'And you want to collect the insurance from it,' Nate concluded for him.

Summer jumped in surprise as Nate emerged from the shadows. He gave her a quick nod in greeting, but his primary focus remained on Daniel.

'Through our investigation, we learned about the insurance policy that you took out in the event of the business's failure,' Nate told him. 'And we also learned that you attempted to make a claim on the policy this morning.'

'An insurance policy in the event of the business's failure?' Nelson echoed in confusion. 'We don't have an insurance policy for that.'

'*You* don't,' Daniel rejoined, 'but *I* do.'

Nelson gaped at him.

Daniel gave a derisive snort. 'You clearly have no idea how much money that kind of a policy pays out. If you had joined in it with me, you could be on an extremely nice vacation with your son right now, and you wouldn't have had to work again for a very long time. But instead, you stupidly kept trying to find new investors. You thought that it was simply bad luck when they repeatedly fell by the wayside. Except it wasn't bad luck. It was me convincing them not to invest! And it worked perfectly until the last one. I couldn't dissuade him, because I didn't know enough about him. He was traveling in a camper van rather than living in the area, and you had all of your dealings with him electronically. When he finally arrived on the premises, and I realized that he was intent on rescuing the Green Goat rather than letting it collapse, I was forced to take more drastic measures than I had in the past. So after you had your meeting with Collin in the office, I had my meeting with him in the wine cellar.'

'The second set of footprints,' Summer whispered in horror.

Hope was stunned. The second set of bloody footprints belonged to Daniel. Except they were in actuality the first set and had come before Nelson's, because Daniel was the one who had murdered Collin.

Amber made a gurgling sound. She may not have known anything about the bloody footprints, but she had no difficulty comprehending the meaning of Daniel's words and their end result. The red spots reappeared on her cheeks, and she stammered some feverish, incoherent syllables.

'Be calm, dude,' Erik said to her.

Lucas once more put a comforting hand on her shoulder.

She took no notice of them. She glared viciously at Daniel.

'You–you–you—' Amber's face contorted with fury, and her voice rose until it became a thunderous roar. 'You . . . killed . . . Collin.'

Then she charged at him, screaming ferociously at the top of her lungs, hurtling through everyone in her path. It happened with such speed and so little warning that nobody could get out of her way, and like a row of dominoes, one after another, they all lost their balance and toppled down the hill.

Erik fell first, then Lucas – with his stovepipe top hat flying in the air. Rosemarie, Percy, and Nelson plunged next. Daniel was the last and had the most time to prepare, but when Amber reached him, she was in such a wrath that she plowed straight into him. He tried to grab Megan for support, but she had already begun to move to safety toward Hope and Summer, and she was able to evade his grasp. Amber pulled Daniel down the slope, clawing and scratching and pummeling him as they tumbled together.

Nate – after hurriedly checking that Summer was unharmed – rushed down the slope with his colleagues.

'Stay here,' Dylan commanded the sisters and Megan.

None of the three offered any dispute. They were quite happy to be out of danger on high ground, and they intended to remain that way. They stood at the edge of the hill and watched as Dylan waded into the deep grass and followed after the others.

There was a scrum below in the pumpkin patch. Unidentified limbs flailed wildly. Frenzied voices rose in the din. The police were shouting instructions. Amber was bellowing. Rosemarie was wailing. Percy was howling. If there had been any rats in the vicinity, they had surely fled from the chaos.

Some lights began to appear amid the pumpkins, and a buzz spread through the mint-green crowd on their blankets and chairs. *Had the visitors arrived in their spacecraft?* More lights appeared – police flashlights and phone flashlights – and there was another buzz, less enthusiastic this time. *It wasn't the visitors, after all. It was only a rowdy group of partygoers in the patch. Richard would be displeased.* In reality, Richard didn't seem to care much. He stood next to Hope for a long minute, clucking his tongue and murmuring once again about the need for guard rails and warning signs. Then he wondered aloud whether there were any bratwursts left over, and he wandered off in the direction of the grills.

Eventually the commotion subsided, and enough flashlights were switched on to allow those above to more clearly see what was happening below. Rosemarie had stopped wailing and was holding a panting Percy, whose bumblebee suit was stained orange with smashed pumpkins. Rosemarie's butterfly wings were partially detached, but that gave Nelson – who had lost both his hat and his cape – the ability to wrap his arm more closely around her. Erik was using all the *dudes* in his arsenal to console a quietly sobbing Amber. Dylan was resetting Lucas's shoulder, which had apparently been dislocated during his fall. Nate and his colleagues were putting handcuffs on Daniel.

As the police led her former boyfriend up the hill and toward the driveway, Megan sighed. 'It turns out that I really was dating a murderer.'

'Oh, Megan . . .' Hope gave her hand a sympathetic squeeze.

Her lips quivered, and her eyes were damp. Then she swallowed hard, and Megan Steele steeled herself.

'C'est la vie,' she said with a rueful shrug. 'It's a Halloween that we'll never forget.'

Hope squeezed her hand again.

'There's one thing that I'm curious about,' Summer mused.

Megan gave a little smile. 'Who stole the party punch when we need it the most?'

Hope laughed. 'Ain't that the truth.'

Summer laughed, too. 'Yes, but I'm also curious about what Nate and Dylan's Halloween costumes were going to be.'

There was a pause.

'Maybe we'll find out at next year's party,' Hope said.

Acknowledgements

I am grateful to my wonderful editor Laurie Johnson and the amazing team at Severn House.

I am also grateful to my lovely agent Kari Stuart at CAA, along with her assistant Alex Johnson.

And as always, I am grateful to my dearest family and friends. Thank you.